It could only happen to the crew of
HMS ORCA

by

Ian Franklin

**Grosvenor House
Publishing Limited**

This book is published by
Grosvenor House Publishing Ltd
28-30 High Street, Guildford, Surrey, GU1 3EL.
www.grosvenorhousepublishing.co.uk

CIP catalogue record of this book
is available from the British Library

ISBN 978-1-78148-583-5

Dedications

To my daughters, for persuading me to put a number of my submarine "dits" into print.

ooOoo

HMS Alliance was my first submarine. It now lies within the submarine museum, standing on concrete blocks. As the main exhibit it takes visitors back in time and is enjoyed by them all. At the moment it is undergoing a major refit to enable it to continue for many more years. All those buying this underwater adventure will be contributing to the significant cost.

Foreword

A somewhat special breed of men has always served in the Royal Navy's Conventional Submarines. From the first *Holland* Class at the turn of the 1900's, to the last small class of *Upholders* in the 1980's, these submarines operated alone - to use the RN term – as Private Ships. Without addressing the obvious hazards of their calling, the lives of these submariners were cramped, claustrophobic, damp, dirty, and they smelled continuously of diesel. Yet they relished their image of scruffy, bearded pirates. They were intensely professional and very proud. This pride went beyond national borders, submariners from other nations were no different, and when crews met these bonds were reinforced with admiration and respect.

At the end of the 1960's there were still a number of conventional submarines based in the squadrons at Gosport, Devonport and Faslane. However, the halcyon days of further squadrons in Halifax and Malta had passed, and the last submarines were about to return from Singapore. Indeed, the advent of the Nuclear Submarine, with the build of *Dreadnought*, then *Valiant*, *Warspite* and the *Churchill* Class meant that an era was about to come to an end. It was a fundamental change. It meant the passing of a culture of young crews uninhibited by the normal rules of the service, but fiercely professional in their own right. It also saw the end of a structural fabric including the demise of their beloved headquarters and main training base at the submariner's ancestral home *HMS Dolphin* (on the Gosport side of Portsmouth Harbour).

Today there are just the two bases for the reducing Nuclear Submarine Flotilla; Devonport in Plymouth and Faslane on the Gare Loch in Scotland. The current HQ is shared with the Fleet and the RAF at Northwood.

Many of the incidents attributed to the fictitious *HMS ORCA* actually happened in a number of boats across the years. However, to aid the flow of the plot, times and places have been changed. All characters are fictitious albeit some characteristics are based on well remembered models of the time. No personalities have been directly transposed onto the page.

It was a privilege savoured by all those who served in Conventional Submarines. *HMS ORCA* captures those days.

Note: To enable the flow of the story the use of some naval jargon has been inevitable. To help the reader the first use of such jargon has been put in italics and an explanation of the respective term has been included in the Glossary of Terms at the end of the book.

CONTENTS

ILLUSTRATIONS

Sketches extracted from Lt Toby Johnson's sea journal

FULL DIVING DEPTH

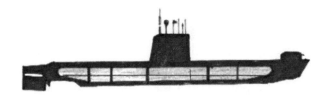

Missing Life in Submarines?

Lesson 1 on recapturing the old days:-

Four hours after you go to bed, have your wife whip open the bedroom curtains, shine a torch in your eyes, and say "Sorry mate, wrong pit"

2035 Sunday 21 October

In the depths of the lower motor room the noise of the auxiliary machines penetrated everything and made Toby want to cover his ears. It also felt bloody cold and damp. There were no signs of actual water in the bilge, but it was pretty murky and definitely not a place to spend a Sunday evening. Imagine a closed space packed out with electrical machines producing as many forms of electrical power as you could think of. It was far from a brilliant design, and yet in the confines of the submarine there was little choice. As he clambered between the machines Toby's thoughts turned to Judy, probably glass in hand at the end of a good day at the sailing club. It seemed an age since she had dropped him off that morning. He ducked under the port main motor cooling pipes to check the for'd systems and noticed that the defective 400hz machine in the aft corner which was awaiting spares, had a cover left off. This was tardy and stooping low he crawled past one of the bigger auxiliary machines to sort it out. As luck would have it he could see one of the wing nuts had dropped on the deck. Stooping to pick it up … everything exploded, and with a blinding pain filling his head, he was thrown across the compartment by an icy cold torrent of salty water, ending up in the bilge with his senses numbed to all but the overwhelming noise of flooding water and the increasing muddled panic that he was drowning in freezing seawater!

The explosion had been like a large calibre gun going off, followed immediately by the sound of what seemed like shrapnel ricocheting around the compartment. With his ear drums ringing, blood streaming down his face and feeling as if he had been kicked in the stomach, Toby became aware that he was soaked to the skin and shaking uncontrollably from shock and the cold. High pressure water was spraying all around him and he had been knocked onto the deck. His feet were desperately trying to find a grip as he sloshed around in the bilges which were quickly filling with oily black water. To top it all the lighting had failed and visibility through the salt water mist was barely possible under the emergency lights.

Gradually he regained a sense of awareness and became conscious of the *Polto* yelling from the other side of the compartment.

"*Control, Motor Room, Flood, Flood - Flood in the Lower Motor Room*". PO Miller shouted into the mike while trying to get Toby back into the land of the living. After getting an acknowledgement from the Control Room he continued to shout at Toby and eventually started to bring him back to reality and the need for immediate action. Calling him all the names he could think of to get his attention, he yelled:

"Lecky, Big L, Toby, can you hear me? Are you OK? Can you hear me?"

He hadn't been yelling for long when Toby at last managed a response. "Polto, I'm OK but I have no idea what has happened."

"Sir - as fast as you can - port after quarter - shut the after services discharge hull valve. Keep talking as you get there. Yes that's it, put your weight behind it ... no it's not stuck ...great it's turning, well done, ensure it's tightly shut."

It took all Toby's strength, but the Polto's clear direction made it possible. As the valve gradually seated the noise slowly subsided and the pressure mist began to disappear. Suddenly it was eerily quiet, and he found himself sitting in six inches of cold mucky bilge water, wondering if he was going to throw up while looking up at the smiling P.O. whose cool mind and actions had not only saved them both, but probably a major incident for the boat.

"Thanks Polto, what the hell happened?" Before the P.O. could answer they were both knocked violently over against the pipe work yet again, as the deck suddenly took on a major angle with the boat surging towards the surface. Toby's head was screaming and lying flat out back in the bilge he managed a brief look at Polto as they both grabbed the nearest pipes to clamber up against the steep bow-up angle. No sooner were they stable than their world turned turtle once again and they hung on for dear life, as the boat dropped back down onto the level with a major jolt. They found themselves once more sprawled on their backs gasping for air in the freezing, black, flood water. Gathering their wits together after one last effort, they struggled, soaked to the skin, finally to find their feet and, pausing to mentally adjust, began to understand what had just happened. The emergency climb from full diving depth had sent the boat surging up through the surface at a steep angle, the bow leaping out some way before crashing back onto an even keel, and sending them both flying. They had ended up on their backsides sitting up to their waists in black bilge water, literally freezing their arses off. Gradually both realised that the excitement had come to an end, and what a bloody sight they both looked. PO Miller, iconic Polto and hero of the hour, looked as though he had just surfaced from jumping over the side of a sinking oil tanker. His beard and hair looked some way from their best, both soaked with a foamy mixture of salt water streaked with oil and grease. Toby's appearance was even more graphic with the deep gash on his head still profusely bleeding down over his right shoulder. Despite his increasingly searing headache Toby stopped to take stock. They both knew the drama was now over and sat silently for a while unable to stop either the shakes enveloping their fingers or the crazy grins which were spreading from ear to ear.

"Oh my God, whatever next. Just look at this. Christ I'm a bloody mess" groaned Toby.

"Come on Sir. Let's get up top and sort ourselves out. Is anything broken? No - OK up you go we need to clean you up and stop up that wound." Guided by the emergency lighting, and supporting each other, they waded through the sloshing, oily bilge water to the ladder at the far side. The compartment now looked a complete mess, with the sheets of readings floating amongst the debris. A wet and bloody Electrical Officer was guided up the ladder by the P.O. to be greeted by concerned smiles, a blanket and a large mug of steaming tea.

Sitting on the motor room bench while his head was being cleaned up and bandaged, Toby's mind lost its way and all he remembered thinking was "how had they made the brew that quickly", but with his mind still reeling he didn't pursue it. The tea tasted good and really hit the spot; albeit his head continued to scream while he waited for the painkillers to take effect. Within a few minutes all the urgency of the incident had passed. The pain killers began to kick in and the pair were sharing a second cup while the watch sent a team below to clear up the mess. The Polto was covered in oily streaks and his face looked as though it was covered in camouflage paint, Toby didn't look much different. It took a while to get everything sorted, as they sat there, oblivious to the passing of time, slowly regaining some form of mental order. Peter the XO paid them a visit so that he could both confirm their state of their recovery to the Boss, and also to ensure that Toby didn't need any of his personal needlework to patch up the wound. Not that he relished the idea having only ever practiced on oranges during exercises. In the meantime the Motor Room Watch pumped out the bilges and had the Engineer Officer, John, and his team come back to survey the scene to find out what had happened and whether there was any further damage.

Finally Toby was taken back to his pit to sleep it off and allow the drugs to really kick in. He clambered up into his top tier bunk and snuggled deep into the sleeping bag. As he drifted off the events of a long day whirled around in his head and he found himself bouncing along in the MGB with Judy at the wheel.

ooOoo

0435 Sunday 21 October

The day had started with Lieutenant Toby Johnson, Electrical Officer of HMS Orca, a conventional Oberon Class submarine, waking to his alarm at 0400 on that cold Sunday morning. His current abode was on the Portsmouth side of the Harbour, below Portsdown Hill in Farlington Avenue. A humble Lieutenant's married quarter at the bottom of the hill, and a far cry from the opulent piles in which the gold braided brass resided at the top. As ever, in service life everyone had to know his place … and Toby's was at the bottom of the hill.

That early on a Sunday it took barely thirty minutes to charge around the Harbour from Farlington to Gosport. Cramped into the MG, and with Judy driving, they weren't hanging about. Even at this early hour she had ignored shoes, and wore the merest suggestion of a skirt ....he flattered himself that it was her way of giving him a fond farewell.

They drove into HMS Dolphin and followed the coast road past the escape tower before turning into Fort Blockhouse to park alongside the green outside the Wardroom. The Wardroom hall porter on duty that morning was Tom Suffolk, very much a lady's man, so much so that he ignored most of the officers themselves, who often wondered why he was there. However, spotting the long legs, he rushed to give Judy his full attention and she was soon seated with a small pot of his special coffee. In the mean time Toby was reluctantly gathering his gear from the boot and forcing as much as he could into his pusser's grip. Extracting the final bits, with the grip in one hand and a mucky but full suit cover over the other arm, he joined Judy for a final coffee. At that time in the morning a meaningful good-bye was just not possible but they did their best. An enjoyable full body clinch, as much for the crowd as for him, and she departed with a quick wave driving the MG up through the base.

Gosport was cold and uninviting, and the six boats at their berths on the trots alongside in HMS Dolphin all had that "night after" look following the festivities of the Ladies' Dinner the previous evening. Vague images of the lonely Trot Sentries, hiding in the igloos above their respective main hatches, were visible in the gloom of a bleak, damp and misty Sunday morning. HMS Orca appeared the only boat with any life. Large white fume trails churned out from her diesel exhausts into the cold morning air as the overnight charge continued to top up the batteries.

HMS Orca sat on the outboard trot and PO Price, the *Second Cox'n,* and his team were clearing the casing and getting ready for the departure. PO Price was a real character, but he had one burden in life- his height. He was only five foot three, and unfortunately for him they had another Price on board who was six foot two. He had, therefore, learnt to live with the nickname of "Half the Price", with his name sake understandably being called "Twice the Price". It hadn't held him back. He had used it to good effect and had become one of the trusted stalwarts in the crew.

Crossing HMS Onslaught, the inboard boat, and stepping onto Orca's brow Toby halted to attention on the casing, a brief form of salute given his armful of personal gear. Once over the side he made his way across to the main access hatch, dropped down the grip, and then turned to clamber down the ladder. The vertical access was never easy especially when you were overloaded, but he managed to get to the bottom without ripping the suit carrier. That familiar "eau du diesel" smell attacked his nostrils as he bent to gather the grip. It made him reflect just how familiar this strange life had become.

Turning aft to the Wardroom he was immediately accosted by Petty Officer "Smudger" Smith, the Torpedo Instructor, or *TI* as they called him,

"Sorry Sir, but the fish we need for the training firings weren't available yesterday and now we will have to get them from the armament depot at Coulport when we get up to the Clyde Base. It may mean moving around to the Coulport Jetty on Loch Long. Hope the CO doesn't blow his top; it will almost certainly mean an extra night in Faslane.

"Christ TI", Toby replied. "That's all we need. Did you manage to ensure they are the ones with the new guide wire dispensers?"

"Yes Sir, with a bit of luck these may even work! I'll bring a draft signal requesting them from Coulport along in the first dog watch after tea."

Turning aft Toby diverted into the Wardroom and swung his grip onto the top pit - his private space and the only bunk which didn't have to be cleared away for breakfast. A luxury which allowed him all of an extra ten minutes in his own cramped space before joining the others each morning – he had even been offered genuine folding money for that pit.

"Morning Toby" John Bulmer, the Engineer leaned in, "when did you hear that we had drawn the short straw?"

"Just as the port was going around last night, at least it was the good stuff put down by HMS Acheron's wardroom on paying off." Toby responded.

"The word is that Porpoise was due to clockwork mouse, acting as a target, for the Frigates working up in the Rosyth operating areas from Thursday, but has blown the Turbo on her port diesel. She'll be out for a number of weeks. Why they forced us to sail two days early – and on a Sunday at that- and didn't just call up one of the SM3 boats already at Faslane beats me." John was clearly pissed off.

"Has the running period been extended, or are we going to come back early?"

"No such luck, I've been told to add on the annual deep dive before you have fun on the weapon's range off Raasay" he muttered.

Toby shook his head. "Why does it always happen to us? – We'll need to re-jig the programme. Can we go over it later? I must go and meet the new Polto who has arrived at only four hours notice" Toby's mind was racing. Brilliant planning as ever, the usual bugger's muddle. Why should Russia tremble? And yet somehow the RN always seemed to muck along and come up trumps.

ooOoo

A conventional submarine, HMS Orca was part of the First Submarine Squadron (*SM1*), based at that ancestral home of all conventional submariners HMS Dolphin. It was here that submariners qualified in the escape tank for their extra submarine pay - much to the disgust of those in the surface fleet. Orca's crew was a motley bunch of sixty eight misfits, average age just under twenty two.

The "old man" (he was 36) led the marine engineering team, affectionately known as the *plumbers*. This was Lieutenant John Bulmer, an old school *Janner* who joined as a young rating in Plymouth straight from school. Despite a lack of education his quality soon shone through and he advanced as a fast track Artificer to become a Special Duties Officer in his twenties. John was a classic old school conventional submarine Chief of the Boat and master of his trade. His additional role at the moment was mentor, or as the Wardroom members called him, "Sea Daddy" to Toby, his younger engineering partner in crime. Without his support Toby, despite doing well, would have been struggling. There had been a few incidents which could even have been somewhat hairy but for John's guidance. Despite this significant difference in age and experience John and Toby had also gained the reputation of being joined at the hip with no back-biting. A somewhat refreshing partnership, given the many clashes of personality amongst the engineers in most of the other boats. They had become affectionately known as "the terrible twins" in the squadron, and invariably as a result had decisions fall their way when it came to choices for the squadron staff...

Toby, the junior partner, was the boat's Electrical Officer. As he put it he was the first, and probably last, of a long Naval line, as none of his family had ever been career officers. He joined up at the suggestion of his Godmother by answering an advert in the Sunday Telegraph after a family lunch. Before he had realised what was happening he found himself in the middle of a series of interviews (which he naively thought were fact finding missions) and ended up with a sixth form scholarship at grammar school, which funded a motorbike. Unfortunately when he asked if he could defer entry and go to University before joining up the answer was no unless he paid back the scholarship ... and having just blown the big-end bearings on his Matchless 350 ...he had no choice.

His first term at *BRNC* (Britannia Royal Naval College) in Dartmouth was awful. He ended up calling it the prison on the hill, seeing its sole purpose to turn reasonably bright and mature eighteen year olds into very immature nineteen year olds. Unfortunately it was occasionally rather successful and produced classic officers fit for a peace time navy with crisp white shirts, creases you could cut your fingers on and shoes you could see your face in. Fortunately, somewhat by chance, it also nurtured a number of independent rebels who were the real fighters of the future. Many of these were to become house hold names particularly during the Falklands conflict.

During those first two years, apart from his two terms at BRNC, he had had a ball, spending eighteen months in the West Indies. The frigate he was in effectively cruised the Caribbean, although the formal term was showing the flag. As a sun-tanned Midshipman he had fallen in love with a series of beautiful dusky maidens, the point of affection changing as the ship visited island after island. Once back in the UK at the Naval Engineering College he had learnt to fly and was destined to join the Fleet Air Arm as a flying engineer. Then Dennis Healey cancelled the new Fixed Wing Aircraft Carriers and his career took a dive, not just figuratively. He opted for a complete change of direction and became a Submariner.

Toby and John were not just good partners, they complemented each other, and as a pair were a force to reckon with.

ooOoo

0535 Sunday 21 October
Going aft through the control room melee, Toby ducked through the engine room hatch entering what was affectionately called the *donk shop* and passed down the passage between the two large diesel engines into the motor room, the domain of the Polto.

The regular PO Electrician or Polto was PO Stan Merriweather an experienced Scouser worth his weight in gold, who ran the electrical propulsion team, both men and machines, like clockwork. Unfortunately, as the officers were enjoying the mess dinner the night before, he was entertaining his brother, a Royal Marine. In the full traditions of the service he provided his brother with the very best of submarine hospitality, and ended up with a leg in plaster. A tearful *Polto* is a rare animal, but his pleas for forgiveness on the phone were genuine. As he said, at least he had given his *Bootie* (Royal Marine) brother one hell of a run ashore.

"Good Morning, Petty Officer Miller I presume - did you volunteer, or were you pushed? No, don't answer that- four hours notice for a five week trip says it all." Toby greeted the new man with a genuinely warm handshake.

"First of all, Welcome on board. I apologise for the brevity, but as we set sail in forty-five minutes can you and the team give me the latest update on our readiness for sea? I'll come back and we can introduce ourselves properly and fully brief each other over a coffee once we are underway." Toby sat down, picked up the Motor Room log and turned to listen to the team.

"Thanks Sir. Despite the notice I am happy to be here. ....From what we've reviewed we are ready to go. Only one issue and that's the outstanding operational defect on No. 2 400 Hz machine, which is still awaiting spares." Miller was a big man, with a deep low voice which seemed to be muffled by his overly full ginger beard.

"Good, hopefully they should be waiting for us once we are alongside in Faslane. Nothing else? No." Toby turned to go. "In that case I'll come back aft around 0730 once we've all had breakfast and we can get properly introduced and both get up to speed. Thanks again for taking the pier head jump so well, your positive approach is much appreciated."

Short but fortunately sweet, he looked a pretty solid man. Toby reflected on the change as he nipped in behind the switchboard to a gap in the electric power panels which he had made his private wardrobe. He grabbed his working uniform jacket to ready himself to go up top and greet the CO with John. It was cold outside so they would both be dressed in their standard garb, No 5's the formal Naval Officers uniform, but in this case with submarine sweaters rather than shirt and tie.

"Toby, it's 0550, time to go up top," noted John as he tidied away the last of his gear in the wardroom. Toby followed him for'd and they clambered up the main hatch onto the casing. John acknowledged the XO's wave from the bridge and they formed up together for'd of the fin between the brow and the fin door. Their timing was just right, no sooner had they stood formally at ease than Captain SM and HMS Orca's CO, Lieutenant Commander James Olliphant, appeared out of the squadron offices. Captain SM never missed a departure; the tradition of seeing each and every boat off was one that he had, as yet, not failed to perform in the two years of his time. These measured strolls were

First Submarine Squadron on the "Trots" at HMS Dolphin

important for all the boats, it emphasised a sense of belonging and enhanced their respect for the man. As they approached the Second Cox'n's team manning the brow came to attention, and after a farewell handshake from Captain SM the skipper walked up onto the casing and was piped on board

"Morning John, how is Ruth?"

"She's fine thank you, Sir" John responded with a crisp salute mentally thanking the Boss for remembering that he had left a wife recovering from appendicitis at home with two young sons.

"Engineering Department ready for Sea, no OPDEFs"

"Very Good. How's the *Polto* Toby?"

Toby saluted and replied "Feeling very humble and a little sorry for himself, Sir. Electrical Department is ready for Sea. Petty Officer Miller has stepped in at four hours notice to replace him. I will bring him along to your cabin mid forenoon. We still have the OPDEF on the 400Hz machine but I have been promised the spares in Faslane, and I regret that we will probably have to go alongside Coulport to take on the four exercise *Mk 23's* we have been allocated for the firings on the practice range ."

"The squadron filled me in." the CO responded. "I'm not fussed, with luck they should bring them around to the base in Faslane, in which case it should only take four hours. OK Gentlemen, thank you," and with that he disappeared into the fin. It was a standard ritual but one the submarine community all rather enjoyed, with each occasion opening another chapter in the life of HMS Orca.

As John and Toby clambered down the hatch the order *"Let go for'd. Slow Ahead Together"* came over the broadcast and a gentle rumble could be felt throughout the boat. It slowly edged away from the jetty and started the turn out past Fort Blockhouse into the narrow main entrance of Portsmouth Harbour. Once round and in the main fairway the revolutions were increased and Orca rapidly accelerated to twelve knots heading out into the familiar but busy waters of the Solent.

ooOoo

0645 Sunday 21 October

It wasn't long before she had made her way out past the Nab Tower, around the east end of the Isle of Wight and had St Catherine's Point coming fast abeam. The crew were a fairly experienced team, only having three *Part III* submarine trainees on board for this trip, so everyone quickly settled down into their own individual routines.

By now, apart from the pilotage team and those still on the bridge, everyone had changed out of uniform into their personal pirate rigs. Toby's was a relatively simple denim shirt, covered by a submarine sweater, cord jeans and cowboy boot *steaming bats*, nothing noteworthy. Back in the *donk shop* there were some real gems. One star performer, Leading Stoker Jenkins, had really done himself proud this trip. His outfit was always based on his favourite white grandpa tee shirt (with a string lace-up front), white jeans and the ever present Seventh Cavalry cap. However, this time the whole outfit was covered in stencilled arrows and on the back was emblazoned "HM Prison Orca". Full marks for cheek, but it wouldn't be long before all the oil and grease soon converted his latest outfit into the standard jet black. Toby wondered what motivated them to do it. Not all did, but it was part practical reasons and part tradition. They certainly didn't need badges of rank, they all knew each other and irrespective of rank had been trained to ensure mistakes were immediately rectified, even if it meant a junior pushing a senior out of the way to stop a dangerous error. There was also their somewhat erroneous piratical reputation, further enhanced by the established routine of boats returning from war patrols with Jolly Rogers flying - a standard had even evolved for the symbols denoting the respective targets sunk.

This culture was also partly due to the restricted amount of water available for washing both bodies and clothes on board the boats. Tanks were finite in size and they were only able to distil their own water under strictly benign conditions... To use the distillers on operations was the equivalent of sending out a siren noise signature indicating exactly where they were. So the alternative was strict water rationing, and it was strict. The Part III's were taught how to wash themselves all over in one six inch basin of water - and then *dhobi* a pair of socks in the same water as a finale! The only showers in the boat were dry and involved talcum powder, perhaps followed with liberal splashes of aftershave lotion for the more flamboyant.

"*Blind pilotage team stand down*" came loudly over the main broadcast.

The weather and visibility were bucking up, and it was time for breakfast. None of the Wardroom had eaten anything as yet this morning and were feeling somewhat ravenous. The Navigator was the first on watch up top, so the rest gathered for a cosy breakfast keen to get the brief from the CO on the changes to the trip following their enforced stand-in for the Third Submarine Squadron boat HMS Porpoise. Making his way out of the control room Toby squeezed past the ongoing watch and turned into the Wardroom. The name sounds very grand; in effect the space was the size of a large cupboard, about eight feet by twelve. In this six of them lived - the best accommodation on board! It had two sets of two-tier bunks and one set of three, the spare was for any Rider or a Part III officer under training. At the far end there was a small cupboard chock full of single malts which served as their bar, probably the most important space after the bunks. Beside it was a counter where food and papers were laid out and below that a two drawer filing cabinet affectionately known as the Ship's Office (it was also the stowage for a small type writer). This desk top also doubled as an extension to the bar on social occasions and above it was hung a rather impressive Bernard Buffet lithograph which had been presented to the boat on commissioning. For reasons Toby could never fathom, what he considered to be a rather fine painting was universally hated by the rest of the wardroom.

All the gear had been neatly stowed away and the Wardroom table was set for breakfast. The Sonar Officer and Fifth Hand were already seated as Toby pushed past to his regular place in the corner.

"Morning, Frank, Julian, how are the hangovers?" was met with a pair of winces, but before they had a chance to reply John and the XO, Lieutenant Peter Ince, came bounding in followed quickly by the Leading Steward.

"Well Leading Steward what delights do you have for us this morning given that is not yet 0800, it's Sunday, and by all that's just we should all be in our own beds tucked up beside our wives?" demanded the XO.

"Your favourites Sir, specials are *Yellow Peril* or *Shit on a Raft*!"

"Brilliant - I'll have Shit on a Raft with extra beans - and remember I like two slices of fried bread, the CO will have the same, he won't be long" XO replied.

"Same for me" said John

".. And me" added Julian, the Fifth Hand, followed quickly by *TASO*. (Our Sonar Officer affectionately known by his old title TASO – Torpedo & Anti- Submarine Officer)

"How you chaps can take offal and deep fried concrete beats me". replied Toby. Shit on a Raft was in fact kidneys on fried bread.

"I'll have the Yellow Peril Leader ... with two poached eggs on top of the smoked haddock. Presumably chef hasn't had time to bake any rolls yet?" Toby continued.

"Fraid not Sir. What will the Navigator have? I'll need to put something aside for him."

"He's a fish man like me, he'll have the Yellow Peril. But don't cook it until he comes down. Julian, are you going up to relieve him after breakfast?"

"Yes, I won't be long."

Toby poured a cup of strong tea and sat back to review the Sunday Times as the smells from the galley added to his hunger and anticipation.

"Morning Peter, Gentlemen, what's on for breakfast?" the CO swept into the room taking his normal seat by the door, sounding far too cheerful for the rest of us. Like John he also had a young family he would miss and was probably putting on a show of muted leadership to boost his reluctant heroes.

"I've ordered Shit on a Raft with the works for you, Sir. Hope that's OK?"

"Just right. It will dilute last night's excess and set me up for the coming surface passage. John has probably told you why we were bounced and had to leave two days early. Porpoise is unlikely to be back in harness for some weeks, and the impact will affect *SM2* in Devonport and *SM3* at Faslane as well as ourselves. For us it simply means we had to forego the alongside *Fast Cruise* planned for Monday and Tuesday, but the rest of the programme is basically unchanged. Captain SM sends his apologies, but considered us to be in good fettle, hence he had no concerns over the missed training. He also suggested by way of a carrot that we might like a break in Portree after our weapon firings on the Raasay range. He will signal approval once Faslane have made the arrangements."

Not too dramatic then, thought Toby. The brief was interrupted at this point as overflowing plates of kidneys, fried bread, and baked beans were thrust in front of the CO and XO, shortly followed by those for the TASO and Julian. Toby's smoked haddock and poached eggs were not far behind, and a warm hush enveloped the assembly as they devoured a damn fine breakfast.

Eventually with appetites satisfied, discussion of the trip began again.

John started, "Do you intend a surface passage all the way up to the Clyde areas, Sir? Peter will want to sort out the trim and I am keen to get the deep dive done before we are enmeshed in Toby's weapon games on the range … the weather doesn't look that good and, although it doesn't have a big impact at our full diving depth, the detailed inspections, particularly of the lower areas, would be easier if it wasn't too lumpy."

"Yes I agree John, we have some *Water* off Portland, then off Falmouth and in the SW approaches; other diving areas have been scheduled at our discretion in the

Irish Sea, and finally in the Clyde areas. SM1 packaged it so that we could be flexible and suit ourselves. Let me look at the time/distance and the MET forecasts and I will decide later this morning, although my instinct is to get it over while we are still off the south coast."

"In the mean time Sir, I'd like to get back into our routine. Are you happy to fall out Special Sea Duty-men and close up the first watch for Passage Routine?" added the XO. "If we are likely to dive before the *Dogs* the lads would appreciate knowing before all the bunks get turned out and they settle down in their pits following lunch."

"Peter, given our unplanned departure have you had time to work out the new trim after the maintenance period?"

The XO replied with a nod.

"In that case I would like to prove it as soon as possible. The Water we've been allocated in the Portland areas would be ideal. We'll be there before mid-day; lets plan on diving at 1100 for two hours to finalise the trim and get ourselves fit for any diving opportunity, routine or otherwise." the Boss replied. Then in a more measured tone added "*Fall out Special Sea Duty-men, close up the first watch for Passage Routine*"

"*Passage Routine Sir.*" No sooner had the XO left the wardroom than he was on the main broadcast calling up the on-watch team, and warning the crew that they would be diving at 1100. There were a few grumbles from the sluggardly bunk rats, where the loss of thirty minutes shut-eye was a major event. For the rest you could sense a return to normality, albeit a rather unusual normality. It was far from normal and the isolation from family and friends was hidden away as a mental no go area by this small band of misfits. In a similar manner those at home were settling down to another matriarchal period alone without male influence, parental or otherwise. Few of them addressed it, it was far too difficult. How could any of them justify this self imposed masochism? Dodgy ground - and most of them kept well clear.

Replete from a good breakfast, Toby made his way aft to the Motor Room to have an impromptu Plan of the Day with his senior team. This comprised the Chiefs responsible for the Communications/Radar, Sonar, and Weapon Systems, plus the new Polto for the high power Propulsion Motors and the Main Batteries. Sunday or not, they needed to know what the plan was, then they could all ease into their routine and try to forget their missed weekend.

ooOoo

1100 Sunday 21 October

"Officer of the Watch"

"Yes Sir"

"Clear and secure the bridge. Come below. Dive the submarine."

"Clear and secure the bridge. Dive the Submarine - Aye, Aye Sir."

Most of the first eleven had assembled before the formal pipe to "Diving Stations". Indeed, they were all at their posts when Toby and John entered the Control Room. The Cox'n was seated on the after planes, Second Cox'n on the fore planes, and the *Outside Wrecker* on the trim. So the sound of the klaxon came as no surprise.

The Fifth Hand vacated the bridge, shutting and confirming the clips shut on the upper lid as he came down the tower. He then went straight to the CO at the chart table, confirming the boat's position and reporting all the surface contacts. It was clearly very quiet being Sunday, apart from a yacht race slowly creeping around Portland Bill before the tide turned. As Orca was well out from the Shambles they shouldn't come anywhere near her. The XO reflected that yachts could be a real pain for a submarine because they are small and difficult to see from a periscope plus when sailing they are silent and cannot, therefore, be tracked on the sonar. There had been many a near miss with lone yachts in some of the operating areas.

At the same time the XO was diving the submarine and hoping that his trim calculations were going to be close to the mark.

"*Five degrees of bubble and passing fifty feet*" declared the Cox'n.

"*Fifty feet, Roger*" the XO replied.

"*Keep one hundred and fifty feet*" the CO ordered."*Let me know when you are happy with the trim XO*"

"*Aye, Aye Sir*"

One hundred feet came up pretty quickly but they were slowing and the bow was starting to come up rather sharply. The XO was convinced that they were heavy and was pumping out of "O tanks", but the bow was still rising - they were light for'd. Toby then realised that the XO had probably not been told about the cancelled torpedo outload. To avoid embarrassing them both in front of the CO and the whole crew, he sidled up to him and whispered that they were four fish light and that the *Torpedo Operating Tanks (TOTs)* had little water in them.

The XO caught Toby's eye, nodded, and crisply ordered "*Fore Ends, Control. Dip the Port and Starboard Torpedo Operating Tanks.*"

It took them a couple of minutes and then the TI's dulcet tones came on the intercom.

"Control, Fore Ends. Port TOT one hundred gallons, Starboard TOT, one hundred and fifty gallons"

Each fish weighed about 2500lbs, so the boat was very light up there. However, the speedy addition of 500 gallons on each side soon sorted it out. Some fifteen minutes later, after fine tuning with the odd fifty gallons, Peter was happy and the boat was slipping along at an easy four knots at one hundred and fifty feet.

"Happy with the trim, Sir. Depth one hundred and fifty feet, keeping four knots, on a heading of 270. Sound room has no contacts"

"Thank you XO. Ten degrees for'd bubble. Keep sixty two feet. Stand by for'd periscope"

Back up to periscope depth. Having just dived they knew there was nothing close. However, this was always an evolution which heightened the crew's senses. Between one hundred feet and fifty feet was no man's land, with the real chance of a missed sonar contact and a resultant collision on coming up to periscope depth. The yachts mentioned earlier were a classic case. A number of well known incidents from operations across the submarine flotilla had resulted in boats sneaking back to their bases with crumpled fins and bent periscopes, hurriedly covered over with black painted hessian to hide their embarrassment from prying eyes.

"Raise For'd Periscope." Crouching, the CO grabbed the scope as soon as the handles slid up from the deck, and then executed a continuous all round look as they approached the surface.

"Breaking - Depth?"

"Sixty four feet, Sir"

"Keep sixty two. Nothing in sight. Watch Diving. Electrical Officer raise the after periscope and take the watch"

The watch on was Toby's. Each watch dived had two officers and he shared his with the Navigating Officer. It took two of them to deal with the periscope and maintain the vital visual watch, ensure the trim especially when snorting so that the diesels could be run at periscope depth to charge the batteries, and manage the overall operational state of the boat at any time. Fortunately for them diving this late in the morning they would only be on for about forty minutes and then it would be lunch.

The after scope was binocular (whereas the for'd was monocular) and the view on this Sunday afternoon was very pleasant. They decided that, given the good light, they would split the watch and do twenty minutes each on the scope. In fact it was a very pleasant doddle. The after scope had a turntable seat which once engaged enabled you to drive the rotation speed with your right foot. Altering the eye pieces to his settings, and with arms akimbo over the scope handles, Toby rotated the scope gently anti-clockwise as they poodled past Portland with the distant yacht race and the end of the Bill their only companions.

The pair handed over to John and the Fifth Hand at 1230. Toby was conscious that he urgently needed to get rid of his breakfast and immediately rushed aft to the heads. The officer's trap was number one - the luxury heads replete with wash basin and hand held shower (although the latter was invariably tagged out to ensure no overuse of water). No sooner had he sat down than he heard John announce over the main broadcast, *"Stand by to Snort"*. Thanks buddy he thought, why was it always him caught out with his trolleys around his ankles? Snorting is the routine whereby the diesels are run and the batteries charged while dived. It is a routine which requires the crew to raise the snort mast and suck air into the submarine to feed the diesels. This routine is involved but not complex and comprises draining the mast of sea water prior to starting the diesels. This was where Toby's embarrassment came in, and at the appropriate time he opened the door of the officer's trap, unwound a valve over his head (trolleys still around his ankles) and formally announced "*Snort Drain Two Open*". The crew always enjoyed this little ritual, it was a point of honour to catch as many of the wardroom "mid-george" as they could. Privacy in a conventional submarine was something that did not exist and individuals just had to learn to live with it.

Anyway, ritual over, Toby completed his ablutions or almost. For some reason the pan just would not clear. New comers often had problems with submarine heads, the valve routine is awkward, and the contents go into the affectionately named shit tank –or formally – the slop drain and sewerage tank. However, although Toby was completely au fait with the routine, try as he might he could not get it to pump out. Eventually, with some significant embarrassment he was forced to seek the *Outside Wrecker*, the Chief responsible for the auxiliary systems and explain his embarrassing problem. The Chief grinned but understood and said he would see to it at once. A somewhat chastened Electrical Officer retreated meekly, and made his way forward for lunch in the wardroom.

ooOoo

1430 Sunday 21 October

Orca surfaced at 1300, and continued her passage on the surface across Lyme Bay at a steady fourteen knots. Toby was the only one still at the table reading the Sunday papers when John came in for his late lunch. No sooner was he tucking in when the Outside Wrecker knocked on the door and asked to speak to him. Not wanting to spoil his meal John nodded at Toby and invited the Wrecker to come in and sit down.

"Sorry to disturb you Sir, but it's trap one. We don't seem to have got rid of the problem we had last running period. The Electrical Officer couldn't clear the pan this morning. I sent in two of my lads and they completely stripped it down. But on re-assembly it still would not clear. We've come to the conclusion that it is something internal to the tank. It's not something I would wish on anyone but I think we should open up the tank and send someone in to find out what the problem is."

"God, Wrecker, that's a bit extreme. Are you really sure?" John replied without pausing to tackle the Yorkshire pudding in his belated Sunday lunch.

"Yes, Sir, I am afraid we are."

"In that case you'd better seek out a credible volunteer. We'll have to do it on the surface. I'll have a word with the Boss and let you know when. Whoever goes in will need a full diving suit with air feed. God help the rest of us, the stench will be appalling. Thanks Wrecker - great timing"... and turning to Toby finished with "I hope the pudding's good."

After his figgy duff they both retreated to their pits. John drifted off first and there was soon a background of gentle snoring from his bunk. He really needed to get his nasal passages reamed out thought Toby as at times the vibrations even reached his pit two up from John's, being the traditional Engineer's bunk at the bottom of the three.

ooOoo

1630 Sunday 21 October

John and Toby came to, overcome by the wonderful aroma of fresh baking. Tea was laid out on the wardroom table and the source of the aroma was a large fruit cake being cut by the leading steward. It wasn't long before the full team was assembled to devour the cake. In typical male fashion their friendly banter soon turned to work and the options for the programme while on passage up the west coast to Faslane. In two hours the boat would be entering the operating areas off Plymouth. The alternatives for the deep dive were reasonably simple, being dependent on the depth available. To cut the overly long discussion short the CO and John eventually decided to do it early in the deep water off Falmouth, rather than delay and be forced to avoid the heavier surface traffic in the Irish Sea. So much for a quiet Sunday on surface passage, let alone the one which should have been spent at home cuddled up in front of the fire.

ooOoo

2000 Sunday 21 October

Orca dived again at 2000 and, as a result of the earlier trim dive, quickly caught the trim and settled quietly back up at periscope depth. John and the engineers had gathered the mass of deep dive forms together in the control room and after a short broadcast explaining the routine, had them sent out to each compartment. A deep dive is an annual routine, not that exciting but it does get the juices flowing. The boat is taken down from two hundred feet in hundred foot steps to full diving depth. At each level all the compartments and specific hull valves and systems are monitored. It is fairly straightforward, given that the hull and the systems are designed to two and a half times full diving depth. However, small leaks are invariably found, particularly where bearings are worn on the shafts and periscopes, even, on occasions, on the pumps and valves in the sea water services.

Toby made his way back aft to the Motor Room to join the Polto and his team as they settled at two hundred feet for the first set of readings. It wasn't an involved procedure, each team basically followed a check off list, mainly checking for leaks but also for Toby's team a series of electrical earth readings, and then each compartment reported in turn to the Control Room before going down another hundred feet to repeat the procedure. The only light hearted element was the watch Leading Hand's own depth calculator. He had strung up a length of twine attached to fittings diametrically opposite each other on the pressure hull, pulled it taught across the compartment, and hung a small cuddly smiling monkey from it. Initially the monkey was way up in the deck head, but as they went deeper so the string sagged and gradually the ghastly grin came closer into view. A very visible reminder to them all of the how much the pressure hull gets squeezed by the increased pressure with depth.

After a number of iterations they at last reached full diving depth. To date there had been no real problems only weeps from a couple of valves and a thermometer pocket on the after services cooling system to the port electric main motor. At this stage, partly for their own satisfaction and to ensure that they both had a good feel for their systems, the Polto and Toby personally took up the check sheets and went down below. They clambered down into the lower motor room and started a slow and thorough inspection of all the equipment and systems. It was balls-aching but worth it.

Despite being three years into her commission the boat was in pretty good condition. After checking the main systems Toby called up for the duty LEM in the Motor Room to take a final set of insulation readings for both main motors as they often varied significantly with depth. The routine measurements were taken either on the surface or at two hundred feet, so this series at hundred foot intervals was somewhat special.

.... Unaware that his world was about to literally blow up in his face Toby turned to squeeze past the 400 Hz machine and noticed the missing cover....

ooOoo

2230 Sunday 21 October

The lively discussion around the Wardroom table brought Toby back from his deep slumber. He turned over in his sleeping bag, got stuck half way and realised that his head was still thumping. Gradually the catalogue of events and the dramatic culmination sorted itself out in his mind and he became aware of the discussion going on in the wardroom. Dried out and back in the land of the living he climbed down from his pit and joined the assembly gathered around the wardroom table. As he sat down to warm words of concern, and with a large mug of tea thrust into his hand, John began to explain to them all what had happened.

In fact the Polto had been on the ball from the first bang. It turned out that the thermometer pocket which had been weeping had been suddenly blown out like a one inch diameter bullet across the compartment. The sound of shrapnel had been the brass pocket ricocheting around the lower level. Being further from the blow out, and realising what it must have been, the *Polto* had quickly informed the Control Room of the flooding and then shut the *after services* inlet hull valve. However, not being able to get past the water jet coming out of the pipe, he had had to get Toby focused and then up and moving to shut the outlet valve. Success on all counts, he had been outstanding and Toby was the first to tell the Wardroom so.

So much for a quiet Sunday. Let alone one where PO "Dusty" Miller had only been given four hours notice to go off with a strange crew! Toby said a quiet prayer for the quality of people it was his privilege to work with.

In good humour the XO said he would let Toby off any watch overnight, which was something of a back-handed compliment as they were staying on the surface and the only surface watches Toby ever did were Film Night ones, as a kindness to the Seaman watchkeepers.

After these asides John continued his brief. Everyone assumed that repairing the pipe, or replacing the thermometer pocket, was beyond their resources until they were back alongside with full workshops support. Or so they all thought. Continuing, with most of the gathering losing interest, John then came up with the term "Pot Mender's Weld".

"Whatever's that John?" said the CO.

"It is very simple really. Do you remember how itinerant traders of pots and pans used to effect their repairs? No. Well, in repairing a hole all they usually did was to plug it with a nut and bolt, using a lead washer to achieve the seal. I propose to do the same on the after services."

"Are you serious?" said the CO.

"I most certainly am. The Outside Wrecker is doing it now and we hope to have it back fitted within the half hour. All we'll lose then is the ability to take temperature readings, and we'll have no limitations on use of the port main electrical motor."

"That is almost unbelievable! Yet, because it's you John, I do believe it." said the CO "What about testing?"

"I suggest we continue on the surface overnight, and then I can see if it is holding. If it still looks good tomorrow we can test it dived. That way we will not lose

Passage Routine at its best

passage time and will be able to keep all our options open. It also gives me time to see if the rest of the Deep Dive was OK"

"Fine John. Well done, full marks for ingenuity. In that case let's stay up top, set Passage Routine, and continue around the Lizard and Land's End and up into the Irish Sea."

ooOoo

0945 Monday 22 October

To cut a long story short the Pot Menders Weld worked a treat, and the crew found themselves with St David's coming up fast on the starboard side as the dawn started to break. They staggered out of their pits the following morning, fighting fit, and ready to tackle another of those submarine breakfasts - what better way to start another day serving the Queen.

With the probable need to repeat elements of the deep dive once a formal repair of the offending pipe had been completed the CO decided to stay on the surface up through the Irish Sea and get ahead of their planned passage. The weather was pretty reasonable with the wind no more than force 3 to 4, no white horses and little water coming over the casing. There was even some sunshine. So full of the joys of spring John announced that the Outside Wrecker's team would attempt to resolve the blocked heads scenario during the forenoon.

A young stoker called Frensham had been volunteered for the job. Everyone's guess was that he was the only viable member of the Outside Staff, being small and wiry, and thus able to get into and manoeuvre in the tight space once inside the tank. They got him rigged up in a full dry diving suit with the smallest air set they had, fed by an external air source. Fortunately Frensham was a qualified diver so there were no unwarranted risks there. Once he was rigged up John got on the main broadcast and warned the ship's company of what they were about to do ...and of the impending stench that was about to envelope their small, fully contained little world. The standard routine even on the surface was to use the snort system to feed air to the diesels. Unless they ran "shut down" (during bad weather with the hatch up into the fin shut) it created an enormous draft that swept through the boat. Indeed, given the circumstances a draft was just what they wanted, and the bigger the better.

It took the Outside Wrecker and his staff at least twenty minutes to get the top off the tank. By the time that had been achieved some of the crew were already gagging as the appalling aroma penetrated even the most distant corners. Given the integrated ventilation system there was nowhere to escape it. Frensham managed to enter the tank, not without difficulty, and albeit slipping and sliding on the contents, was soon exploring the depths of that unmentionable space. He came back up ten minutes later and with some difficulty (he understandably refused to take his mask off) made his requirements clear by shouting before disappearing back into those murky depths. Those close enough to endure the smell soon heard bangings and crashings and wondered what the hell he was doing. After a few minutes Toby, feeling personally responsible for the whole episode, could endure it no longer and disappeared back aft where the draft to the diesels was strongest and he could at least breathe.

The activity took almost half an hour and then the poor lad emerged. He was literally covered in shit! Those closest were having a bad time but John had prepared for the worst and had a hose rigged up to wash him down. Eventually an air of normality returned, the tank top was replaced and sealed, and John brought the small team forward to reward them with some refreshments in the wardroom.

Toby and the XO were already there having a late morning coffee when John brought them in. Frensham understandably looked pretty pale, and the others had clearly been throwing up. John sat them down and grabbed a bottle of the best Grouse, pouring stiff measures all round. At last with some colour returning to their cheeks Toby could wait no longer and asked the question all of them wanted answering.

"John what was the problem and have you managed to fix it? How come all the banging and crashing?"

"Well Toby, you will be relieved to know that you were not totally responsible. The problem, however, was only with trap one, our wardroom heads, and it had clearly been coming for some time, in fact you could say it had been building up over the last three years."

"Go on"

"It was a frigging stalagmite! The damn thing had built up so much that it was actually blocking the outlet from the trap down into the tank. It was absolutely rock solid and Frensham had to attack it with hammers and chisels to break it up!"

"It must be the quality of shit produced in the Wardroom" added the Outside Wrecker, chancing his arm while quickly downing his large Grouse whisky.

"Oh, no" said the XO "It's those bloody breakfasts - too much "Shit on a Raft!"

PLAYING POSSUM

Missing Life in Submarines?

Lesson 2 on recapturing the old days:-

Set your alarm clock to go off at random times through the night. When it goes off, leap out of bed, get dressed as fast as you can then run out into the garden and break out the garden hose for the fire exercise.

0525 Tuesday 23 October

Bridge watch-keeping was normally the province of the Seamen Officers. HMS Orca was rather unusual in that John and Toby, despite being Engineers, had both qualified and gained Bridge Watch-keeping tickets during their time on board. Nonetheless, they kept their independence as department heads alongside the XO, and only undertook watches as favours when it didn't impact their other duties. In this way the Seamen Officers could occasionally have a break as a group, eat together and take in the odd evening movie. In reality John and Toby would volunteer for a watch when they actually wanted to enjoy being up top, alone on the small bridge at the top of the fin with the world to themselves. This was one of those occasions.

The west coast of Scotland is pretty dramatic; it is especially so from the sea, and the outstanding scenery starts much further south than many realise. On their occasional visits to Faslane it had become Toby's habit to take the surface watch as they entered the outer Clyde, knowing the area rather well from his sailing experience. He had taken over at 0400, it was now coming up to 0530 and had just finished a cup of *Kai*. Although initially warming his hands, it had gone cold by the time he had finished the last dregs. The sun was now just making an appearance with the Mull of Kintyre to port and Ailsa Craig some six or so miles ahead. Gannets were whirling around everywhere, frenetically diving for breakfast. The noise was fantastic. You definitely got the impression that this was not just eating to live, it was fun and the birds were having the time of their lives. His companion was a young Able Seaman called Tomlinson. He and Toby had got to know each other during many such watches. To his surprise and delight Toby had discovered that Tomlinson was quite a Twitcher. It all started in a somewhat embarrassing way. Late one evening off Norway with the two of them alone on the bridge, Toby had referred to the vast numbers of "Shite Hawks" around that evening, particularly those following the trawler close on the starboard side. Tomlinson's response had been polite but firm, "Those aren't Shite Hawks, Sir. They are an unusual mixture of Fulmars and Kittiwakes, with the odd Gannet."

So started Toby's long term course in practical Ornithology. Despite his age, Tomlinson was only eighteen, he was a good and very enthusiastic teacher. Over the last year Toby had volunteered for the watches on the bridge when Tomlinson had been on duty and as a result had enjoyed some dramatic times around the UK and European coast, particularly Norway.

Around them there were a number of small fishing boats taking advantage of the good weather to capture quite a harvest from the shoals that had gathered in the relative shelter of the outer Clyde estuary. Each was being mobbed by its own flock of gulls and gannets. As the sun rose Ailsa Craig began to glow a deep red, within which you could see the continual movement of the thousands of gannets, manically shrieking with the delights of a new day. The false light had turned them all pink as if they had been gorging all night on flamingo soup.

As they passed abeam the stunning backdrop of the hills and mountains of South Argyll started to come into view. Breaking from his trance Toby noted that the first morning ferry across to Broddick on Arran was going to come rather close - and ferries altered for no-one. After a small alteration to starboard and a wave to those on

Ailsa Craig from the South

the bridge to make light of the potential problem, the pair's senses were quickly diverted by the smell of bacon sandwiches wafting up through the tower. Fortunately the watch below had kindly seen their need as primary and a great plate of grilled bacon rolls appeared, together with large mugs of trencherman's tea. A meal fit for a king, together with a view second to none. Life couldn't get much better.

As it turned 0600 it was clear that the world was starting to wake up. Goat Fell on Arran was standing up proud abeam and Toby took a fix to ensure they were right on track. Given his sailing experience he knew the area rather well, and had spent some great week-ends in the waters around Bute exploring the Burnt Isles and the passage up the East Kyle to Tighnabruaich. He had even seen shoals of basking sharks up there. As a result the CO accepted him taking them up the Clyde and even through the Cumbraes, without closing up Special Sea Duty men, providing it wasn't too busy. At the very least it gave the Seamen lads an extra hour in their pits. Finally Toward Point was approaching and he got the plot to call up the CO and give him their position, together with the request to close up the *SSD* team.

As ever, most were up and ready. The CO and the Navigator arrived on the bridge within ten minutes and having turned over the watch Toby repaired below to get ready for a busy morning alongside in Faslane, with every probability of the afternoon alongside the armament depot at Coulport in Loch Long to collect the four fish they had missed in Gosport.

ooOoo

0700 Tuesday 23 October

They were soon past Gourock and turning north to enter the Gareloch. With the attractive town of Helensburgh spanning the northern side of the entrance to the Loch, they negotiated Rhu Narrows and saw the Faslane Naval Base appear on the north eastern side. It had been some years since the Submarine Depot ship had finally departed. The Base was definitely growing, with the added impetus of the additional squadron of four Polaris submarines. Cranes were everywhere as the building works continued apace. To the north was the old breaker's yard and you could still see the great gun mountings lying on the jetty which they had taken from the old battleship Vanguard. She had been up here for some time and had understandably taken some years to break up. Another old legend departing for good.

With ten minutes to go before they tied up alongside John and Toby took up their traditional tasks - setting up the bar. As with the departures, arrivals had their own tradition in submarines. A visiting boat, however small, could expect all the base VIPs onboard as soon as it got alongside, and first impressions were always gained on two things; the manner and professionalism of coming alongside (i.e. not scratching the paint), and the hospitality in the Wardroom ...hence the bar. John and Toby laid out their finest single malts and the leading steward brought in a fresh plate of bacon wedges. It looked pretty good.

The first down was Captain SM3, leader of the Third Submarine Squadron, escorted by the CO who had met him on the casing. John and Toby were warmly greeted by name and the CO was soon being thanked for sailing early and helping out the team up north.

It always came as a surprise to Toby that submariners all seemed to know each other. With the squadrons spread around Faslane, Devonport, Gosport in the UK, and the few boats still left in Singapore and Halifax, all seemed to be of one company. The total number of submariners was less than six thousand, with no more than six hundred being officers - about the size of an army regiment - which meant knowing your compatriots was quite feasible.

It was still dark and quite cool in the early morning air, but staying dry to the relief of the crew working up top. Faslane and the surrounding area is very rich and green, but only because it can sometimes rain there for around 300 days in every year. Most of the visitors had not yet had breakfast so the regal mix of coffee, single malts and bacon wedges was going down rather well. Having tied the boat up and organized the brow and casing access, the XO left the casing to the TASO and hurried down into the wardroom to warmly greet Captain SM and his team.

"Hello, Sir. It's a grand morning, what have we done to deserve being granted a berth behind Repulse, one of the new *bombers*? And why has she got that weird paint scheme? Did you see her Toby, she looks as if a flight deck has been painted on her rear end."

Captain SM turned to the boss with a grin on his face. "James it's probably time for me to come clean to your team and let them know the real reason for their short notice deployment from Gosport. Gentlemen, we've brought you up here for a rather special exercise in which Orca is going to be the focus. Some of you may be aware that with the addition of the Polaris boats we gained a bonus from their size in that they are large enough to act as Motherships to the USN's *DSRV* or Deep Submersion Rescue Vessel. This beast is a mini rescue submarine which resides in San Diego, but weighing only 50 tonnes, is able to be flown around the world in a USAF Galaxy aircraft. Well it arrives in Glasgow at mid-day and you are the ones we are going to rescue!"

At this point his deputy Alastair Cameron, Commander SM, took up the brief. "We are going to deploy you at 1800 tomorrow evening and get you to settle on the bottom of the deep trench just north of Arran. Given the fishing boat activity we'll have a safety boat in attendance at all times. This isn't that artificial as in a real situation there would be a number of surface craft in attendance. Once settled on the bottom we will get you to release one of your escape buoys. The radio signal from this will be the initiator of the exercise. The DSRV will arrive later today - it's so large that we cannot allow the Galaxy aircraft to sit on any part of the airport at Glasgow for more than 20 minutes before we offload it or the Galaxy will sink into the tarmac. Then it gets transferred here creating havoc on the road by going the wrong way around most of the roundabouts. Once it arrives we have one of the only six 200 tonne mobile cranes in the UK to transfer it onto the back of Repulse. It goes into a cage sat in the middle of the aft casing, or flight deck as Peter so quickly termed it. The modifications were fitted during Repulse's recent refit so she is our first boat capable of being a Mothership. She will then deploy to the outer Clyde areas and release the DSRV from a depth of about 250 feet. The Water is pretty good there so she should have a fair amount of room to manoeuvre if needed. Our intent then is to conduct four rescue transfers. There are a number of other details but my team will fill you in on all these tomorrow forenoon at a brief in the squadron operations room. We will only be using your for'd escape hatch and there is a jazzy paint scheme like Repulse's for you to put on just to help those US Navy guys, who are frankly only used to the clear waters of the Pacific off San Diego. This is their first visit to Europe." Commander SM finished his one man brief.

"So there you are Gentlemen, all you are being asked to do is play possum for a couple of days. You can even watch the odd movie and make all the noise you want to help them find you" added Captain SM. "The most arduous part of the exercise will be the party onboard Repulse tonight. Once we are finished, then you will be free to go up to Raasay and continue your fun on the torpedo ranges."

"Will any of our lads get a ride in it Sir?" asked John

"Oh most definitely, after all you are the ones being rescued." continued Commander SM. "I think she can carry up to twenty four but they may reduce that for exercise comfort and safety. We will let you fill half the places and I suggest you plan on a dozen lads for each trip. The remainder will be taken by our experts from the Submarine Escape Tank at Dolphin, and some of their US counterparts"

Peter was clearly excited: "The lads will be queuing up - I'd better set up a draw this for this evening so those involved will know before we sail. Presumably we will have a number of riders from the Dolphin team so I'd like to leave a few ashore, that is if any want to miss the fun."

"Peter, we are getting down to the detail, I suggest you and your TASO come ashore with me and we can go over everything you need to do today. The others can then come to the formal combined briefing later. Many thanks for the hearty Scottish breakfast, I think we had better leave you in peace, you'll have much to do now you know the real plan." He turned to Captain SM, "Come on Sir, I'll see you back to the morning brief in the Ops Room."

With that farewell, Captain and Commander SM were escorted off the boat and Orca's Wardroom settled down to finish breakfast and come to terms with the new plan.

ooOoo

0945 Tuesday 23 October

"This is more like a bloody Op Order, Sir, than a paint scheme" coughed "Half the Price", the Second Cox'n, after being given a very impressive folder by the TASO. "Lots of Go Faster stripes and Keep Off signs would be just as good!"

"Don't get cynical Second, we've got to help them find the for'd escape hatch and ensure that they don't bump into the fin. I know it appears somewhat artificial, but this is the first time they've operated with us, and it will be pretty murky down there." responded TASO

The casing team had stretched out significant lengths of masking tape, and were setting to with a will applying vast quantities of white paint. After a couple of hours the fruits of their labour were soon becoming evident as indicated by lots of white stripes but as yet no clear pattern. Having been dulled by their normal painting scheme, namely the application of pusser's black on all parts of the casing, hull, and fittings, this unusual opportunity gave them a welcome freedom. In fact they were soon acting like a group of budding Renoirs, progressing the job but leaving vital sections to the end, so that the final scheme only became apparent as they added the last flourishes.

As a finale, having carefully removed all the masking tape, they assembled to show Orca in her new glory, and to have their efforts recorded on film. The overall final image was further enhanced by the physical presence of this team of rogues whose overalls were embossed with liberal quantities of white paint, topped with faces wreathed in impish grins, and much ribaldry. Definitely photogenic, and very fetching.

A final personal touch, purposefully orchestrated by the Second Cox'n after the photo, was the addition of a skull and cross bones above a Keep Off sign on the back of the fin. TASO, somewhat bravely decided to leave it, but had left out a pot of black paint to cover it over in case it was seen as a step too far by the XO. In the event he need not have worried, both the XO and CO laughed it off in the spirit of the exercise and it remained. Probably just as well, as events turned out.

ooOoo

1530 Tuesday 23 October

That afternoon Toby managed to create some excitement with the lads in the Motor Room by exchanging their somewhat B list of movies for half a dozen of the latest releases on the basis that Orca was the focus of a very important exercise. The stowage of these and additional victuals for the extra riders gave an air of anticipation. It came to a head when the XO conducted the draw for those who were to be "rescued" via the DSRV. Lots of excitement, and to his stunned surprise Toby's name was one of those to come out of the hat.

With inquisitive thoughts as to what it would be like, he gathered up his wash gear and at sea "Run Ashore" plain clothes outfit, and trundled through HMS Neptune to the shore base Wardroom. Those in conventional submarines were always treated to accommodation ashore whenever they tied up alongside, because normal life on board was so frugal. No one in their right minds would live in an oily sardine tin. The officers lived in an enlarged cupboard, and that was the luxury accommodation. Showers were forbidden, although they were allowed to cover themselves in talcum powder, or foo foo powder as they called it, in lieu. Their run ashore clothes may well have looked very fetching, but the down side was they stank of diesel. It permeated everywhere. In a previous trip to Faslane where he had been the Part III Officer trainee on another conventional boat for only three weeks, Toby had returned south on the Inter City train from Glasgow. Fortunately he had found an empty first class compartment well before its leaving time. As he sat there, one passenger after another came in and joined him and then left within a few minutes. At first he did not realise why, then it gradually dawned on him that his personal diesel cologne was the problem. It turned out to be a blessing. He had been exhausted by the extra effort needed as a trainee on board and, being shattered, had been able to lay flat out and get a good kip as the sole occupant the whole way, despite the numbers bulging outside in the corridor.

ooOoo

1830 Tuesday 23 October

Toby was soon enjoying the luxury of a proper shower with plenty of hot water and soap suds everywhere. He flattered himself that he scrubbed up rather well, and wandered down to the bar to meet John before they both set off for Repulse and the party. Faslane was the home at this time to the Third and Tenth Submarine Squadrons. The Tenth being the new Polaris Missile Submarines of the Resolution class or bombers as they were called and the Third being a mix of some Porpoise, and Oberon Class conventional submarines and the early Nuclear Hunter/Killers. So they were quite used to "eau de diesel" from the likes of John and Toby in the wardroom living quarters.

John was already in the bar and had obviously downed his first pint. Rather than joining him for another he willingly accepted Toby's suggestion of going on straight away to the party. Toby had never really come to terms with the ghastly taste of English beer, nor for that matter the lagers that were coming out of the continent. His early time in the West Indies had led him down quite a different path. His drinks had to taste good, and look good – a rum base lifted their appeal; add an umbrella and extraneous fruit, and the scene was set for a drink to savour. Not like a pint which he saw as being downed quickly to avoid the taste buds being polluted. Knowing Toby's humble tastes John realised that Toby would be much happier at the Cocktail Party compromising with a "Horse's Neck" or some other Naval favourite, so they set off through the Naval Base.

On passing through the security gate they caught up with a number of the Squadron Engineers who were escorting a team of US Naval Officers, clearly those that had come over in the USAF Galaxy with the DSRV. To be fair they were suffering a bit from jet lag, but were making a great effort to join in.

Crossing the brow they got a sense of just how big Repulse was. They were ushered down the fore hatch and passed aft along the main thoroughfare. It was a pretty sizeable passage where you could actually stand upright and walk side by side - something hitherto unknown in submarines. The infectious hum from the party enveloped them as they reached the Wardroom, but they were directed onwards into the Control Room where a somewhat larger variant of the typical Royal Naval Submarine party spread out before them.

The navigation plotting tables were decked out with drinks and canapes, and the excited revellers were entwined around the lowered periscopes. Some of the older guests were seated on the watchkeeping position seats, and the glamorous wives and girlfriends had added to the Trim Panel by hanging their chic hand bags from the control valves. It looked like the makings of a great party.

Toby soon found himself, Horse's Neck in hand, talking to a Lieutenant from the US Naval team. His name was Rich Hallbrook, and he was one of the DSRV pilots – a term which flattered the maneuverability of the DSRV.

"Toby this is something else! You guys certainly know how to live. We have some great parties on the base back home, but the idea of allowing them afloat, let alone in a "Boomer" with its nuclear missiles just the other side of that bulkhead, is off the wall."

At this point the wife of the home team's XO, having overheard his remarks joined in: "You don't want to be fooled by all that serious nonsense. Remember we are a relatively poor country and couldn't possibly afford all those missiles. My neighbour's understanding is that all we've done is to buy one outfit of missiles which the crews onload, and then before deploying they go into Coulport again and take most of them off. After all they've got to store all that beer for the patrols somewhere. This lady lives on the edge of Loch Long opposite the armament depot and assures me that's what they do!"

He looked at her and really could not believe what he was hearing. Clearly XO's wives did not utter such subversive ideas at home. She was starting to respond and explain that her neighbour was getting confused with the movement of the missile stowage liners used to outload the missiles, when she suddenly cried out, threw her gin and tonic all over him, and rushed off with a pained expression on her face.

"Toby what did I say for her to do that?"

Toby was as stunned as he was, and helping him to wipe down his dribbling jacket made it clear that he had no idea. "Rich, I think we need to ask her. Hang on here and dry yourself off with this, and I'll be back."

Looking around, the Control Room was pretty well packed by now, and Toby couldn't see any sign of her so he pushed his way out to the Wardroom and there she was berating Repulse's Engineer.

"Vic, don't you dare do anything like that again. Just behave for once and take that stupid grin off your face."

At this point she saw me, came over, and apologized, asking how the American guest was.

"Rather soggy," I replied "But at least it was a G and T so it won't stain."

"I'm so sorry, it was that bloody Engineer (excuse my French). He snuck up behind me and pinched my bum just as I was about to say I didn't believe my neighbour. He caught me unawares and I ended up jumping out of my skin and depositing my drink all over the poor man. Where is he? I must go back and apologise".

So saying she returned and the last Toby saw of them was a relieved US Navy Lieutenant laughing out loud …and hitting his head on a low pipe … forcing a guilty lady to screech with mirth at his further misfortune. They were now fully in the swing and it would be a party neither would forget.

A number of Horse's Necks later, Toby was cornered by John and Peter and told that they were all off to a little Italian Place at the head of the Loch affectionately known as Disgusto's. Its' real name was Augusto's. The proprietor was an Italian who had married a Scottish lady and settled up there. His party trick was to overtly seduce each and every lady who entered his establishment, falling madly in love with large and small, young and old. It was a good party piece, complemented by some excellent Italian food. They all had a good night and staggered back to their cabins ashore well fed and watered.

ooOoo

0745 Wednesday 24 October

Despite somewhat foggy heads they were all up early the next morning, and gathered over a full Scottish breakfast of Arbroath Smokies and oatcakes with lots of coffee. Rich and his team joined them and full of the best of Scottish breakfasts were then led across the base to the Squadron Offices for the joint brief. More coffee and introductions to both the crowd from Repulse and the guys from the Escape Tank down in HMS Dolphin completed the gathering of the exercise members.

The brief was somewhat detailed and went on for a couple of hours with presentations from each of the players and then the Squadron summed it up with a timetable of the planned events. In simple terms the exercise was emulating a real scenario as far as possible, subject to proving the technical capability in a safe manner and ensuring that everyone learnt as much as possible.

The role of the DSRV was to provide a quick reaction worldwide submarine rescue service independent of weather down to 2000 feet, although the beast itself could go much deeper to about 5000 feet. As explained earlier it was normally delivered in a USAF Galaxy to the nearest airport and thereafter transported to the Mother Submarine to be installed on the after cradle. The Mother Submarine then piggybacked the DSRV to the accident site, for the beast itself to implement the rescue of the crew from the stricken boat. As the DSRV descended to the disabled submarine it would use its' sonar to detect the stricken vessel's distress pingers. It was also able to view the fin of small boats through its large thick glass windows illuminated by some strong underwater lights from about 50 yards under good conditions. The goal was then to achieve voice communications via the

DSRV Avalon being loaded onto HMS REPULSE

emergency underwater telephones. Once achieved it would position itself over the directed escape hatch and pump out the water thereby providing a strong watertight seal enabling the crew to escape and transfer into the after hulls. After some trimming to allow for the extra weight, the DSRV then made the return trip to the Mother Submarine. The whole transfer being conducted with all three vessels underwater, allowing several trips in any probable emergency scenario.

Well, that was the game plan!

ooOoo

1730 Wednesday 24 October.

After questions and a short discussion they made their farewells and returned to Orca. As the initiating distress Submarine it was up to them to get the show on the road and to be frank, they were looking forward to the unusual and somewhat unique role. Once on board the XO took the Second Cox'n on a tour of the casing to ensure that all protective plates and covers were securely in place. Given the nature of the exercise they had fitted special safety covers over most hull fittings to ensure that the planned exercise had no chance of turning into a real event. Bottoming a boat can be dodgy at the best of times, but adding a submarine "mating" exercise created an extra level of risk. The Second Cox'n reported that all was well, and as the extra riders from the Submarine Escape School had all made their way on board, they were soon singling up.

In their traditional manner John and Toby fell in on the casing to greet the CO, who acknowledged their reports, and made his way up to the bridge. They set off on time at 1800 and made their way out of the Gare Loch with the Tug Archer as escort. It was a clear evening and they were soon past Rhu narrows, turning to the West into the outer Clyde. Although they were at Special Sea Duty men, almost all the crew were informally closed up for the short passage, eagerly awaiting Diving Stations and the bottoming drill in the Arran trench. Some years ago bottoming had been a regular feature of life in conventional submarines, but these days it was pretty rare. Only a handful of those onboard had experienced it before, John had, but Toby certainly had not, and they both knew the CO hadn't done one during his time in command.

Orca slowed and turned NW above Arran, dispatching the safety tug to clear a small fisherman from the area. She soon dived, sorted out the trim at periscope depth and after a couple of runs up and down the trench, to get a feel of the depth and ensure that they were positioned correctly, she made her way down into the depths of the trench. A meaningfully slow affair so that she would stay aligned to the grounding spot ahead in the deep trench.

With everyone closed up in the Control Room the CO ordered them down to 200 feet, with the XO maintaining as close to a stop trim as he could. Bottoming had to be gentle, and it was best achieved by having a bow down attitude carefully controlled by managing the water in Q tank.

"*XO take us down to 300 feet, and keep 5 degrees bow down.*" ordered the CO.

No one was breathing. They were all waiting for that bump.

It came surprisingly quickly and was more of a prolonged thud, with a bit of a sludgy slide on the sandy bottom.

"*Stop Engines, flood 400 gallons to O's*"

Silence enveloped the boat and as it gently settled on the bottom they all started to breathe again. After a pause of what seemed like a minute she suddenly tilted over to starboard, eventually stopping at about 15 degrees. Finally, with no more movement or groans, they all relaxed and came to terms with the reality of the exercise.

A controlled evolution? Yes, but still pretty hairy, not something any of them would wish to do on a regular basis. God knows what the realities of a genuine accident would be like. Fortunately for the RN, it had been some decades since the last boat had gone down (apart from the HMS Artemis incident alongside in Dolphin). Although there were still serving members who had been in a few close calls.

As directed, they let go their for'd escape buoy, hoping that the checks they had conducted during the maintenance period would ensure that it did its stuff. The buoys were notorious for failing such tests. There was no way of telling whether it had successfully erected its aerial once on the surface and had started the series of transmissions which would initiate the exercise. Only then would the frenetic activity start with Repulse getting underway, the DSRV piggy-backing on her rear end awaiting its special role.

Unbeknown to the crew, the ball had been set rolling successfully and awaiting all the excitement, they settled down and closed up to a variant of watch diving. This meant reducing all the internal machinery to a minimal load on the batteries that would allow them to sustain sufficient power for the exercise plus a margin for any real emergency. It resulted in an atmosphere which although comfortable, would soon become increasingly warm and close. The crew quietly settled down to their evening meal enjoying the enforced relaxation, augmented by an after-ends film show of the first of the special movies Toby had managed to purloin from the Tenth Submarine Squadron.

Watching a movie in the Wardroom was somewhat different. Imagine six of them sitting in a cupboard with a full size Bell and Howells projector whirling away, projecting its image over the vast distance of four feet to provide a screen size of twelve by eighteen inches. Really atmospheric! Given the lack of space, one specially chosen member of the audience was allowed the extra excitement of sitting on the speaker ... providing a full interactive buttock massage totally in tune with the sound track. Very few lasted a full movie, and none were able to enjoy a beer without some spillage. At least these specially chosen movies had reasonable plots and were credible entertainment. Their last patrol had been a bit of a challenge movie-wise. They had had three where the wardroom had come to the end of the second reel (with another to go) when the credits appeared and no-one had noticed any discernable change in the plot. Being Film Officer, Toby had been on a hiding to nothing from the whole crew. In the wardroom he had the additional burden of having to expound the plots of the most interesting films to a pretty drongo audience, whose mental qualities made you wonder how they had passed through Dartmouth. Although to be fair, perhaps it had more to do with their exhaustion factor and a sleep routine whereby they worked two hours on watch and four off for up to five weeks when dived at sea. The average period asleep ended up being about three and a half hours. At such times they all lived on the edge, relying on an adrenalin rush to get them to react in any emergency.

But this film was a good one. Raising their moral with a half of bitter - freshly drawn from the chief's mess bar - they settled down to await the frenetic activity playing out above them as a result of the escape buoy's transmissions. If all went well they would also get a few hours in their pits before the action started.

ooOoo

2230 Wednesday 24 October

But it was not to be a quiet night.

The film had only just finished when they all heard (or perhaps one could say felt) transmissions from the Underwater Telephone through the hull. Hastening into the control room Peter and Toby could hear their call sign coming over from the UWT speaker. It was being repeated over and over by a rather anxious voice playing out his role for real. They had the script ready, but rather than using the normal operational UWT they responded via the emergency set in the fore ends weapon stowage compartment - amongst the outfit of torpedoes. The response went as follows:

"This is Orca, Orca, Orca. Major flooding in after section and control room. Party of fifteen survivors in fore-ends. Emergency CO2 scrubbers operational but only eight refills left. O2 burner operational with five candles remaining. Compartment pressure slowly increasing. Estimate compartment habitable for twelve more hours when will attempt compartment flood and emergency escape"

It sounded pretty real!

It was at this stage that they realised that the UWT transmissions were not, as thought, from the exercise tug but from Repulse herself. She made it clear that the DSRV would be deployed within the next couple of hours and they would be kept continuously updated on progress and the steps they should take to prepare for its arrival.

Clearing away the projector, those off watch sat around the wardroom table and over a pot of coffee discussed the events unfolding above them. Their best guess was that Repulse had positioned herself to the east of Arran where she had enough water to stay comfortably at about three hundred feet. That gave her the room to deploy her piggy backed mate into the murky depths. Her role was the Mothership, available to launch and recover the DSRV as it either rescued bodies and or supplied escape stores for those still left onboard. Not an easy evolution as the DSRV was supported by four pylons and sat on a metal skirt around the after escape hatch.

This would be the route in and out for people, stores, and if the event became prolonged, the cables for essential re-charging of her batteries.

ooOoo

2330 Wednesday 24 October

After about forty minutes the UWT transmissions started again. This time to inform Orca that the DSRV had been deployed and would be taking over the communications UWT link.

Sure enough, five minutes later a distinctly American voice began transmitting:

"Orca, Orca, this is the Avalon. Am circling you to assess best approach. Do you read me? Over."

"Avalon this is Orca we read you loud and clear. Have turned on distress pinger. Will await your instructions"

Having read up all the technical details of the DSRV they realised that at this stage the DSRV would be using their sonar to locate the emergency pinger to establish the best path before mating. For the close quarters stuff they relied on a visual approach looking through the major glass panels under the glare of four powerful floodlights. In theory the DSRV should be able to detect the fin of the distress submarine from at least fifty yards. From what Rich had told them at the party it was a very maneuverable beast, could turn on a sixpence and had excellent depth control.

More transmissions told those in the Control Room that the DSRV had located the for'd escape hatch seat and were about to land on the casing. That surprised Orca as it was still very quiet. Given the way any noise easily passes through the pressure hull from surface vessels passing close, they thought that they would have

DSRV Avalon in "Home Waters"

heard the DSRV's motors by now. They concluded that the electric motors made her very quiet and hoped that their paint scheme would stop her bumping into the fin.

"Orca, Orca, have mated to your forward escape hatch. Am draining down the mating skirt. Stand by to drain your upper hatch cavity."

Each member of the crew was on tenterhooks, this was exciting stuff. The first underwater transfer between US and UK submarines - the sort of thing to tell your grand children. The guys in the fore ends were all closed up and awaiting instructions with the first "escapees" ready and mustered in the passage flat just outside the fore ends. They waited for the order to drain, and waited, and waited, until finally they began to wonder if something had gone wrong. Perhaps they should have responded before. An urgent re-look at the Op Order showed that they had followed the script and done their part. What was it?

After some twenty minutes of pregnant silence the UWT burst into life again:

"*Orca, Orca, have minor failure. Must make immediate return to Mo ship. Will recharge batteries and return soonest.*"

Nonplussed they had no idea what had happened; but were concerned that no significant problem would put paid to the exercise. Given Orca's position they had no alternative but to be patient, sit tight, and await their fate. The idea of another movie did not appeal and the general consensus was that pit time would be the most sensible thing. So reverting to a diluted watch diving routine they all settled down in their bunks ...waiting somewhat less anxiously for the next episode in the rescue saga.

ooOoo

0045 Thursday 25 October

Toby couldn't sleep, and after thirty minutes of tossing and turning, slipped quietly out of his pit. Given the situation he went back to the motor room to check the state of the charge on the batteries and to make an estimate of how long they could remain "playing possum". It was more something to do than an urgent need, as the answer turned out to be several days. At least he would be able to give the CO chapter and verse as he was bound to ask the question yet again once they were all closed up. The team on watch made him a coffee and they talked about the exercise. There was soon quite a gathering as the lads were understandably very interested. As he couldn't answer all the questions Toby went for'd and retrieved the file from the Wardroom which showed photographs of *Avalon*, the DSRV that had come across from the US. The shots were very good and some dramatic pictures showed the pilot's view out through his front screen. The best were from a previous USN exercise, showing the actual mating phase with the disabled submarine. The cockpit was more like that of an aircraft and the package of sensors and controls were pretty impressive. The beasts themselves weighed about just under the fifty tonnes flying weight and were in fact made up of three interconnected spheres which formed the pressure hull, surrounded by a fibre glass outer hull. That came as a surprise, although Jackson, the watch leading hand, did remind them that their casing was also fibre glass. The spheres had hatches for movement of the crew between them, with the for'd one being the control cockpit and the after two being able to accommodate up to twenty four survivors plus two DSRV crew men. Under the centre sphere was a hemispherical skirt and shock system which allowed the mini-sub to mate over the escape trunk and hatch of the disabled submarine. It also confirmed that the propulsion was electric with shrouded propellers and ducted thrusters enabling that impressive maneuverability Rich had spoken about. They now understood why they had not heard anything when the DSRV was coming in to mate. It could also attach itself to boats inclined up to forty-five degrees, so the slight list to starboard was not going to be a problem.

It wasn't just those who had won a place to be rescued in the lottery that were interested. Almost all of them were eager to see the shots, and Toby made a note to tell Peter so that he could put the photographs on the main notice board for the other messes to see.

Eventually the crowd dispersed back to their messes and Toby was about to go himself when he heard (or again felt through the hull) more UWT transmissions.

HMS Repulse with DSRV Avalon

Guessing that Avalon was on her way again Toby made his farewells and scampered through the donk shop back into the control room to catch the end of the message. Yes, she was on her way and the first group of rescuees were being mustered in the fore-ends. He went forward to join them.

ooOoo

0145 Thursday 25 October

They all had their fingers crossed that this run would be successful. The Escape Tank riders and the Second Cox'ns team were ready to man the escape systems, while the escapees bunched themselves on the empty torpedo racks. The excitement level was rising and there was a defined tension in the air.

Jumping out of his skin when the UWT started up again, Toby had failed to realise that he was standing right beside it.

"Orca, Orca, this is Avalon. Approaching from the east. Will circle once and then approach for mating."

"Avalon, this is Orca, message understood. Will await instructions after mate"

You could hear a pin drop. Then to the surprise of the group assembled in the Control Room they started to hear her maneuvering above them. In fact they could actually tell where she was as she passed by on her initial circuit. It faded and then became stronger as she made the final run in. They all held their breath as she closed in, and then clearly moved some way for'd.

"God, I hope she's seen my keep off sign on the fin," muttered the Second Cox'n

With all eyes pointing at the deck head, the noise of her motors slowly came back moving for'd and, without a break in the hum, they heard the additional sound of pumping as she started to clear the water out of her mating skirt.

"Orca this is Avalon. Have successfully mated. Drain your upper escape hatch cavity and report on completion."

This was definitely it. With the eager members from the Escape Tank watching, the Second Cox'ns team did their stuff, and the fore-ends team was soon brought back to earth with a soaking from the salty mist arising from the bilges.

"Avalon this is Orca - hatch drained and free to rotate."

The ladders were in place and as they all stood clear, they witnessed the amazing site of their for'd escape hatch handle turning ... whilst sitting on the bottom! Within seconds the hatch was open and a shadowy figure filled the space uttering an unreal command in a deep southern accent,

"Yo'all ready to come up and join us?"

It was a great leveller, and it brought everyone back to their senses. The assembled escapees started to ascend the ladder, and were soon ensconced in the central sphere. The first pass was going to be a limited number to ensure that any hiccup would put only a few, and all of them experts, at risk.

"*Avalon, Orca. Six men transferred. Escape hatch shut and clipped. Ready for you to flood the skirt.*"

"*Orca, Avalon - flooding now.*"

...and they were away. Almost routine ....but unexpectedly those in Orca could definitely hear them go.

The exercise was based on four rescue trips. Three in rapid succession and then a pause while the routine for re-charging the DSRV batteries was conducted, and then a final pass before the mini fleet returned to Faslane for a formal wash-up and a joint run ashore in Glasgow.

Having had his name come out of the hat Toby was due to go in the next trip and at that moment was soaked to the skin. It was clear that he was going to get soaked again, and couldn't take a change of clothes. The answer lay in shedding his current outfit and donning a dry pair of elegant long johns, a set of number eight fatigues and full foul weather gear with baseball boots in lieu of wellies. It was getting close to dawn and a round trip was only taking an hour, so a large mug of tea later and he was making his way back to the fore-ends.

It was only the second trip and yet everything seemed familiar, almost going like clockwork. She was soon mated and Toby was invited to be the first of their batch to climb up into the sphere. On entry he was met by the crew and immediately ushered through the hatch into the after sphere. As you would expect it was very spartan. When he entered the atmosphere was cold and damp, but cuddling up to another six bodies in a space any normal person would say was only fit for three soon warmed them up. It actually became misty. The loading took less than ten minutes and with Orca's escape hatch shut the pumping started. However, before they lifted there was more activity as the weight of the additional survivors was compensated for by the pumping of more ballast out of the DSRV. From inside Orca this phase had not been appreciated, melding in with the noise of flooding the skirt.

The trip back was more about appreciation of the little boat's motion than having visibility of its control. It was, nonetheless, an experience to savour ...and over all too quickly.

The Mo-Sub mating was the same again, but being in the actual DSRV gave an insight into the delicacy and skill of the pilots in controlling Avalon to very fine tolerances. They did bump a bit, but Toby was certainly not going to criticize them. The entry into Repulse was a new experience. Once onboard they were ushered past the manoeuvring room, through the tunnel over the reactor, along the upper deck of the missile compartment ...it went on forever .... and eventually along their main passage into the wardroom. In all about three times the length of the main arterial passage in Orca.

Awaiting them in the wardroom were the SM10 staff and a fantastic breakfast spread. How the other half lived. The seventy five to eighty five days they spent away on patrols did justify having some special comforts. Toby was ushered to a seat for breakfast alongside their Weapon's Engineer and being of the same cloth became quickly engrossed in talk of his systems.

The bacon and eggs were starting to disappear when the Lieutenant Commander OIC of the Escape Tank came and sat opposite them, having been briefed by Repulse's CO and the USN team in the control room. He looked puzzled and Toby asked him why? Wasn't everything going well?

"Oh yes, we couldn't have had a more successful exercise. My only issue is the rather strange response I got when I enquired after the fault which caused the Avalon to return without mating on the first run. I don't believe it to be an issue but I really didn't get an answer - they seemed to just change the subject."

"Ah," said the WEO. "I can fill you in on that; it's all a bit embarrassing for them. They went off very confidently, found you guys very quickly and were soon reporting locking on. What they were reluctant to tell you was that when they opened the hatch all they saw were three large limpet shells looking at them! They hadn't found you at all … they'd mated onto a large rock bed some four hundred yards to your north. So much for clear water sailors. They were bloody embarrassed and Rich told me very quietly when the others weren't around. I suggest you don't push it further, it could be something they don't want to get back home."

They all looked at each other and burst out laughing. The TASO's paint scheme may well have worked after all, particularly the "Keep Off" sign …perhaps they would never know.

TRAINING, TRAINING, TRAINING

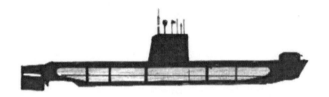

Missing Life in Submarines?

Lesson 3 on recapturing the old days:-

Build a shelf in the top of your wardrobe and sleep on it inside a smelly sleeping bag. Remove the wardrobe door and replace it with a curtain that's too small.

0730 Friday 26 October

After all the excitement "bottomed" in the Arran Trench, Orca surfaced without incident, and fell in just behind Repulse to follow her back up the Clyde to Faslane. As the senior Orca visitor, Toby was very privileged to be invited to join Repulse's CO and Navigator on their bridge for the short passage through Rhu narrows and on up the Gare Loch. The difference was dramatic. The fin towered over Orca's and the shape and size of her bow emphasized the power of her reactor in pushing 7500 tonnes of streamlined submarine along at an even 10 knots. The bow wave rose right up over the casing but left little wake. Leaning out over the side Toby could see the expanse of the casing over the missile compartment, the sixteen large missile muzzle hatches standing out very clearly despite the presence of the DSRV mini-sub stuck on her back like an offspring catching a ride. This beast was a world apart from their humble O Boat – but from the little Toby had seen of life on board he still would not have missed his time in Orca. These days all submariners would end up in Nuclear boats eventually, but starting in conventional boats was special, and an increasingly rare privilege. Another difference Toby noticed was the mandatory use of tugs to tie up alongside – he couldn't remember the last time they had even been offered one. He concluded that it wasn't just size, these boats were serious business and a significant national investment ... scraping the paint may have been OK, but anything more would not have gone down too well.

Once alongside Toby returned to Repulse's Wardroom for a final celebration drink with the home team and the support staff who had been invited onboard for the continuing party. By this time, despite all the hospitality, he was desperate for a shower and some clean, dry, clothing and once Orca had tied up astern he quickly gave his farewells. With a promise of a few drinks and a tour of his cramped home (for those in Repulse who hadn't been on a Conventional before), Toby made his way out of the fore hatch.

It was the little things which made the lives of those in Repulse totally different: a main passage which actually allowed you to walk past each other, hatches which you could pass through without doubling down and bashing your head, and the overall deck height headroom which allowed six footer's to walk normally. Even double cabins for most of the wardroom – their cup definitely runneth over. So on walking down their brow and along to Orca's berth Toby prepared himself for a return to that familiar "eau de diesel" smell and the cramped conditions of his home from home.

ooOoo

0715 Saturday 27 October

A restful night in his cabin ashore followed by yet another full Scottish breakfast set Toby up for the long day which followed. All the excitement of the DSRV and bottoming was now over and the crew had to re-focus back onto their original programme of weapons training, culminating in four firings all under the critical eyes of the submarine sea training staff. Those guys had a reputation not only for high standards but also for catching you out. Their forte was hitting crews with big unannounced surprises, so Orca's crew would be under the cosh and needed to keep their wits about them. Toby's role wasn't about being heavy handed and making lots of noise, supposedly leading from the front.

The crew of HMS Orca were an experienced team and knew their individual parts in the complexity of a torpedo action, albeit they needed the practice not having actually fired any fish for over six months. In fact Toby's real role was to manage the spy system keeping tabs on the riders, so that his team would not be caught cold by their pranks.

The armament depot had been good to them and by sending the exercise torpedoes around to the base by truck had saved the crew yet another trot move down the Clyde and across to the jetty at RNAD Coulport in Loch Long. Nonetheless, it was still an early start. By 0700 they had the rails rigged down through the forward torpedo hatch and were well on their way to moving the resident few warshots to the outer stowage berths in readiness for taking the practice fish on board. The two training CPOs assessing their loading skills were already with them, one on the jetty and the other down in the fore ends, watching them rig the rails and move the fish about.

Loading fish is a bit like a game of Solitaire. Crews always have to have a space available so that they can move them around as easily as possible. The knack was getting the pattern right so that they were able to load the right weapon in the right tube as quickly as possible. In the middle of an action, especially with the boat manoeuvring, it would be hairy enough moving several tonnes of fish around. Have the space in the wrong place and they would end up shuffling fish ad infinitum, with potential dire consequences.

Toby had just received the call from the Police at the North Gate that the weapons truck had arrived in the base and was on its way to their berth, when the XO popped his head into the wardroom and asked Toby to join him and the CO in the latter's cabin.

"Morning Toby, we must be in favour," greeted the CO as they squeezed into the space at the end of his sofa bunk, "I've just received all the routine signals we missed after sitting on the bottom for the last few days. It appears that we've been chosen to loose off the annual allowance of Mk VIIIs in a live firing. Unfortunately there isn't a spare hulk for us to send to the bottom – so it won't be a SINKEX. Much to my amazement we are being directed to fire at Cape Wrath and remove a bit of North West Scotland instead. The weapons truck you are expecting has these extra four warshots on board."

"Does Captain Sea Training's team know?" Toby asked

"I believe so – but they won't be with us for the firing. The only rider we will have at the time will be a range safety officer. He should join us just before we leave the torpedo tracking range off Raasay, when the trainers get off."

"In that case, Sir, I had better go straight up for'ard and let the TI know. This will mean re-arranging the load pattern ... probably taking the warshots on first so that they are out of the way for the training and range firings. Excuse me for now and I'll get them going. I'll catch you both later in the dogs to get the full picture and read the signals."

"Fine Toby – make sure the trainers are aware of the extra weapons, we'll see you later."

Climbing up the fore hatch Toby thought it never rains but it pours, as the Argyll weather added insult to injury by letting rip with a heavy deluge. Oh to be in Sunny Scotland. He just managed to brief the TI, the Trainers and the Fore Ends crew as the weapons trucks arrived on the jetty. Explosive safety rules had meant that each truck had to be constrained to two training and two warshot fish, the second truck parking at some distance until the first was offloaded. Fortunately, the TI's load plan only required some minor change so they were able to get the first onload underway pretty sharpish. As the crane took the strain of the first warshot and started to swing it up in the air prior to arcing it across to the loading hatch, the TI abruptly, but very formally, stopped the lift and directed it back on the truck.

"What's up TI?" asked Toby.

"Sorry, Sir …these aren't MkVIII's …I think they're the Mk IX surface equivalent. I've never seen these in a boat before, and I don't know if they can be discharged from our tubes."

"My God – what now. Have you CSST guys been briefed on this? No! In that case I had better go up to the squadron offices and see if I can get some answers. TI please explain the reason for the delay to the team and the depot staff. I'll be back as soon as I have a way ahead."

Getting to the bottom of it all took over an hour, mainly finding the right people in the Squadron down in HMS Dolphin and up there at the Depot. As it turned out the two weapons were effectively the same. The only slight difference was the trip mechanism for starting the fish up as they left the tube. The correct "mod" had been done so all was in fact well. But how were the crew to know? Despite the pain of the stop start nature of the morning, with the team impatiently hanging around twiddling their thumbs, they did get a chuck up from the trainers. The TI's courage in stopping the outload as soon as he recognized the different weapons was highly commended. Those early browny points would not go amiss, and the crew set to loading the remainder in an even temper.

At last they completed the outload and were finally all seated in the Junior rates mess at 1500 for their training debrief and assessment. There were a few minor comments, but despite the delays Toby's lads had done well, and with the early chuck-up they were set to perform really well on the Raasay range.

It had been another long day and they were all out on their feet. Toby himself, desperately needed a long shower and set off through the penetrating drizzle back up to the inboard wardroom. It would be their last night ashore for a week or so and he wanted to call Judy. Calls home came in several forms – they always wanted to call their loved ones but it was not always easy. The most basic was what they called the "check report". A submarine "check report" is a very short signal basically saying it has not sunk. You have to send them within certain time frames. If they were not received the awesome SUBMISS/SUNK procedures got underway – and they were serious and at best embarrassing if all was well. Often the crew only had time for something similar when calling home – a basic, blunt message, but a similar assurance that all was still well. Many used it as a cop out. Once away, most of them occupied a mental dream world, not necessarily positive. It was a survival mechanism which set aside the reality of the appalling life they were actually leading. Calls home broke the spell. Despite the bravado, most men are cowards when it comes to communication, especially where emotions are concerned and the resultant pressures are at the forefront. Toby and the crew were no different.

In the event all was well, and as ever the call was what he needed. Judy's job continued to be interesting and fun, the sailing off Hayling Island was still the highlight of the week and she was even considering booking them in for the frost bite winter racing series – He tried hard not to sound too negative, but it cheered him up. His fears were set aside and he came off the phone buoyed up by Judy's infectious enthusiasm. Three and a bit weeks to go. Time for a beer before dinner.

ooOoo

0600 Sunday 28 October

It was 0600 when the last line was let go and they slipped quietly away from Faslane.

True to form Captain SM3 and the CO of Repulse (Starboard) were on the jetty, bidding farewell after Orca's part in their DSRV antics. Fortunately the drizzle

Leaving the Clyde

had eased off, but there was a lingering damp mist which made the Gare Loch somewhat uninviting. The route was now becoming familiar as they passed the married quarters and then negotiated the narrows at Rhu. It wasn't long before the sea front at Helensburgh was abeam, then the Clyde opened up with Kilcreggan and Loch Long disappearing to starboard and the early Greenoch ferry to port. Once around the corner passing between the Isles of Bute and Cumbrae, and Orca was on her way. An independent, small black object, home to a motley crew, whose pirate rigs were starting to meld into conformity as the increasing number of oily stains took their toll.

TASO had taken over the watch on the bridge from Simon, the Navigator, who climbed down the fin and, having taken off his foul weather gear, joined Toby on the chart table on the starboard side of the control room.

"We haven't got much time to get up to Raasay so we are going to stay on the surface until we pick up the CSST team of riders off the Crowlin's at the southern end of the weapon's range. It gives them the shortest transfer from their base at the Kyle of Lochalsh. Not that being nomads they really have a base, the Kyle is actually the range base for all the tenders and other small craft. If the CSST team had a base at all up here I'm sure they would vote for the "Craig 'n Darrich", one of the small hotels in Plockton. It is their home from home and the bar stays open whenever they are in residence. It is also the one place they seem to be able to get a meal at any hour in the Kyle area. Actually it's rather a good spot, have you been there Toby?"

"No. I have heard the stories of the "Plockton Beltway," the single lane road from there to the Kyle.

Is that where the famous Raasay range helicopter, or "petrol budgey" as it is affectionately known, is kept?"

"Yes, that's right. I've had one trip in it. It's bloody small, and makes a hell of a racket. Your whole body vibrates in that thing. If you ask me it's a pension trap waiting to happen. Plockton itself is a delightful place. They have tropical trees and ferns on the waterfront, which survive because of the mild climate caused by the Gulf Stream coming into that area. If you get the chance it's a great place for a romantic long weekend – pending the weather." Simon enthused.

"Changing the subject, the Boss has a little excursion in mind. Rather than going outside Islay once we are clear of the Mull of Kintyre, he wants to go up through the islands. I've suggested the Sound of Islay – between Islay and Jura. But what he really wants to do is go through the Gulf of Corryvreckan – do you know it?" Simon's face screwed up in concern.

"I've heard of its' reputation. Doesn't it have fantastic tidal rips?"

"That's right- the local yachting guides strongly recommend that nothing below 50 tonnes ever goes up there. I'm hoping he'll accept my suggestion that the Sound of Islay is a quieter, but just as scenic an alternative. Corryvreckan is not somewhere any fisherman up here would choose to venture through. But if he is adamant, and we stay at this pace, we will go through very early tomorrow morning."

"Simon, surely you know him by now, he may have put the proposal in a gentlemanly fashion but that usually means he has already made up his mind. Show me on the chart. I may volunteer for the bridge watch if it is all you say it is."

"Yes, you're right. I had better do my homework and look at the tides. They will be critical. Look it's here at the end of the Sound of Jura, between Scarba and Jura. Any yachts going up the west coast to Oban or Mull usually go around Luing and only with the tide. Have you got the weather forecast? That may be the decider."

"The weather is definitely on his side, Simon. It looks pretty good from this evening, once this front has cleared away. "

"That's it then. I'd better accept the inevitable and get on with preparing the passage. At least we'll see some interesting parts of Argyll. Look we'll pass Machrihanish, then Gigha, and then once through, out either past Colonsay, Mull and Tiree, or up the Sound of Mull. Give me half an hour and I'll have some alternatives we can chew over at breakfast. Are you happy to be my sounding board before I give the Boss his options?"

"Certainly, what shall I order from the Leading Steward for you? I heard he had got hold of some more of those lovely smokies?" Toby replied ever conscious that breakfast was the most important meal of the day.

"Sounds good. See you later." Simon turned and gathered the tide tables and charts together.

Putting his head into the wardroom to place the order for their breakfasts, Toby left him to it, and went up to the fore-ends to check on the pre-firing preps with the TI. The fish were all correctly secured and all the gear had been neatly stowed away, so the TI and he talked about the LIVEX. Toby still had some unease at doing a 2000 yard shot at a cliff with a salvo of four live fish, particularly ones which were designed to be fired from a surface ship. It would have to be a periscope depth shot, but instinct made him think that surfacing before they hit might be a sensible precaution. The TI tended to agree. Toby decided not to raise it in the Wardroom until he had spoken to the CSST team who would be with them on the range. They had significant experience and would be able to advise him. But now it was time for breakfast, and he needed to ensure that he could take the watch for the passage through the Gulf of Corryvrecken.

ooOoo

0715 Sunday 28 October

The smokies hit the spot, and with fresh toast and a couple of mugs of tea the day looked much better. Simon quietly let Toby know that his time /distance calculations meant that they would turn into the passage between Jura and Scarba at about 2030. So, feigning innocence, Toby raised an offer to do the film watch that evening. Julian, the Fifth Hand, was due to be on the bridge and warmly accepted the kind offer, he even volunteered to show the movie in Toby's place. Not that this one was any great shakes as they had had to return the good ones to Faslane after the DSRV exercise. Those that remained all looked pretty dire. That night's choice had been made by the XO and was an old horror flick.

Staying on the surface was becoming rather more of the norm than many of the crew would have liked. Nonetheless, it meant they had more time to prepare for the firings and make sure that the weapons team were up with the drills and the weapon prep details. Firstly though, Toby had to conduct morning rounds. It was a practice that had become routine for him and his department. He did it every morning at sea (except when actually on watch dived), no formality, just a round of the electrical and weapon spaces. The logic was to keep abreast of the activities and particularly give him a chance to talk to the team in an informal, semi-professional way. It gave time for them and Toby sensed they valued the chance to be quite personal, discussing everything from the programme to intimate details of their individual home lives. He started back aft in the Motor Room, not a quiet space when the boat was on the surface. The roar from the donk shop through the for'ard bulkhead door meant that they often had to shout at each other. These lads occupied the after mess and without these frequent trips Toby would see little of them. On this trip Polto and he went down to the lower space to check on John's "Pot Mender's Weld", only to find that a full repair had been completed whilst in Faslane. A shiny new thermometer pocket stood in its proper place, marking the scene of Toby's ear blasting, soggy escapade.

After the mandatory mug of coffee, he carried on completing the rounds down in the gyro room, not really a room but at least a space he had carved out for himself in the auxiliary machinery space (AMS) below the control room. He had created a small desk area with some limited shelving which equated to an office. Even though you couldn't stand up or spread your arms out each side it was still recognized as his office, and he cherished this very private space, albeit broom cupboard sized.

Toby spent the next hour going over all the range routines. Practice torpedo firings were a bit artificial. They were OK if you were just doing a periscope attack with a salvo or single Mk VIII. The crew simply went through the circus act in the control room with the CO leading on the attack periscope, and then discharged the weapons. It was pretty straightforward, unless they ended up on the beach. In one particular case early in the commission one weapon had finished up on Whitsand Beach around the corner from Rame Head outside Plymouth - an unfortunate incident, but not one Toby wanted to either remember or repeat.

This trip was not to be as simple, the goal was to fire four individual Mk 23's, each at separate targets on different runs. These were wire guided torpedoes with a complex discharge arrangement. It also meant the launch of the special targets which were controlled by the range, so, all in all, the crew had to be on the ball just to get an attack underway, before contemplating any success or otherwise. Hence Toby's cramming.

His concentration was eventually interrupted by a broadcast, "The smell of burning is coming from the galley", sadly, one that was all too familiar he thought, but thinking of his stomach again, it did remind him that lunch was due. He packed up and climbed back up into the Control Room. A glance at the chart showed that they were close to rounding the Mull of Kintyre and a look through the after periscope showed he could see that Scotland was starting to look much better. The clouds were clearing and the sun was coming out. As he made his way back up to the wardroom a feeling of expectation and excitement washed over him in anticipation of the rather special evening cruise.

ooOoo

1615 Sunday 28 October

As had been explained before the crew's sleep cycle started after lunch. So when Toby was shaken awake for tea he was not quite so chirpy as he had been that morning. His face looked and felt all puffy, and before he could embrace any tea and cake he had to go and scrape his tongue and teeth in the heads. At least, after that, part of him was somewhat fresher. The cake was a chocoholic special, made by Mandy, the CO's wife. It looked very good, but sadly Toby was not a chocolate person, something often described as a failing by the ladies in his life. As he often stated not everyone could be perfect, at least he professed to be saving himself for supper. He just hoped it would be worth it.

Well it was. A kind donation in Faslane from Repulse's XO had been some wild fowl he had shot on his brother-in-law's estate (a rather large piece of Scotland). They had pink feet but no-one was meant to notice that. Something to do with what you can and cannot shoot during the season, but they tasted really good. The guys in the galley had created a magical gravy (they called it a sauce and it probably merited the description particularly after the addition of the whisky). Together with roast tatties and some fresh greens it was bloody good. The wardroom even treated themselves to a large glass of "Red Infuriator", the special cheap vintage they bought in one and a half litre bottles, supposedly Italian.

So, replete, Toby gathered his foul weather gear together and prepared himself for the evening on the bridge. The chart showed that Simon's plan was spot on. Another half an hour and they would be turning to port to transit the magical Gulf of "C". Once through they would leave Mull to starboard and make their way up past Tiree and Coll, then Muck, Eigg and Rum, before going up to the Inner Minch to round Skye. Quite an evening cruise, although Toby's watch would only see part of it.

An all round look through the after scope showed Toby that the weather had continued to clear and the evening sun was promising a grand sunset. As he stepped onto the ladder to climb up into the fin, Simon called to say he and the CO would be up in twenty minutes. Not much room up there so it was going to be cosy. By the time Toby reached the bridge he had to admit that he was panting a bit. It's quite a long haul with an awkward transfer from one ladder to another one behind you half way up. Frank, the TASO, was pleased to see him. Being a very tall, well built, rugby type, Frank was always hungry, and whatever the offerings he devoured every meal as if it was his last. The handover didn't take long. Toby knew where they were, and where they were going. Their only companions were a couple of small fishing smacks which were disappearing back down the Sound of Jura. So being content, Toby released him and Frank slid out of view back to the damp, smelly depths below.

Unfortunately, because Toby had wanted this particular watch, he wasn't sharing it with AB Tomlinson – his friendly Twitcher. The lookout was another young lad called Jones, who actually was Welsh and understandably played rugby for the boat. He was pleasant company and was unaware of the special transit they had ahead of them. So Toby was able to brief him all about it and the reputation of this stretch of water. Toby had heard all about the Gulf of Corryvreckan when he had been sailing in this area. His route had been the safer one which most yachtsmen take from the Clyde to Oban. Cutting off the Mull of Kintyre via the Crinan Canal saved a long haul around the peninsula, then it was a dash through the Dhorus Mhor, with the tide in your favour, to get up to Oban. Even then it was pretty spectacular. The Clyde Cruising Club pilot was direct in its' advice, no yacht should take the passage through the Gulf of C, it was simply too dangerous.

With ten minutes to go to the turn, Toby took a series of bearings to get a fix on the chart. No sooner had it been plotted than he was informed by the helm that the CO and NO were on their way to the bridge. Time to squeeze up, so he had the radar mast tagged off and Jones ducked under the back of the bridge into the radar mast well.

"Evening, Sir. We couldn't have had a better one. Not a cloud in the sky now and hardly a breath of wind. The tide is with us and shouldn't be full until we are clear of Scarba. Are you happy for me to start the turn?"

"Yes please, Toby. Once you are on course I will take the ship."

"*Aye, aye, Sir. Helm – Bridge, Port 15*"

Toby waited until they were at least half way round then directed:

"*Steer 275*"

It took a few minutes for the boat to steady up, "*Steady on course 275, Sir*" came the reply from down below.

"*Very well. I have the Ship*. This should be quite an evening Gentlemen." said the Boss, quietly taking over.

It all started very gently. The views were stunning. Ahead of them they could see some form of tide rip and there were a number of gulls and some ducks floating around. Then slowly they became aware of the breeze stiffening, with a background hum. The sides of Jura and Scarba were both very steep. Toby vaguely remembered from the chart that they went down sheer to a depth of about 600 feet. Orca was now actually in the passage and Toby became conscious of their speed increasing. Then suddenly he saw a tufted duck overtake them on the starboard side. It was incongruous. It was clearly on a back eddy and had come around half a circle on a fast rip which accelerated it up the side at some 6 knots faster than them. This impossible image had just registered when the boat slewed violently to port. Some two thousand five hundred tonnes of submarine was being spewed through the passage. By now the wind was up and howling, they were on their way. Fortunately the boat was reasonably aligned so no dramatic steerage action was needed. It was genuinely awesome, and they just drank it all in. Nature had taken them, with all its power, and they were simply willing spectators. It hardly seemed any time at all before they were literally thrown out at the other end and suddenly all was still with not a breath of wind again. If they hadn't been there together they would not have believed it. Quite magical.

With that the CO and Simon left Toby to enjoy the remainder of the sunset and disappeared down off the bridge into the fin. Jones came back out of the radar well and recognized that there was little to add. They spent the rest of the watch with vacant, grinning expressions on their faces. Finally with Muck, Eigg and Rhum in sight under a waxing moon, Toby turned over to Peter for the middle watch and clambered back down the tower to a hot cup of Kai and the warmth of his pit.

ooOoo

0600 Monday 29 October

The passage through the night took Orca around Skye and back south over the deep water range to the east of Raasay. As 0600 arrived the boat was drifting just off the Crowlin Islands awaiting the team of riders from CSST. Their tender was on its way and those of in the Wardroom were setting the scene for a working breakfast with them. It was time for Toby to be on his toes and get the intelligence network active. The CSST team were led by Lt Cdr Ernie FitzSimmonds, a Lecky like Toby. He had a reputation for always being one step ahead and coming up with surprises when the boats least expected them. That said, he was a warm and very approachable person. Everyone liked Ernie, which made it difficult to be standoffish with him. Toby and his team had discussed their approach with the CSST team. They were recognized as quite an experienced crew and had to be careful not to be over confident. They certainly needed the practice, but did not want to be caught out and shown up by Ernie and his team. There was one approach that an ex CO of Toby's had used with trainers a couple of times, he called it "the calculated fuck up". His classic example had been at the culmination of his practical tests to become a professional RN Navigator. They were going down Southampton water in a Frigate and he was waiting on tenterhooks for the next drill failure. Eventually he could wait no longer so he initiated his own – a gyro failure. It was so well done that the examiners thought it had been a real failure and he passed with flying colours. He had used the approach ever since ...and had yet to be caught out. Toby and the team discussed it as a real option but in the end decided that discretion was the better part of valour, and set it aside.

Few people have ever experienced, or seen, a submarine personnel transfer on the surface. They are not pretty. The bulbous tanks present a slippery, smooth surface which the participants have to climb. They have to be tied up with a safety line around their middles, but it only stops them being lost over the side. It doesn't prevent the slipping and sliding, often ending up with the innocent party up to his waist in cold (Scottish) water, hoping that the rescue team drag him up onto the casing bloody quickly. Invariably they have no change of clothes as they only intend staying for the day. So meeting and greeting after such an evolution requires tact and sympathy. However, these guys did it all the time, so they were worldly wise (and had some spare gear), but most important of all they knew it wasn't the crew's fault if they had a bit of a dip.

Ernie and his team duly appeared clambering down the tower ladder to be checked on board in the Control Room. Shedding life jackets and safety harnesses they made their way to the various messes - Ernie to the Wardroom, and the Chiefs to the Senior Rates Mess. Following the tradition of sea riders they came armed with a welcome pack of the morning papers, and some mail – you don't get deliveries to ships at sea.

"Morning all. Good to see you guys again," breezed Ernie, and immediately settled down to breakfast having deposited his gear on the spare wardroom bunk just outside in the passage.

Pushing his plate aside he was chatting in a general way when he asked, "Toby, could you let me have a small bar of soap? I forgot to bring any with me."

"Sure. Is that all? Do you need any other toiletries? If so I'll get the boat's Naafi shop to send some up." Shop" was a bit of an exaggeration. It was basically a locker which stored a very limited number of Naafi provided items such as snacks, toothpaste and toiletries.

"No. That will be just fine. I'm OK for the rest. As you are aware, it will probably be a long day. My aim is to get two runs done this morning. The first will be a pull

Orca's For'd Tubes

through, with the second being a live run including the actual deployment of a target. Is that OK with you?"

Peter responded, "Yes. That's what we anticipated. Toby's team realise your Chiefs will want to see the guide wire dispensers hooked up so they have frozen the drill at that point and are ready to re-start when your chaps say so."

The Mk23 guided torpedoes were complex and full of problems. The previous year had been dubbed the year of the torpedo in an attempt to bring out all the faults and sort them out. Orca had spent a significant time off Norway and, being one of the few selected boats, must have fired about fifty fish in all. They had gradually overcome all the drill and procedural errors, but a lot of failures were still occurring, most being with the deployment of the guide wire dispensers – they kept parting the wire. This resulted in the weapons immediately stopping and practice torpedoes would then rise to the surface with their flotation collars inflating. The real issue was that if they had been warshots any boat would have been forced to have two weapons in the water at the same time just to ensure success, which was at best wasteful.

Hence the emphasis that these guys placed on their training approach, every crew going through the Range being subjected to the same rigour.

It took a couple of hours to check and confirm the dispensers. Then the fore-ends team went through the paces with the Range, initially positioning themselves so that the boat, the target, and the weapon could all be tracked simultaneously. Then they did a dummy run pretending that the Range was deploying and running the target. After two rehearsals everyone was content, so Ernie directed the start of live run one.

As explained these being training scenarios they had by nature to be somewhat false in that the whole gamut of the acquisition and tracking phases of the target had to be set aside. Nonetheless, a live firing did get the adrenalin going. Locating the target was fairly straightforward for the boat and having established its' track Orca launched the first weapon. At this point Toby's role became very visible, a single point, success or failure. It was his task to guide the weapon with direct control on a panel called the TCU (torpedo control unit). The telemetered data showed on the TCU once it had gained contact, and after a period of consolidation, Toby was able to release the weapon for the final stages of its attack, again all this being fed back and displayed on the TCU. To ensure that the CO and attack team knew what was happening all his actions had to be repeated over the net and local broadcast. It started pretty well, but as the attack developed he got quite excited and his voice started to pitch higher and higher. The control room team were well used to this and took it in their stride. None of them ever commented, but it was all recorded, and Toby used to shrink with embarrassment on listening to the playback.

The first run was a visible success. No guide wire breaks, thank God, and a successful attack on the guided target. They were all feeling pretty good and at that point Ernie agreed a short break for the Range to set up the next run and prepare the next target. So far, so good.

The officers grabbed some sandwiches in the Wardroom, full of confidence at their success so far. As this was happening Toby saw Ernie sneak back off towards the control room with a large white bag in his hand. In response Toby quickly put down his half eaten sarnie and was leaving to follow him when the CO grabbed him to ask whether he had discussed the LIVEX with CSST. Unfortunately he hadn't had time yet but assured the CO that he would grab Ernie before the latter caught the tender back to the Kyle after the firings.

At that moment the XO came over the broadcast: *"The next run will commence at 1300."* They only had ten minutes, so Toby wolfed down the rest of his lunch and joined the others back in the Control Room.

This run was a bit more complex. The target was quieter and it took the crew some time to get a credible track. As they were about to fire Toby noticed Ernie move across to his side of the Control Room. Ernie looked relaxed and was clearly finishing a mouthful of lunch.

"Fire Two" – the weapon was in the water and all Toby's concentration was focused on getting it to a

position where it would acquire the target. A bit more positioning...

"*Target Acquisition*" – he yelled into the ether and the tapes, his voice going way up in pitch. Then all hell let loose ... Ernie suddenly started screaming at the top of his voice, collided with Toby and started to grab at the wiring in the deck head above him. It was as much as Toby could do to maintain focus on the torpedo control. Fortunately he managed to retain enough composure to release the torpedo to complete its own final attack, then Ernie staggered across the console with his mouth foaming and bits of cable protruding from his teeth, "Christ, what's happening to him," Toby thought while desperately trying to focus on the torpedo and its' attack.

Ernie slumped to the deck and started twitching, "*Safeguard, Safeguard, Leading Writer to the Control Room,*" came over the broadcast as Peter, supported by the Outside Wrecker and then the Leading Writer (the crew's formally qualified first aider) arrived and they struggled to get Ernie under some kind of control.

"Sir, it must be some form of epileptic fit. I don't think we can move him yet," said Peter to the CO.

"I agree. Look after him while we sort out the range issues. *LO report state of the weapon.*"

"*Weapon engaging target, accelerating to attack speed.*" Toby replied.

"*Abort the run, Abort the run - TASO pass to the range that we have a Safeguard situation and that the run has been aborted. LO keep reporting the state of the weapon.*"

It took some ten minutes for them to bring the range situation to a stable conclusion. By that time Ernie was looking very bad. His face looked really milky, foamy dribble was around his chin, and he still had bits of cable sticking out of his mouth. At least he had stopped twitching. The XO and team were now getting him into a stretcher to take him into the for'd mess, which the crew used as an emergency sick bay. Everyone was pretty shocked, none of them had witnessed an actual fit before and it was not a pleasant experience. As they took him away he was clearly coming round and gave Toby a somewhat brave but rueful smile before disappearing through the hatch.

The crew managed to bring the run to a formal conclusion and, with the weapon sighted safely on the surface with its buoyancy collar inflated, that concluded their interaction with the Range for the day and the CO gave the order to surface. Once up the CO disappeared into the Comms Shack to establish whether the petrol budgie would be available for a stretcher transfer if required. He returned as they were blowing round to stabilise their buoyancy and called Toby over to the chart table.

"Toby, are you aware of any medical history with Ernie? Any scuttlebutt amongst the greenies?"

"Not as far as I know, Sir. I would have thought that any history of epileptic fits would be a no, no, for staying on active service. Not something anyone would advertise."

"That's what I was thinking. TASO are you ready to take the watch on the bridge? Good. In that case Toby, let's go and see the patient."

By now they were both anticipating the scene in the Wardroom. There was Ernie, all grins, cleaning himself up and devouring a large mug of tea.

"Ernie I am not a crude man …but what the fuck was that all about!!!" yelled the CO, getting closer to being out of control than Toby had ever seen him.

"Just me doing my job, Sir." Ernie replied, looking definitely defensive. "I knew you guys were pretty good and I decided the only way to test you was to create a diversion. So with Toby's soap in my mouth to set me foaming, and with liquorice layered up amongst the deck head cabling as dummy wiring, I acted out my fit. Grabbing and eating the wiring really brought out some awesome looks from your team – at least I broke their concentration. I tried hard to stop Toby in his tracks by slobbering all over him, but tripped getting near and fell on the TCU instead. He managed to fend me off and still acquire the target – pretty amazing. So I then went into the full fit routine which you all saw. I am afraid I can't fault your response. You certainly managed a good balance between what you saw as a real medical emergency and a live weapon firing. Well done, Sir, to you and all the team." He stopped and you could see he was really quite nervous as to the CO's reaction. Rightly so, the man was out of this world.

There was a prolonged and very pregnant pause.

"Lt Cdr FitzSimmons, I have considered my response and believe the very least I should subject you to is a stretcher ride on the Petrol Budgie, which is on its way. But I can be considered a lenient man and your alternative is a fine of a beer for every man on board, to be paid and delivered personally during our visit off Portree on completion of our time on the range. The choice is yours."

A big and very relieved grin spread over Ernie's face. "Thank you, Sir, it will be my pleasure." Holding out his hand he offered it to the CO, and was visibly relieved to have it accepted.

God, everything people said about him just had to be true! After that the rest of Orca's range time was a complete anti-climax. Both weapons the following day had their dispensers fail with wire breaks. So they ended up finishing early. By 1600 the boat was nicely entering the bay off Portree, with the crew looking forward to two quiet days with shore leave for those off watch. At 1700 the bars were opened and beers were dispensed in all the messes courtesy of Ernie.

TIME FOR HOROSCOPES

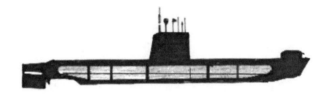

Missing Life in Submarines?

Lesson 4 on recapturing the old days:-

Wash your underwear in a bucket every night, and then hang it over the water pipes to dry.

1730 Thursday 1 November

Anchoring in a submarine is a pretty rare event. Not that John and Toby thought the seamen weren't capable, they were all trained and able. Indeed, many of them were able to trip the training off the tongue at the most unlikely times; such as ... *"How much cable should you pay out when anchoring?"* Their glib answer just sang out *"two route two times the depth in fathoms in shackles."* John questioned whether that was English, or some underground nautical code? From long experience he knew it was just the RN living in a world in which cricket pitches are measured in chains, and the length of an anchor cable in shackles ... God bless them.

So why was it rare? The point in submarines was that anchors and cables were loose noisy great lumps of metal, and survival in a submarine depended on achieving the lowest underwater noise signature possible. As a result the cable and the anchor (they only have one permanently rigged unlike their surface counterparts) were stowed in a permanently lashed-down state, with rope and canvass under the lashings to prevent rubbing and noisy rattles. Removing it all to anchor was a pretty lengthy process, one which the Second Cox'n and his team avoided at all costs. It was wet, grimy, and required a considerable time on their bellies or backs under the casing. Not nice.

But this time they were smiling. They were going to have a long week-end anchored off Portree, the "capital" of Skye. It was a dramatic setting. Beinn na Greine towered over them and the delightful town promenade looked really inviting. For the lads the added attractions of a Ceilidh, with a clutch of nurses from the local cottage hospital, and a chance to unwind with a few beers made life complete. In addition the aficionados of Scotland's amber nectar would be able to venture only a little further along the coast to the distillery at Talisker – a peaty brew, with a strong following.

By 1830 Eric had honoured his debt and most of the crew had enjoyed their well earned beers. He and his team of riders, along with those venturing forth for a steamy night out, caught the tender to take them ashore at 1900. These included a small wardroom team led by John who was determined to sample the odd wee dram. For Toby no such luck. He had the duty, not that it was too demanding. His Duty PO was the TI, and as the tender took those in luck on their "run ashore", Toby and the TI conducted the routine nightly rounds to ensure the boat was clean and stowed away for a quiet night at anchor. They started for'd in the weapon stowage compartment and made their way gradually aft through the mess decks, control room and *donk shop* to the after ends mess. All was pretty clean and tidy with no significant issues, thank God. After the last few days all they needed was another minor drama.

Having finished rounds, each had time for supper and a coffee before it was time to go up top to say good night to the Queen. Their simple ritual, conducted whenever they were either alongside or at anchor, was to salute the lowering of the white ensign from their stern and the union jack from the bow as the sun dipped below the horizon. Toby really rather enjoyed the custom. It was an institution with ships and submarines from Navies all around the world conforming wherever they were. For once it wasn't raining so Toby's romantic side was in full flow. On completion he made his way for'd on the casing to clamber around the fin, prior to climbing down the main access hatch to make his way below. The walk way around the fin is only about twelve inches wide. So you have to hang on to the handrail provided to ensure you don't go for an inadvertent swim.

Toby was only half way around when the TI suddenly appeared in front of him with a weird expression on his face, and a crude body motion that was either a mating dance or he'd lost his marbles.

" Oh, I'm all in a dither Sir! Do I block your passage or toss myself off!!!"

Toby was somewhat gob-smacked. In fact he didn't really take in what the TI was saying until the over familiar leer returned and the TI started winking at him. Mind you the TI was always winking at him. In fact Toby was never sure whether it was a tick in his eye, or whether the TI fancied him. The chance of it being the latter was too much and not something he could frankly face – the TI was just a bloody moron, whose behaviour was not just outlandish, but totally beyond the pale.

"Sod off, you prat!" was Toby's officer like response.

It worked. The TI winked once more and shuffled away pretty quickly before Toby could literally put his steaming boot up that very ample arse. Toby reflected that having characters in the crew was good news, but you did sometimes wonder.

The evening passed with a forgettable film in the wardroom, and then the long wait for the return of the tender at 2200 and then 0100 in the early hours. The last one arrived without any untoward behaviour, although it was clear that most of the lads had really enjoyed the Ceilidh and were only just under control. However, as John came off he asked Toby to join him below in the wardroom, in a rather serious fashion. It transpired that although the Ceilidh had gone rather well, a couple of

John's stokers had taken a fancy to two likely nurses and had been rather too forward. Their advances having been turned down, they became somewhat disillusioned and had ended up idiotically going to the cottage hospital ...where a window had been broken. John had smoothed things over with the staff, and as a gesture of good will – and to be frank a visible apology – had ordered some flowers, via the landlord of the pub on the front, to be delivered by hand the following morning. He would like to do it, but was taking over the duty from Toby ...so could Toby do the honours?

Toby reluctantly agreed provided he was able to get some sleep. In fact that was it for the night. Having checked the anchor bearings, and made sure the duty quartermaster was on the ball Toby was able to call it a day. Another quiet night at sea? Fingers crossed. It was beautiful up top. A filling crescent moon was beaming across the bay and their little black home, lying quietly to its anchor, was lost against the spread of the surrounding mountains. A hammock in the fresh air would have been magical, but Toby accepted the inevitable and made his way down below to that familiar warm foetid atmosphere to grab some shut-eye before rising early for the sunrise.

ooOoo

0700 Friday 2 November

The following morning was surprisingly different. The atmosphere on board was very relaxed – those that had been ashore were quiet, but not overly subdued from too much alcohol. The rest of them were looking forward to stepping ashore themselves and enjoying the treats of one of those rare Argyll Island townships, of which Portree was in the top bracket. But first Toby had to undertake his little chore. He decided that a bit of formality was probably the best, indeed John had been honest enough to admit that those in the hospital might not be that warm to any attempt to "deal" with the unhappy incident without some genuine remorse and apology. So dressed in a blazer and grey flannels, and armed with a large bunch of flowers he was fully equipped to set the scene. As he landed from the tender, he really wondered what John had let him in for.

The walk from the front up to the small cottage hospital did not take that long, and as Toby approached he saw a number of faces watching him make his way up the drive. As he came up to the front two ladies in uniform and a gentleman opened the door and greeted him in the entrance. It turned out they were the duty Doctor, the Matron, and the duty Sister. Not a bad turn out with the weekend beckoning. In fact such an obvious welcome immediately put him at ease, and he was able to be absolutely straight with them, apologise for the unfortunate behaviour, and sort out the cost of the window. As it transpired, the duty Sister had been at the Ceilidh and admitted that the contribution from the lads in the crew had made it a really good evening. So all was sorted pretty quickly, not that Toby was allowed to leave until he had been given the mandatory tour and they had all had lunch together (complete with wine – where that came from in such a small hospital he never fathomed). Toby offered invitations to dinner onboard the following night, but clearly none from such a small set up could really spare the time. So he suggested early evening drinks and a short tour of the boat. Both Matron and the duty sister jumped at it. So job done he returned on board with a wry grin on his face to let John know of his forthcoming guests. After all it had been his lads who had upset the apple cart.

In fact they duly came unannounced that very evening but were delightful, entertaining, company. The tour highlight turned out to be their exposure to the basic nature of submarine ablutions. Inadvertently it was very basic – with one young stoker undertaking a full body scrub and brush-up – absolutely starker's in full view of the main passage. The sight of female visitors didn't put him off at all. As they passed he had finished his all over in his allotted six inches of water, had dried off but was still naked and hard into scrubbing his smalls and socks. He charmingly passed the time of day and the ladies noted that they were a very clean crew!

They returned to the Wardroom with radiant smiles to enjoy a bottle of the wardroom wine and some nibbles – Orca's officers could put on the charm when required and the leading steward had cleaned the place up nicely. Mind you with the Wardroom being so small it was no great task. Peter, being a sociable XO, kindly joined them and soon had the visitors describing their favourite Skye walk. It led out of Portree up to the top of Beinn na Greine. He looked over at Toby and the latter nodded – what better way for the two of them to spend their free day on the morrow. The guests even told them where to get the best packed lunch and offered to have a map ready at the hospital reception the following day. So Peter and Toby were all set.

As the discussion rolled around, Matron turned to Toby with a rather unexpected question – which was: why wasn't he dressed in uniform for the visit? It came as a surprise. It had never occurred to either John or him that those in the hospital were really looking forward to a visitor in uniform. In fact the damage to the hospital had never been a problem – it was a visit from the sailors in the submarine that they really wanted to enjoy ...so Toby's somewhat staid blazer and flannels had not been quite up to the mark. He apologised profusely, but remarked that he had arrived with that genuine and unmistakable submarine perfume eau du diesel. Their response was laughter and forceful comments that they had certainly noticed it.

ooOoo

0900 Saturday 3 November
Peter had allowed crew leave the following morning to start when the first tender came alongside at 1030, but his and Toby's various duties kept both busy so they didn't make it. It was late morning by the time they managed to get ashore. As promised the map was waiting for them and the sandwich selection at the local bakery was pretty impressive. So armed with a sizeable picnic and a flask of coffee in one ruck sack and some drinks in the other, they set off out of the town. It wasn't long before they were passing the last house, and about a mile later turned off the coast road to take a rough track across the lowland cattle grazing area. Their luck was definitely in, and although it was pretty nippy, the skies were clearing and before long the sun appeared. Scotland is a land where you have to take as it comes, but today fortune (and the Sun) were shining on them. It was a complete contrast from their cramped, airless abode. Each breath was intoxicating and they were soon tackling the first gradient with a boyish vigour, enjoying their unexpected escape from both the boat and the

responsibilities that went with it. As they climbed the view of the bay became even more impressive. Due to Toby's evolving interest in birds, he was aware that Skye was one of the few places in the UK where there were Eagles, so every now and then he did an "all round look". Sadly he had no luck, although at one point he became very excited until Peter told him that it wasn't even a bird but a light aircraft.

It took them just under three hours to do the climb. They enjoyed a rather late lunch, but it was worth it. The view was stunning. Below them their smart little vessel lay calmly at anchor, and little was definitely the word. It looked so small in the empty bay, set against the backdrop of some serious Scottish Mountains. Mind you finding a dry patch to settle for lunch was not that easy. Toby found it amazing that he was walking through deep, peaty bogs, with the mucky brown water coming over his boots on the top of Beinn na Greine. He had always assumed that water flowed downhill, but clearly not in Scotland.

ooOoo

1330 Saturday 3 November

Having devoured their lunch, with a couple of beers inside them (Toby having compromised with a weak lager) and the sun still out, they felt pretty good. The light was very special, giving some amazing views beyond Raasay, south across Skye to the Cuillins, and east above Applecross on the mainland. They sat mostly in silence and being honest with himself Toby admitted to feeling a bit low. These moments never seemed to come at the right time. The time away and the inability to share life with Judy was starting to take its toll. Without the need to say anything both Peter and himself were aware that each felt the same. So gathering up their belongings they donned their packs and slowly set off for the descent back down into Portree. Once on the move they regained their spirits and were able to make the most of the fresh air. It was about 1830 by the time they reached the centre of Portree, still just light but the Pubs would be open for some healthy refreshment.

So with glowing cheeks, after pints of bitter and shandy respectively and a local amber chaser, they returned on board for a quiet supper. Simon, Frank and Julian (the junior seaman trio) had all disappeared ashore together, so the Boss, Peter and Toby had a bit of space around the table and, with John (on duty) joining them, were able to eat in relative comfort. In fact it was a very passable steak pie with some excellent "clacker" around the edges. They even treated themselves to a civilized cheese course with a small glass of port – living well in the field as they called it. As the mugs of coffee were served John and Peter decided that they were going to give Toby's movie selection another chance. Toby declined to join them but helped them rig the projector, and as he was leaving to retire to his so called office, the Boss asked him if he would join him in his cabin.

"Toby please make yourself as comfortable as you can in my luxurious abode. Put your coffee on the desk"

Not easily done as there was hardly room for two. This height of luxury was more the size of a broom cupboard, with a six foot bunk taking up over half the area – but it was the best onboard.

"As you are aware it's S206 time, and I prefer to have a chat before I put any words on paper. You've done very well this last year and now that you have been with us for two years there is an outside chance that you could be moved on before, or shortly after, we go into refit at Chatham. So I wanted to make sure that I reflect any preferences you have for your next job."

"God I had forgotten it was report time," Toby thought - being somewhat caught out - although he had known that time was coming up.

The S206 is the Naval form for Officer's reports. In fact it is pretty good. On two sides of A4 it creates a very succinct package which has all the data to judge the performance and potential of officers across the spectrum. The S206 has been the bane of Naval Officers for years. In the zones for promotion they are written every six months and the recipient's prospects depend on it. Zones from Lieutenant Commander to Commander, and then for the stars, to Captain, listed candidates against each other according to seniority. It was harsh, competitive, nail-biting stuff. Fortunately as a lowly Lieutenant, Toby's was more about career progression, but important nonetheless.

And yet it was a bit of a sham, as Toby was to find out later in Naval life. It had hidden meanings and codes and was not what it seemed. Many reporting and appraisal systems are the same. After all, the main purpose is to make the recipients feel good, valued and supported. Being bluntly honest would simply break all that up. The RN had a good system and it worked, after a fashion. Everyone, well almost everyone, got a good report. However, if you looked at the marks (they were out of 100), no-one ever got more than about 76. The hidden codes defining the real judgement, particularly for promotion, were simple but very effective. Credible promotion candidates got 74 for early promotion, 76 for normal, and if anyone was given 78 they were over marked. Given a 74 to 76 mark, the essence of the hidden code was the tense used in the recommendations. "This man thoroughly deserves promotion" actually meant he was unlikely to get it. Whereas – "I strongly recommend this officer for promotion NOW" was just the ticket.

At this stage of their careers it was unlikely that any of them, even the CO, was aware of the special judgements applied by their masters in the Squadrons and at FOSM's HQ in Fort Blockhouse. So being innocently unaware of these nuances, and being many years away from the phase of competing for promotion to Commander, Toby's report was either an annual or, as the Boss had intimated, an end of appointment one.

"What thoughts and preferences do you have for the future, Toby? Any specific preferences?"

Despite being caught on the hop, as an Engineer, Toby was keener on getting a deeper technical qualification rather than doing a general staff course. The latter came at respective levels depending on rank. So Toby reflected his thoughts to the Boss and they discussed the various options. There were a number of attractive technically based MSc's at either service colleges or civilian universities. Although Toby was not fully informed, discussions with counterparts in the squadron, and on other boats had given him a good understanding, so he was able to lay out some preferable options. They discussed these for a while and then the Boss laid down his cards much to Toby's surprise.

"Toby, you and John are a rare pair. In the squadron you are seen as a very strong team who rarely disagree, are always supportive, and frankly joined at the hip. It's unusual and stands out because, sadly in most boats, the engineers end up as competitors. Despite being the junior member of this partnership you have personally done a lot to create and maintain this team work. As well as this and your clear technical ability, you have also become a very rounded submariner, as evidenced by you working for your bridge watchkeeping ticket. So I want you to go away and consider what I am going to say. Have you ever considered changing branches and becoming a General List Seaman? If you did, I am very confident that you would get a place on *Perisher,* with every chance of an early command."

Toby was stunned, what an accolade. The Perisher was the Holy Grail to submarine seamen officers- it was the Commanding Officers Qualifying Course. He sat quietly for what seemed an age. His mind was in freefall. All he could do was thank the Boss for his trust and kind words and request that he be given the chance to discuss it with Judy before he gave a reply.

"That's fine Toby. I was going to suggest that you waited until after your leave to give me a firm answer. That way you can discuss it at home and take whatever counsel you need to make up your mind. I would ask that you keep the proposal confidential and if you want to ask anyone ashore on a professional basis you clear it with me first. In the mean time well done and keep up the good work"

The Boss gave him a warm, sincere, handshake and Toby quietly withdrew. Avoiding the duty watch in the control room, Toby snuck down into the AMS and his micro office to reflect on the cataclysmic career crossroads he now found himself facing. To bring some order back to his thoughts he tried to enmesh himself in drafting the reports on his senior team of Chief and Petty

Officers, but his mind would not wander far from his mental crossroads. Ever since that first interview at fifteen he had only ever considered being an Engineer. Mind you, if he was frank with himself he had little if any knowledge of the Navy before joining and had certainly never been aware of the pre-eminence of the Seaman specialization in terms of Command. In his confused state his ideal future looked like one appointment as a Seaman, in command of a Conventional Boat, and then a return to Engineering. He doubted, however, whether that would be credible. Christ, he just didn't want to think about it. It was clear that he wasn't getting anywhere with the reports, so in fairness to the reportees he packed up and returned to the Wardroom. He needed a diversion.

Well, John as ever provided it. Seeing that Toby was a bit off colour, and goading Peter as an ally, John jumped in at the deep end.

"Well ship mate my guess is you've just had your Horoscope read. A nice chat with the Boss going through your S206? Come on now what was his judgement? If it was me, I'd put you down as - *I would not breed from this officer*"

"Oh no", said Peter, joining in-"I would put Toby as – *He has carried out each and every one of his duties to his entire satisfaction*"

"Thank you both for your vote of confidence." Toby replied. He poured himself a black coffee and offered to top their's up, but they wouldn't stop.

Peter suddenly buried his head in the locker under his bunk and re-appeared with a couple of A4 sheets of paper. "How about these John? – *His men would follow him anywhere, but only out of curiosity…. or …I wish this Officer would understand that nought is a mark*"

"Where did you get those Peter?" John asked taking the first page from him.

"During a trip to a friendly *Appointer*, he tried some of them on me, and then gave me a copy of the Naval ones and this report from an Infantry Regiment in 1813. There are some great ones here, this is my favourite: *"All Irish, promoted from the ranks, low vulgar men without any one qualification to recommend them, more fit to carry the Hod than the Epaulette"* The great thing about it is the simple way the Regimental Colonel grades them, the star of the regiment is described as - *An Excellent Officer* – no more than that, straight to the point with no doubts. In the middle he describes some as ...*All Good Officers* ... and further down others as ...*Merely good – nothing promising* . At the other end of the spectrum one poor wretch of an Ensign gets the prize: ..*The very dregs of the earth, unfit for anything under Heaven. God only knows how the poor thing got an Appointment* ... . I have to say I think this Colonel's concise judgement and style takes some beating."

John was enjoying this and found more on Peter's Navy list of report comments: "Here's one for that Wren Officer who is Captain SM's assistant: ... *When she opens her mouth, it seems that this is only to change whichever foot was previously in there* ....or here is another ....*She sets low personal standards and then consistently fails to achieve them...*"

"Come on now she's not that bad." Toby replied, but John was on a roll and as a Special Duties Officer who had come up through the ranks he relished the chance to poke fun at the caricature of career General List Officers like Toby and Peter.

"Hey, this is one of the best. It hits the mark for most Naval Doctors I know: ...*This Medical Officer has used my ship to carry his genitals from Port to Port, and my Officers to carry him from Bar to Bar...*"

Toby snatched the list from him and quickly found something appropriate

"John is this you? ...*raised from the ranks, ignorant, vulgar and incompetent...* No, even I think that is a bit unkind ...but if the cap fits then this must be it ...*When he joined my ship, this officer was something of a granny, but since then he has aged considerably....* No violence now... Peter, defend me!"

Fortunately having sat behind the Wardroom table for supper and the movie, John couldn't get out around the projector to physically get at Toby. So Toby escaped with a number of expletives. They gradually settled down and over a final coffee had a chance to examine both documents at leisure. Peter clearly had been given a couple of gems.

The episode certainly did the trick for Toby and as he settled into his bunk he drifted off, clear that fortune had smiled on him and that his only concern was judging which of these opportunity paths he should take.

ooOoo

0630 Sunday 4 November
A combination of John's snoring and the breakfast smells brought Toby to the following morning. By the time the table had been cleared away and their humble home was fit for sea it was close to 0700 and he made his way into the control room just as "*Special Sea Dutymen close up*" was piped over the main broadcast.

Taking the after periscope he could see the Second Cox'ns team bringing up the anchor cable. It was almost there and they would be underway pretty soon. A measured all round look showed Portree waking up with the first signs of life along the sea front despite it being early on a Sunday morning. The line of his and Peter's walk the previous day was slowly clearing as Beinn na Greine started to appear out from the morning mist. Turning the scope again the outline of Raasay, deep in shadow, showed the relatively narrow passage down to the bottom of the island beyond which they had to make their way back to the end of the Range and an early rendezvous off the Crowlins. It was there that they were to pick up the range safety team for the live firing. A misty start, but the shipping forecast was for a good day. Sea State 3 to 4 with good visibility and little chance of precipitation. It was only about a hundred nautical miles up to Cape Wrath so not an overly long passage. Their intent was to do a number of runs on the noise range and then set off to be ready to fire first thing the following morning, particularly as it would be Monday. It promised to be another of those grand days for cruising off the West Coast of Scotland. Toby's intent was to spend the forenoon with his fore-ends team ensuring that their systems and the four warshots were all ready for the morrow. Then he had orchestrated the afternoon watch on the bridge for some more birdwatching. By that time they would have cleared Skye and be in the Minches, with Harris and Lewis to seaward on the port side and the ragged coast of North West Scotland to Starboard.

ooOoo

0830 Sunday 4 November

Peter and the CO were on the bridge as Orca left Portree. Permission for preparing the tubes and moving the fish around in another of those games of Solitaire had been granted to ensure they were lined up against their respective launch tubes. To this end the TI and his team were setting up the loading rails for the first two of the LIVEX warshots to be placed in tubes one and two. Operations in the fore-ends followed the mantra "slow but sure". The gear up there was heavyweight and moving one to two tonnes of explosive torpedo was not something done without objective and direct control. To a certain extent Toby's involvement was superfluous, but the TI and he had adopted a pattern whereby his extra informed pair of eyes were an insurance back-up where possible during preps. It helped them both feel a little more comfortable. Toby made sure the TI's authority was not undermined and merely created an atmosphere whereby the fore-end teams saw his engagement with them and the TI as normal business.

It wasn't long before the first one was being traversed to line up to tube one. Once aligned, permission was requested to open tube one rear door and the beast was slowly rammed into position to successfully engage with the top stop. During this movement the umbilical had been carefully held to one side without fouling the loading. So now the umbilical cutter was set up and the remainder of the cable locked into the inner face of the rear door and mated to the connector. As these were Mk IX's (the equivalent of the old anti- surface ship gyro-guided Mk VIII's) there was no complex guide wire dispenser, so the drill was pretty straightforward.

"*Control – Fore-ends. Tube one loaded. Rear door shut and clipped.*" One down - three to go.

The loading of the next one into tube two was a mirror image of the first. The team were in their stride and it didn't take long before that too was reported loaded and shut down. Getting the third in was somewhat more problematic. Following their earlier firings on the range they had had no option but to store some of the wire guided warshots (the ones they were required to have on board at all times as an emergency war outfit) inboard of these last two. So a number of movements were needed before they were eventually lined up and loaded into tubes three and four. It then took another half an hour to return the fore-ends to sea configuration. Once this was over the TI checked that the Torpedo Operating Tanks (or ToTs as they called them) had the requisite amount of water in them. These were used to compensate for the weight of the discharged weapon and the water surrounding it. A check on the air tank pressures for the discharge system, and finally a look at the calibration figures for the last water shots, and Toby left them to a well earned stand easy in the for'd mess.

It was second nature to look at the chart as he passed through the Control Room. Not far to the turn at the bottom of Raasay. His thoughts were turning to a coffee in the wardroom when the CEA (his CPO Control Artificer who maintained and, together with Toby, operated the torpedo control equipment at the for'd end of the Control Room) took him aside.

"Checks on the TCU completed Sir. I've also had a word in the Comms Centre to ensure they know the frequencies the range safety team will be using"

"Well done CEA. As belt and braces just check those haven't changed with the Range Safety chap once we have picked him up off the Crowlins."

"Will do Sir. I've got the afternoon watch so the TI and I will catch you in the Dogs to make sure we're all set and ready for the big event first thing tomorrow."

Toby left him and carried on for'd to the Wardroom, where a large pot of coffee was being passed around. Knowing he had the afternoon watch, Simon who, as Navigator, was responsible for the setting up the positioning for the firing, brought in his chart showing the detail of the range area for the LIVEX. As expected the water was pretty deep so getting into a representative firing range close to the cliffs would not be a problem. They discussed the options for the orientation of the boat. A zero degree "down the throat" shot was neither really credible, nor safe. It didn't give them any room for manoeuvre that close to the cliffs, particularly if there was a delay or if anything went pear-shaped. They looked at the geometry and decided that a forty degree starboard shot gave them most freedom. As for speed, that came down to the depth of water they actually had that close to the cliffs and whether they would surface immediately after firing. Their consensus was to get a good trim, keep down to four knots, and surface as soon as the last fish was on its way. Toby reminded Simon that he would be rigging the camera to the after scope, which meant that both scopes would be up for the firing, with the CO controlling the action from the for'd attack scope. Toby's intent was to get some shots of the impact, but he was not sure whether they could surface sufficiently quickly and then have the boat sufficiently stable for some good photographs. They agreed it was a plausible plan and Simon disappeared back to the chart table in the Control Room to set it all down before offering it as their proposal to the CO.

Having to go on watch at 1230 (they staggered the officer's watches by half an hour to those of the lads, just to make sure no hic-cups occurred during changeovers), Toby sat down to an early lunch. As the soup arrived he could hear the sound of astern revs. They must have just arrived at the position off the Crowlins for the transfer. After forty minutes, and a great cottage pie followed by a bit of cheddar, there was still no scraping of a tender alongside. As Toby drained more coffee he just hoped nothing was going to delay them. Before long it was time to get himself kitted up for the outside world and an afternoon on the bridge. He grabbed some foul weather gear and donning his roll-neck submarine sweater, made his way to the chart table to see where they were. Having dressed, he had a quick all round look through the after periscope and then entered the tower for the long climb up the fin to take over the watch.

ooOoo

1230 Sunday 4 November

Once up top Toby was informed that the rider transfer had been delayed for an hour because of a problem with the tender at the base in the Kyle of Lochalsh. Their new ETA was for 1315 so the boat would have to remain at the rendezvous and simply drift about to waste the extra half an hour. Fortunately the tide had only just turned so they weren't being set very much. The weather had cleared but there was a stiff breeze, definitely more force 4 than 3. Once they were clear of the shelter from Raasay and out in the Minch, Toby's guess was that there would be a few white horses. Until then he stuck himself into a sheltered corner of the bridge and scanned the scene with his binoculars. Drifting just to the west of the islands he could see a brave yacht seeking a bit of shelter between the two southerly islands (Eiln More and Eiln Meadhonach). Having sailed up there himself, he knew they had to keep clear of the reef that runs out from Eiln Meadhonach. There were about two fathoms there, but you had to be careful the current later in the tide didn't swing you across the wind and force you on to the putty.

To the north of them he could just make out Applecross, where the underwater range shore centre was based. Getting there by land was a bit of a trek, hence the use of the Petrol Budgie on a regular basis. Just then, as he turned to scan to the East, almost on cue, it suddenly came into view. It clearly had not long taken off from Plockton and was on its way to Applecross. Continuing his scan to the south he raised the Range tender making a speedy ten knots towards them. They weren't going to be so late after all.

"*Control Room – Bridge. Tender in sight; inform the Captain it will be alongside in ten minutes.*"

"*Roger Bridge – Tender alongside in ten minutes*" played back the helm.

"*Slow ahead starboard*". Toby needed to get their head into the wind, and ensure they had little way on for the transfer.

"*Helm – Bridge; transfer party to the casing*"

"*Second Cox'n coming up through the Tower, Sir. Permission to open the Fin Door?*"

"*Open the Fin Door. Carry on with the transfer*"

"*Aye, Aye, Sir.*"

The boat came around slowly and Toby stopped both engines as the tender made its way around the stern and gently nudged along the port side. Both teams were well practiced and did this on a regular basis so the rope ladder was quickly over the side. The tender's bow was secured and the safety line passed across. Two well wrapped up characters clambered up and across from the bow onto Orca's ladder, and with nimble, practiced steps, quickly climbed up into the hands of the casing party to be shepherded through the Fin door and down the ladder to the warmth of the Control Room. The tender didn't wait. They let go at once and waved Toby farewell, turning back to retrace their passage to the Kyle.

"*Riders on board, Sir. Casing cleared. Fin Door shut and clipped.*" Passed up the duty PO from the plot.

"*Roger. Half Ahead together; revolutions for twelve knots. Starboard fifteen. Steer 005.*" Toby replied.

"*Fifteen of Starboard wheel on, coming right to 005*" sang out the helmsman as the boat started to turn.

"*Inform the Captain that the riders are on board and that I am assuming course and speed for the runs on the noise range.*" Toby passed to the messenger.

"*Plot, bridge, stand by to take a fix. Stand by bearings.*"

Using the bridge pelorus (the gimbaled compass), Toby took the bearings for a fix using the obvious features he had noted on the chart before coming up to the bridge. The PO of the watch in the control room was quick to confirm that there was a good three point fix on the plot. So, fix on the chart, underway and making way, it was 1320 and they were at last on their way up the inner sound.

ooOoo

1420 Sunday 4 November

After half an hour the entrance to Loch Carron and the passage up to Simon's favourite hamlet of Plockton, with its tropical sea front and bevy of drinking holes, disappeared well behind them. They were following a directed passage across the range for those in the range buildings to record their noise signature. Despite being on the surface (noise runs are normally done dived) they had decided to do two runs at different speeds. At the end of the first they had to loiter for a while until John and his engineering team had altered the systems to the configuration appropriate for the next run. The role on the bridge was minimal and somewhat boring despite the marvelous setting. Finally they were released at the end of the second run, by which time half of the watch had passed. As they turned and came back onto course, Toby took another fix to ensure they were on the planned track and ordered the boat back up to twelve knots. Applecross was now well past the beam to starboard, and the entrance to Loch Torridon was just starting to appear in the distance. The only company they had out there was the Skye ferry and a small fishing vessel some way to the south. The latter wasn't going to come close. At that distance Toby couldn't even see whether it had its' fishing gear out. So in splendid isolation, with the northern tip of Raasay shortly abeam to port, he had the chance to have a close look at the northern end of Skye beyond the Isle of Rona. A.B. Tomlinson, as ever, was the doubty look-out, and he had been keeping an eye open for them both while Toby had been otherwise engaged. Their fervent hope was to spot a Golden Eagle. It was clear that they still bred on this northern part of Skye, but in recent years the farmers and gamekeepers had hit their numbers hard. On the walk with Peter, they had met a local who confirmed that a couple of pairs still bred in this area, but it would be pure luck to see one.

Half an hour later they were well clear of the Range, and Toby was forced to give in to the urgency of a full bladder after all that coffee. Not an easy task on the bridge of a submarine. However, they did have what was affectionately known as the "*Pig's Ear*". It looked very similar to the voice pipe, only the latter was made of brass and kept well buffed up to shine out. This device was painted black and instead of going down to open up beside the ear of the helmsman, it had an open end in the back of the fin. Getting the two mixed up would have dire consequences initially for the helmsman and then for the person getting it wrong. So Toby carefully aimed his member and achieved relief without any embarrassing moments.

No sooner had he tucked everything away than Tomlinson shouted excitedly that he could actually see an Eagle circling away over the northern point of Raasay. It took Toby some moments to find it against the hills in the background, but sure enough there it was. He had never seen one in the wild before, so this was very special. Even at this range, as it soared in the afternoon thermals, you could see the enormity of its wing span and as it turned the sun caught its golden yellow beak bringing out the shape of that powerful ripping tool. Its talons were hidden but he had no doubt of the shear strength of the bird. It had no enemies, other than man.

They lost sight of it as they gradually left Raasay astern. That had been very special, another Tomlinson gold star. He just had this ability to see what others missed. A good quality in a lookout.

The passage north to Cape Wrath was only about eighty miles and they weren't due off it before 0600 in the morning. This would give plenty of time to dive, get a good trim and position themselves for the firing. So their choices were to either reduce speed or loiter. The CO was not at all keen on the latter, particularly off either Loch Ewe or the entrance to Ullapool just beyond it. The ferries to Stornaway and a fair number of large fishing vessels regularly came in and out of Ullapool, including some very large Russian factory ships which serviced the fishing vessels. So Toby called for Simon to come on the bridge intercom to give guidance as to what he should do. In fact Simon was already kitting up to take over the watch, and after a brief word with the CO told Toby to come down to eight knots. Their choice was to move further out into the Minches, and with plenty of sea room make a gentle passage north slightly further off the coast.

Tomlinson had already been relieved at 1600, so with Toby's watch coming to an end and his stomach grumbling for some tea and cake, the sound of Simon climbing his way up the fin was very welcome. To Toby's surprise he came with a visitor. As the second body struggled out of the hatch way Toby thought it was the Range Officer, but as he held out his hand to introduce himself he could see the newcomer was far too young.

"Evening, Sir. Sub-Lieutenant Steve Frankham. I'm a Part III Electrical Officer and I'm joining you all for the rest of the running period, until you get back to SM1 in Gosport in two weeks"

"Well this is a surprise. Firstly, please don't call me Sir. I'm Toby. Simon has probably told you I'm the LO so I guess you'll want to shadow me during your stay. Simon, when did we know Steve was joining us?

"Another balls-up I'm afraid. Not that it's your fault Steve. SM10 were meant to have told us after the fun with the DSRV. Well you're safely with us now. Apparently it was Steve's imminent arrival which held up the tender leaving the Kyle. At least we have room, although his pit will have to be one of the temporary ones on the racks in the fore-ends. Cuddling up to the odd torpedo can be fun, albeit a little chillier than in one of the messes, but you will have the Range Safety man as company. I'm afraid it is where all the riders have to sleep. I suggested Steve came up here with me for the first dog to give him a watch on the bridge with some dramatic scenery. It could be a last chance for some days with the weather getting up and once we are around the top, the wind off the North Sea is not pleasant." he explained.

"You two can talk later. Toby, off you go, the Leading Steward has saved you some cake" finished Simon. Thus tempted, Toby turned over the watch and bid a quick farewell to clamber back down below.

ooOoo

1645 Sunday 4 November

After tea Toby had arranged to have a "progress chat" with LREM Best, in an attempt to finish yet another of his annual reports before they got back. The large number he had to write up inevitably resulted in some being left over to the time alongside, but with the full docking period coming up Toby was going to be heavily loaded and wanted to get ahead of the curve. At least that was his game plan. Finding somewhere where they could talk alone was almost impossible, and in the end he opted for his little office grot in the Lower AMS. Not quite your normal one on one setting, but it would have to do. Best had been on board just over a year and had done pretty well, but had somehow gone off the boil of late. He was six or so years older than Toby, was married and had some children, although Toby didn't know the details. Professionally he was on the verge of getting the step up to Petty Officer, so Toby was keen to have an open chat and understand his ambition and goals, and basically set out a credible timetable which they could both work to.

Best arrived with a mug of tea, settled down on a stool in the corner and they started going over the normal details at the start of the report forms. Toby felt fairly quickly that something was not right, and a sixth sense told him not to address it straight away, but it just popped out.

"With your seniority and performance you are clearly ready for the next step up to PO – and I'm very happy to fully recommend you. I've got some dates for the respective POREL courses, but before we go into those I wanted to ask you about this running period. At times you just haven't been yourself. Is there a problem with the team in the Comms shack? … or the REA? …or Me? Please be open, if there is something we can do to help let's discuss it."

He sat there in silence for quite some time and then tears started to well up in his eyes and very quietly and slowly he started.

"At the end of the DSRV exercise I received a letter from my wife telling me she is leaving. I've managed to phone her from Faslane and then again from Portree but find it's almost impossible to understand what has happened. We've had arguments but this has come out of the blue. I don't know if it is me, another bloke, the Navy or what. It's blowing my mind and I just can't think about anything else"

"Why didn't you tell me earlier? We'd have got you a rail warrant and back down south straight away?"

"I realise that Sir. But she told me the worst thing I could do would be to charge back home. She was adamant that she needed time, and that I was not to get back before our due return date. At the moment she's taken herself and the children to her Mother's."

Toby sat there listening to all this thinking how the hell can he, at twenty six, married for just under three years, with no children or any thoughts as yet, act as a marriage counsellor and give this guy any advice. Best needed real help and he wasn't sure that he could give it. This was somewhere Toby had never been before.

"Best, have you talked to anyone else on board about this?" He asked.

"No, Sir, and I don't want to."

A brick wall, but Best needed someone else to help him.

"Look this is me being very straight. I can fully understand you not wanting to talk to your immediate boss the REA, he's not always the easiest or most understanding of people. I also realise that you want this to stay very private and not be known around the boat. But I do believe Chief Connelly, who is also my deputy in seniority, is someone who could help. He's a genuine person, a family man who will understand fully the pressures on you and your family as well as your personal concerns and fears ... and I fully trust him. I'd like to tell him and for the pair of you to sit down and discuss what we can do to help. For my part I will do all I can to give you all the space you need for you and your wife to have time for yourselves once we get back. Cut off like this, it's the best we can do. Sharing your problems with someone who we both trust, and has seen almost all the stresses and strains of family life in the Service can only help you. Are you happy with that?"

"Yes, I guess so Sir. I guess it might actually ease the load talking to some-one. I feel some of the pressure has come off just letting you know. Chief Connelly is a good man."

Toby's mind was racing as to what else he could do. "In the mean time I will continue to put you forward for the POREL's course as an early candidate. Having some time ashore might be what you and your family need and it is a pretty lengthy course at HMS Collingwood. It might also help you both in providing a sense of direction, plus show your wife how much we value you. Being frank, at this stage I can't think of anything else we could do right now. Is there anything else you have in mind and would like me to do?"

"No Sir, but thanks for listening." he got up to go clearly still in some distress.

"If you want to talk or think of anything else we can do to help, come and see me," Best started up the ladder leaving Toby in a state of real shock. All the crew tended to be flippant about life in a blue suit, but there were the many pressures of families with constant separation which Toby had only just started to experience. So many of his counterparts had got married at the end of their RNEC Manadon time, and yet a number had already fallen by the wayside. No wonder Judy consistently said that she had married him not the Navy.

So much for his wonderful evening up top. Toby returned to the Wardroom feeling pretty low and sought out Chief Connelly to see how he would take it and if he had any helpful thoughts. It came as a surprise to him, but he took it on board very quickly realising immediately how that had taken the edge off Best's performance. They discussed what Toby had proposed, and he was very frank about his feelings of impotence at being so inexperienced on life and marriage. Chief Connelly was really supportive and told Toby that sympathy and having someone really listen was probably the most valuable help anyone could give in such circumstances - he'd almost been there himself. "So Toby had done well for the lad".

"Lad??? – He was older than me!" thought Toby.

Connelly agreed to let Best know straight away that they had briefly discussed the problem and would arrange to have a long chat with him after the excitement off Cape Wrath was over. Toby thanked God that he had someone as mature and genuinely good as the Chief to help him. So much for the training they all received about being Divisional Officers. It had covered the paper work, and done well on all that leadership stuff, but covered nothing like this. He really felt for the man, and had been humbled by the confidence placed in himself.

ooOoo

0530 Monday 5 November
They stayed on the surface overnight and Toby really enjoyed his "all night in". At about 0430 the boat started to move about, it was clear that the forecast was a bit out and it was going to get quite lumpy as the morning wore on. Toby didn't have a chance to go on the bridge again, but as soon as it was light he had a good look at their surroundings. He also discovered that Cape

Wrath had an interesting name. Apparently it had come from the old Norse "hvarf" being the "turning point" for the Vikings going home. It was also special in that it and Cape Cornwall were the only headlands in the UK which shared the handle Cape. Looking through the search periscope it was pretty impressive, with the smart light-house standing out in its fresh white coat above it. In talking to the Range Safety guy the previous evening, Toby had expressed his surprise that they were being directed to blast a fairly large bit of Scotland off the cliffs up there. The Range Safety guy had explained that the surrounding area was a major military bombardment range used quite extensively by both the RN and the RAF. The range was regularly used for live bombing runs with ordnance clearance up to 1000 lbs of high explosive. It had also been used for major tri-service

Cape Wrath

exercises including landings of significant numbers of Marines. A large area was closed to the public, which enhanced the feeling of remoteness.

Toby could see quite a few white horses, and the sea was breaking heavily against the cliffs. Below these there were large numbers of Gannets and Fulmars. He guessed that the remoteness of the area must have enhanced its attraction for wildlife. Oddly it had large herds of Red Deer which were formally the property of the MoD. Toby wondered which service was able to take advantage of having game on the menu. Probably the Pongos - they aspired to live well in the field. He could just imagine some regiments in a tent, regimental silver all laid out, tucking into well hung fillets of venison.

Toby took advantage of this quiet spell to get the camera fitted to the search periscope. Normally they used the for'd attack scope which was monocular, but the boss would need this for the dummy attack routine. So the Leading Writer who helped Toby with all the photo recce's and looked after the cameras, had adapted their kit to fit to one of the eye pieces of the search scope. It worked after a fashion. You could still use the other eye piece – just. Toby's only concern was whether light would get in to spoil any shots they took. Judicious use of masking tape minimized the risk. He finished by taking a couple of shots to prove the set up.

At 0700, having had an early breakfast, they closed up at diving stations. The Range Safety Officer was stationed on the plot, and they had plugged through a radio link to the Range HQ for him to man on his head phones. He made contact to prove the link before they dived. Anyone watching them go through their paces from the shore would have wondered what they were doing. Normally for a periscope attack, in an attempt to remain covert, they would only raise the very small diameter monocular attack periscope. For this event they were going to have both scopes and the radio mast up. To Naval eyes it would look very unusual. In the event it turned out to be a full house as they added the snort and exhaust masts so they could keep the diesels going, and the Range insisted they raise the radar mast to ensure an accurate range from the cliff target. So it became a "full house" in terms of masts, sadly there were no witnesses to photograph such an unusual configuration.

Although the plan had been to close up to diving stations, dive and get a trim, and then once settled go to Action Stations, the teams had simply all closed up at the same time. Nonetheless, with Peter (the XO) undertaking the dive, the boat slowly settled under the water, coming back up to periscope depth without incident. With all the alterations to the trim and the torpedo movements and loading, it took a while for a good trim to be sorted. The CO wanted to be as shallow as possible without impeding a routine discharge from the four upper tubes. This would ease their ability to have as smooth a surface as possible after firing. Given the weather it would also help to keep his visibility through the for'd scope clear of the wave chop during the attack.

Toby looked around at the gathering. Steve Frankham, their newly joined part III, was pressed into a corner. He was clearly excited, but somewhat stunned to realise how many people were crammed into the Control Room. Toby remembered counting the bodies during one of their routine attack evolutions. He vaguely remembered that the number had been eighteen, just under a third of the crew. Today with their Riders and the additional record keepers, they were way above that number. Yet to their credit you could have heard a pin drop. Despite all this the space around the attack scope was kept well clear, so that the Boss would not be hampered doing his routine.

"*Sir, submarine trimmed and level at sixty feet. We could come up to fifty eight if desired?*"

"*Thank you Number One. No, stay at sixty feet. Pipe: "Action Stations". Starboard ten, come right to 340, confirm speed.*"

"*Starboard Ten, speed five knots*" replied the Second Cox'n on the helm.

The noise level came up a little as they all took up their prime Action Station positions. The trim and overall control of the submarine was led by the XO, with the Outside Wrecker on the trim panel, and the Cox'n on the after planes. John joined his team in the donk shop. This group were those who would ensure the Naval tenets of "Move and Float" or in our case keeping the water out, whereas the "Fight" was down to the CO and Toby's teams in the Control Room and the Fore Ends. The Second Cox'n had just reported "*on course 340*", when the reports from all compartments in the submarine started to come through. The last were the team in the fore-ends - theirs was a relatively long report confirming the status of the tubes and the warshots in them.

"*Prepare to Snort*" ordered the CO, closely followed by "*Raise the radar mast and report range to target*".

The XO conducted the snort drill calmly with the Outside Wrecker and his team: the opening of the snort drains, the raising of the mast and its draining down. Eventually having had permission to open the hull valve and emergency back-up valve they were ready to snort.

The diesels were started and to the delight of the crowded and sweaty mass in the Control Room, a strong guff of fresh Scottish air immediately started to waft its way through the submarine.

"*Crew closed up at Action Stations. Submarine snorting with diesels running on both sides, Sir.*"

Now was time for the Circus to start. A periscope attack is somewhat akin to the running of a circus ring. The CO is the Ringmaster who singly controls every act and nuance in the ring. His support teams are just that, they act out a routine which is rehearsed, and rehearsed, and rehearsed ... until it is perfect. It runs like clockwork. It does not rely on orders, routine or otherwise. It is a script and everyone has to know his part. Not only that but the players are professionals who understand, not only the words, but the workings of all the supporting rigs, jigs and equipment. In a circus it is the high wire – in a submarine it is more complex; the fire control gear, the torpedo tube launch gear, and when the torpedoes are wire guided, all the interactive modes to finally lock it on to the target. This act was a bit more straightforward, but it did have the interaction of the Range and its' safety issues to constrain the overall scene.

"*Range is clear. We have permission to start the run*" announced the safety guy by the plot. All was now ready.

"*Standby target set up*" announced the CO, swinging the attack scope in a quick all round look. "*Come up to fifty eight feet. I need the extra height to clear the breaking waves*"

"*Range 3600 yards. Speed zero, I am 40 degrees on his port bow*"

"*Keeping fifty eight feet*" added the Cox'n.

Four tubes ready to go

"*This will be a four tube salvo, prepare tubes One, Two, Three and Four.*"

"*XO, as soon as the last tube has discharged, following our LIVEX plan, you are to surface the submarine, maintaining course and speed*"

"*Understood, Sir.*"

Despite the twenty or so people crammed in the Control Room the only noises were from the operation of the planes and the occasional adjustments to the helm. After each "all round look" the Outside Wrecker automatically lowered the attack periscope as the CO put up the handles. The latter just stood quietly looking at his wrist stop watch, you could see him counting down the range, this scenario couldn't be closer to a real attack.

"*Up attack.*" As the scope came up he grabbed it about two feet off the deck conducting another all round look as it gradually came up to shoulder height. Taking the target bearing he prepared to "cut" it through to the fire control system via the push on the right handle.

"*Bearing is that*" commanded the CO.

"*Puts you 45 starboard*" responded Toby.

"No. *Make it 40 starboard*" – Toby adjusted the readings on the Torpedo Control Console (or TCC), and these were automatically fed to the fore-ends to adjust the gyros in the fish, giving them their offset run bearings.

Normally the CO would then be using the visual calipers in the scope, set with the targets mast height, to match a double image which gave the range reading. In this case they couldn't do the same for the cliff so they had to use the radar.

"*Range Radar?*" Toby called out.

"*Range 3600 yards*" came the reply.

"*Range set. Salvo interval set at five seconds*" Toby announced.

"No. Make it *four seconds*" the CO replied.

More hush as they crept up to the moment critique. The intent was to fire at about three thousand yards, close enough to the real thing but with sufficient water for them to keep clear of any collateral damage when the fish hit the cliffs. The CO's focus on his chronometer was to match this scenario. Finally he indicated to the Outside Wrecker, who brought the attack scope up. Again he took it very low, doing the all round look.

"*Range is clear. Firing Look*" he added for Range Safety to pass to the Range Head

"*Bearing is that*". He cut it through.

"*Puts you 38 Port*" Toby replied.

"*Set 40 Port. Range?*"

"*Range 3200 yards*" came from the radar shack

"*Range 3200, zero speed, 40 port, with salvo interval 4 seconds …data set.*"

"*Range confirms clear to fire*" reported the Safety guy.

"*Fire One*". The CO immediately replied.

Toby made the push and they all felt the impulse on the boat as the first one was discharged. The others followed at their four second intervals and as soon as the last had gone the XO joined in:

"*Submarine Surfacing. Blow One, Two, Four, Six and Seven main ballast*"

The noise of high pressure air displacing thousands of gallons of sea water from the main ballast tanks just drowned out everything else. They all stood expectantly for the impacts. At this range the run time was just under two minutes. They waited.

"*Stop Blowing*"

They were on the surface rocking quite heavily in the moderate sea. Both periscopes had been left up and the CO was on the Attack, with TASO on the after one desperately trying to look through the one eye piece so that he could get some good shots of the impact.

"*One hit …two …*" They all heard it. " *… three …four*"

"*Excellent, a full salvo*" the Boss took the main broadcast and passed on the news around the boat. Meanwhile TASO was taking continuous shots on the after scope, complete with a running commentary. It was all very dramatic. Toby passed over the TCC control to the CEA and went forward to congratulate the TI and his team promising beers all round that evening. They were cock-a-hoop.

Finally returning to the Control Room Toby grabbed a signal pad and completed the firing signal. The CO signed it with a grin and Toby took it to the Comms Office and waited until they had despatched it into the ether.

050743A

From: ORCA

To: SM1

LIVEX COMPLETED SATISFACTORILY AT 050715 ALPHA.

ALL FOUR WEAPONS DISCHARGED IN SINGLE SALVO .

FOUR IMPACTS.

ALL EXPLODED.

EXERCISE COMPLETED SUCCESSFULLY.

ON SURFACE PASSAGE TO RV IN EASTERN EXERCISE AREAS.

A bland message which brought them all back to earth, after an overdose of adrenalin which certainly set the scene for "Guy Fawkes" day, albeit in somewhat choppy waters.

ooOoo

CLOCKWORK MOUSING

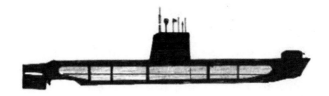

Missing Life in Submarines?

Lesson 5 on recapturing the old days:-

Cut four foot diameter holes in all the internal doors in the house, fit locks & lock the doors; then run from one end to the other through the holes bashing your shins and head on every door.

0930 Monday 6 November

It didn't take them long to settle down after all the excitement. They stayed on the surface and reverted to more relaxed watches under Cruising Routine. Their route now headed East, around the Kyle of Durness, to take them the fifty nautical miles past Thurso, and then passage through the Pentland Firth below the Orkneys. The weather had not eased off and the odd lumpy wave had now turned into a real threat of force six to seven. Eight is gale force, but as yet no warnings had been given from the Met office, perhaps they would just get through in time. Moving about the boat had become very uncomfortable. Toby had a quick word with Polto and the TI to ensure that all their loose gear in the Motor Room and Fore-ends was well lashed down, and then took Steve Frankham, the Part III, into the Wardroom to discuss his training for the next few weeks.

Life in a submarine is like living in a machine. Wherever you look there are pipes, cables and widgets. Hardly any of it is covered over behind screens because any failure has to be tackled immediately by the person nearest to the scene at that moment. To help them there are colour codes on the pipes, denoting the service they provide, and each electrical box lists all the services. Over and above this the environment is a very noisy one. The most noise is from the ventilation system which is pretty fierce. In fact the scariest moment in a submarine is when it goes off and all becomes silent, whatever the time of day or night, everyone wakes up, adrenalin running ready for the inevitable emergency. The system has to push large volumes of air around the boat and through some significant charcoal filters. These take all the nasties out, from misty oils to smoke. In fact there is a lot of the latter because a great number of the crew took advantage of the duty free *Blue Liners* – cigarettes, which considering their price were almost given away. Each person was allowed 300 a month.

Steve's task was to learn how to work in and react to emergencies in this strange, complex machine – which at the moment was starting to roll around like a drunken tube train. He explained that he had completed basic training and the escape tank four months ago. Since then he had been doing application training on the various systems fitted in Conventionals. This trip was one of his last phases before qualification as a submariner and then he would be taking the Nuclear Reactor course at Greenwich College with finally an appointment to one of the new *SSN*s as an *AWEO*

They sat together and reviewed his work book which covered the basic tasks. It was pretty familiar. A cross between systems tracing and practical experience of the drills all of them had to know by heart. As a submariner each and every one of them had to learn the basic sub-marine systems off pat, over and above their individual professional roles. To this end they were required to trace and learn everything from dive and trim systems, to air and hydraulics, to safety systems such as the Emergency Breathing System (EBS) and special drills like snorting. It was a long list, one which at the start all of them found daunting.

Toby would start with the safety systems. As well as being a natural priority, it would force Steve to go all over the boat with the advantage of meeting a great many of the crew. They had all been successfully through this and knew that their success had depended on the help given by their predecessors. It was second nature now to ensure that Part III's got all the help they needed.

As they slowly meandered aft through the boat Toby kept up a general patter explaining the basics of the compartments as they went through. He also made sure Steve was introduced to as many of the on-watch staff as possible. Not that this was really possible in the donk shop, as both main engines were going at a rare pace and it was impossible to hear anything, so communication was via lip reading and sign language. It sufficed for the time being, he could come back once they had dived, the diesels were shut down, and the boat was running on the main electric motors. The noise blew Toby's mind away every time he came through, he didn't think he could ever have worked there, even with the ear defenders they wore. They then loitered in the Motor Room for a coffee and a chat with the team on watch. Steve was, after all one of them, albeit he did have to take some ribbing about wanting to join Nuclear boats and miss out on the pirate life in Conventionals. None of the watch could understand what could possibly lead anyone to actually volunteer for Nuclear Boats.

Toby helped him to make his escape and they eventually arrived in the After-Ends where he gave him the "one and six" tour. This compartment, like its' big brother in the Fore-Ends, combined the roles of weapon stowage and escape compartment. On the weapon side it only had two tubes, but the safety systems were the same. As an escape compartment, although it was considerably smaller, it still had to accommodate the full crew should the worst happen. So it had a full escape system including stowage for escape suits and gear for the whole crew. Steve found the relevant section in his work book, and having introduced him, Toby left him in the very capable hands of LWEM Walsh the local expert.

Making his farewell, Toby turned to leave and hit his head with a mighty thump on the rim of the escape hatch. It clearly hurt, but it was fortunately on the opposite side to his cut from the deep dive incident. He wasn't that tall, being five feet eight and was normally able to walk through the main part of the boat without having to bend. Up here, however, everyone had to bend to get around the tower which filled the centre of the compartment. Toby hadn't forgotten, he just hadn't allowed enough headroom. It was something he did too frequently. So clutching another bleeding brow he staggered back to the Motor Room where the guys patched him up yet again. Just as they were finishing the Polto arrived on the scene.

Grinning from ear to ear he asked: "What have you been doing, Sir?"

"My head hit something harder than it. Don't laugh too loudly." Toby replied.

Passing it off, Toby got him to sit down to discuss the rest of the running period. They both agreed that the next week was what they all needed, a period of calm routine. In fact they were about to have a complete week at sea, almost all dived. The plan was to dive once they had turned into the North Sea, and make their way down to the Exercise areas off the east coast just north of the Firth of Forth and the busy shipping lanes into and out of Edinburgh. This running period had been pretty crammed to date and the idea of settling down to Watch Dived for a week really appealed to them all.

It was surprising how few opportunities they actually managed to get to put into practice their real role, dived and silent on their batteries, albeit interspersed with snort transits to achieve the odd covert entry into new areas. It meant surviving on a two on and four off routine, with two hour watches and sleep periods limited to three and a half hours max. In a masochistic way Toby really enjoyed it. It was what they were about, and they really raised their game as a result. It was the same for the lads, especially in the sound room. Their skills were paramount for the boat's survival and success, yet they could only exercise them when they were dived, and properly functioning in a silent routine. The forthcoming period, however, was going to be a bit drawn out. Orca's role was to play target to a squadron of anti-submarine frigates working up on the east coast. The boat would, therefore, be limited in its freedom of action to meet their needs. It was what the Navy called Clockwork Mousing. Traditionally at the end of these periods the target boat was allowed 24 hours of freeplay, whereby the tables were turned and Orca would be allowed to return the compliment attacking them as and when able. Success for the crew would be one or more surprise attacks culminating in the underwater launch of a green grenade. The classic naval gesture denoting a practice submarine kill on yet another surface target or as submariners phrased it - another *skimmer* put in its place.

ooOoo

1145 Monday 5 November

Having orchestrated the LIVEX off Cape Wrath so that it was conducted around slack tide meant that their passage over the top of Scotland would lead them into the Pentland Firth when the tide was pretty well near its zenith. Simon and the CO were cosseted over the chart table late morning going over the options when Toby eventually passed through the Control Room. They had come to the conclusion that keeping mid channel, with as much sea room around the boat as possible was the best option. They were making good progress and would have Thurso abeam during lunch. So Simon and the CO would at least be able to go on the bridge well prepared for a bracing afternoon to battle the worst that the Pentland Firth could throw at them. Fortunately, the wind had dropped a little and it was visibly less lumpy, so it would just be the tide to contend with. From all they had heard that would be enough.

The prattle over lunch had been started by the leading Steward, The LIVEX had little impact on him and the fact that the boat was about to go through the Pentland Firth was only of passing interest. What he wanted to know about was the forthcoming visit to Sunderland, which was due to take place after the time in the North Sea exercise areas.

"Come on, Sir" he said to the XO. "I need to know what day you have allocated for the Children's Party. These events don't just happen. I have got to get the lads organized."

They all knew that despite his genuine interest in the children – he was definitely a star when it came to these parties - his real interest was the Mums.

"Look, it's on the notice board outside the ship's office. We have a week clockwork-mousing and then the passage to Sunderland will take three days. Once there, we have a cocktail party on the first night, we are open to visitors on the second, we have the children's party on the third day, and then after some lunches on the fourth, make our escape on the fifth," responded a desperate XO.

Oh, God, Toby thought, "I am duty for that open day. Christ, that is all I need, how did the Seaman Officers swing that?" He finished his totally reasonable (that is - small) portion of "apple crumble", and set his plate aside to finish his coffee. Now was not the time to attempt to persuade someone to take his place, they were clearly not in the mood to be persuaded. So, he adjusted his position, pumped up the cushions, and shut his eyes. The world would begin to look much more balanced after a power nap.

Toby came to, as the boat shuddered, with the noise of the screws clearly going astern. What the hell was going on? Rubbing the sleep out of his eyes, he pulled his way around the Wardroom table, and still somewhat groggy, stumbled into the Control Room to join John at the Chart Table.

"John, what is happening?"

"It's the tide rip. My guess is it must be over ten knots, perhaps even up to fourteen. The Boss is trying to steer us around Stroma by using Astern on the relevant screw to keep us heading in the right direction. It's the vibration of the astern revs which is causing the boat to judder in that unseemly fashion." he answered.

"Look," John continued, "We are passing between Stroma and Swona, just south of Ronaldsay. It is here that we will experience the worst of the tide rip. I understand from Simon that this tide rip is infamous, and goes under the name of "Swelkie". It is incredibly strong and depending on the direction of the tide can flow east or west. Today it is behind us, and despite our astern revolutions we are still making a fair speed into the North Sea. It is just our luck after the LIVEX. I think we should be OK once we round Duncansby Head and get out into this broader stretch of the North Sea. Have you looked through the after scope? You can see the seal colony on the north side of Stroma – I am not an expert but I think they are all Grey Seals." He put down the dividers and turned to look at Toby.

"Toby, once we are through this, we can dive and settle down to our week of Clockwork Mousing. God knows, we all need a rest. This running period has been too exciting for the likes of my guys. A slower pace, and a little less excitement will be welcomed by all."

"You're right, as ever, John. My guys have been pretty well stretched and need a break. Playing a dumb target for the skimmers is about the right level for my team. Unfortunately, they are all looking forward to Sunderland rather too eagerly. I smell an incident or two."

At this point the boat shuddered dramatically as both screws bit into astern revs. "John, this is getting scary. It must be incredibly strong" Toby said grabbing the edge of the chart table to stop himself being thrown across the Control Room.

Grabbing the overhead pipes to stop his inevitable passage across the Control Room John replied, "Oh Yes. My guess is that the tide must be over ten knots, perhaps twelve, to throw us about like this. Simon warned me that it has been up to 14 knots just south of Stroma. Have a look a through the search periscope, you should be able to see Duncansby Head to the south and South Ronaldsay to the north."

Toby grabbed the scope and executed a slow "all round look". The mainland and Duncansby Head were clearly visible to the south. Turning further around to the north, the south of Ronaldsay was clear, with the isles of Stroma and Swona fast disappearing astern. They were

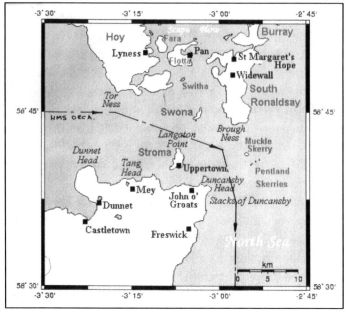

The Route through the Pentland Firth

still going at a rate of knots, despite the use of astern revolutions to keep them heading in the right direction.

Then Toby saw them. They were about four cables off the port bow. It turned out to be a "Pod" of nine Orca's making their way through the Firth. Totally unfazed by the tide rip, they were heading the same way, east towards the North Sea. Their markings were dramatic. The male was leading, he must have been twenty five per cent bigger than each of his harem of females, with the rest of the group being a mix of three young males and the rest females. They were beautiful. Toby could not contain his excitement. He made a full main broadcast to the crew, letting them know that their namesakes were swimming close on the port side. Before he knew what was happening the Control Room was chocker, and guys were queuing up to take their turn in looking at these amazing mammals. Magnificent in their black and white colours.

They were stunning.

Toby ended up being the after scope attendant for the next hour. Then they slowly disappeared, almost as quietly as they had appeared. For most of the crew it had been the first live sighting of their namesakes, a special moment. Quite an afternoon, with the Boss and Simon guiding them through the rip tide in the Pentland Firth by judicious use of astern power, and then the sighting of those magnificent Orca's. Killer whales – a dramatic handle for such beautiful mammals.

Then Orca herself was spewed out into the North Sea, and turned south for the start of the next phase of her trip around the UK.

ooOoo

0700 Tuesday 6 November

They dived the following morning, having spent the night slowly steaming across the Moray Firth. Peter's efforts for the LIVEX meant that the trim was in good shape and it did not take them long to get settled at periscope depth. The boat was understandably a bit light following the discharge of the four warshots, but Peter quickly made allowances for them. Doing four knots at periscope depth, with a good trim, they were soon snorting. Despite the cold North Sea draught rushing through the boat, the fresh air kept them on their toes and they gradually ate up the miles as they slowly made their way around Fraserburgh and Peterhead, down the NE Scottish coast.

"*Fall out Special Sea Duty Men – Watch Dived*" piped Peter once he and the Boss were happy.

At last - "Watch Dived", with every expectation of staying in this routine for the rest of this week you could almost hear the sigh of relief go through the boat. Toby was due on for the first watch. He generally kept watches with Simon, their illustrious Navigator, but this time there were to be three of them. Although Steve Frankham was under training, the extra officer really took the pressure off them both. At periscope depth they took it in turns on the after periscope and trim, changing over every ten to twenty minutes, pending the light and their ability to stay focused. If there was nothing in sight on a dark night their eyes really ached after ten minutes. Steve's main emphasis would be on becoming competent as the Trim officer of the watch. That included the respective drills, particularly snorting. So with the support of those in the donk shop they imposed breaks in the snort passage each time they came on as a watch, so that Steve could hone down his snorting drill. To be fair it didn't take him long. He was fortunate that the seas were now slight - snorting was quite a different challenge when the weather was bad. During exercises earlier in the year they had a particularly bad time. They had been out in the North Atlantic, just below the Iceland – Faroes gap, and the weather had got up to force ten. Snorting in that had been hell. The boat behaved like a drunken tube train, one minute flying on the surface the next plunging to the depths uncontrollably. A couple of the lads back aft had been thrown about quite badly and had broken some bones. It had lasted a week and most of the Officers in the Wardroom had become exhausted. Each time they were shaken to come on watch Toby had found his stomach knotting up with the fear and dread of another two hours of chaos in the Control Room. They had been fortunate not to suffer any significant damage or casualties. Some of the boats had been forced to withdraw and limp back home to Dolphin. It had not been an experience any of them wanted to repeat.

Toby agreed to take the first stint on the after scope. Before doing so he had a good look at the chart and their progress. They were making good time but since leaving sight of land no fix had been taken. That would be Simon's priority, while Toby stayed on the after scope. The team on watch before them had been John the Engineer, and Frank the TASO. As Simon and Toby arrived to take over, Frank was comfortably huddled around the search periscope. He had the roundabout engaged so that his rotation speed was controlled by the peddle operated by his right foot. His arms were cradled over the handles of the scope and, as ever, he looked dead to the world.

"Hi Frank, your relief is at hand, anything in sight?" Toby tapped Frank's right shoulder and he raised his head acknowledging Toby's presence.

"We've just lost sight of the coast. We did have the lights from Peterhead but now the sun is up they have all disappeared. There are two large fishing vessels, both are to seaward of us heading north, about six thousand yards off. Neither is a concern" he replied.

"Fine. Move over and I'll take an all round look" Toby said as Frank vacated the seat. Toby put his visual settings on the eye pieces of the scope and settled down. A quick all round look confirmed Frank's summary.

"*I can see both fishermen. I am happy. I have the periscope.*" Toby formally replied to acknowledge change of responsibility. A simple statement, but quite

The Periscopes

important, given this role was the only one on board with visual awareness of their surroundings. If the person on the periscope missed anything, no-one else was going to see it. The morning light was pretty good just a few white horses, only the occasional wave was breaking over the scope as they made their slow way south. As he rotated Toby could see both the snort and the wireless masts, with the exhaust bubbling from its mast just below the surface at the back of the fin.

"*Sound Room, Search periscope. Do you have contacts running for the two vessels to port? Their range is six thousand*" Toby flicked the comms switch on the scope handle.

"*Control Room, Sonar. We have both contacts, classified fishing vessels*". They replied adding the contact numbers so that the control room team could keep track of them. The crew were definitely back in the groove, and enjoying it. So Toby settled down to concentrate, ensuring that nothing was going to pass him by.

Having checked that the trim, depth and course were all under control, Simon decided that it was time to get that fix on the chart. Out of sight of land he had a few options. *

The most complex was using the sextant in the for'd periscope, to take either a full star fix at night or a "sun – run – sun" during the day. They occasionally attempted the latter but from a dived submarine the errors were pretty big. Their most reliable source was LORAN. This system of radio stations put out signals which they could read, and using the US set fitted on board, translated the information into a positional fix. There were usually at least three stations for them to choose when operating in the North Atlantic and around Europe, so a three point fix was credible.

It came down to the quality of the radio reception as to the accuracy of the fix.

Deciding to use the LORAN set, Simon led Steve into the radar shack and settled down to lock on to his chosen stations. This old US set was an AN/BS7A. Not that the number meant anything to them. It was well worn both in physical and electrical terms. There was definitely a knack to using this old thing. Getting the stations to lock-on required a level of manual tuning. The danger was that the operator ended up tuning to the perceived station signals and not the actual ones. In other words it was quite easy to do what was called - "situate the appreciation".

*Author's Note: In the late 60's and early 70's it was well before the advent of GPS and the satellite systems available to the military in the 80's and 90's

Thereby creating a good looking three point fix with little credibility. The reality was often that the actual signals, being poor, were giving a "cocked hat" fix with each station signal being some way from the others. Some actual fixes gave an area of error the size of a hand on the chart table. Simon's professional pride had occasionally led him up this false path, with him believing he had a good three pointer, when in fact they were anywhere within ten to fifteen miles. As the Electrical Officer Toby felt duty bound to double check the LORAN fixes when they had no other source to turn to. However, at least this time Simon had Steve with him, and in Toby's eyes even a newly fledged "Lecky" should be able to vet what was and was not a good signal.

They remained ensconced over the set for the next half hour, by which time Toby's eyes were losing it and he needed a break. He called over to Simon to say that he needed to be relieved on the periscope.

"I am almost there, Toby. Steve, you take the next spell and that will give me time to get this fix on the chart." He replied, walking over to the chart table.

Keeping his eyes locked to the periscope, Toby called out: "Steve it's your turn then. I'm sure you've been on one of these before, do you know your eye piece settings?" Still sitting on the roundabout Toby turned to give Steve room to enter them.

He applied the adjustments and as Toby vacated the seat Steve slipped across to take his place.

"Quick all round look to start, then a slow deliberate one." He tried to push the scope to no avail. "No, here use your right foot on this and with a gentle pressure you will go around at your chosen speed. Look, this plate here engages the roundabout to the periscope shaft."

Steve quickly got the hang of it and settled down for the all round looks. "Well done. That's it." Toby encouraged him. "Happy with those? Good, now have a good look at the two contacts; those fishing boats on the Port side. You can still see their upper works, my guess is that they are about four miles off now. Remember your horizon is pretty limited looking through a periscope, given the very low height of eye." Toby coached him and went on to ensure he understood the relative positions of the boat and the contacts.

"Our course is 170, can you estimate what theirs is?"

Steve turned up the amplification to get a better view, and after a pause replied; "I would put us just aft of their beam, which would make them about 120 Port, which puts them ... God my mental arithmetic has gone ... no that would be 020?"

Trying to cover up his own shortcomings - Toby tended to cheat and use the analogue settings on the TCC – he replied that he thought they weren't quite as far round as that, "My guess is that they are heading north together, which would put them not quite so far abaft our beam. Remember, they will be moving about a bit if they have still got their gear out. Does that look reasonable?" Toby suggested.

A further more measured look, and Steve agreed. At which point Toby reminded him that the Sound Room had been following them for a while and the *BOP* (*Bearings Only Plot*) confirmed their combined visual assessment.

"When you come off, have a look on the plot, they are contact numbers 023 and 024."

Toby left him to carry on and turned to join Simon, who had just finished plotting his LORAN fix on the *LOP* (*Local Operations Plot*).

"That's a pretty taught fix, Simon. Were the signals good?" The fix showed a small cocked hat on the chart from the three stations.

"Yes" he replied. "It puts us some five miles further out than I had estimated since the last visual fix. Considering the heavy tides we had coming around the corner it's to be expected. Once we are down beyond the Moray Firth they won't be so strong, so our error span will not be so great." He started to draw the error lines either side of their marked course.

"We should enter our allocated part of the Exercise Areas around 1700. The first serial starts at 1900 so we will have plenty of time to get the feel of the area. Then we have a pause overnight before a full day of playing the Hunted Fox." He put the dividers down and looked around the Control Room.

Anticipating his thoughts Toby sent off one of the lads to get them mugs of tea. It wasn't often they had the chance to "have tea together" on watch. Having Steve with them was going to make the next week much more interesting and, hopefully, relaxed. But they had both left the trim for a while so Toby engaged with the lads on the planes to ensure all was well. Their guess was a bit heavy aft, so he transferred some water for'd and waited to see if that reduced their rate of movement. More water than normal was also coming in through the snort system so a short run of the pumps to reduce that helped. They were getting into the rhythm and could feel that everyone was actually enjoying it.

A forenoon watch in the Control Room was always busy. As explained earlier most of the routine work in a conventional submarine at sea is done during that watch, before their sleep routine kicks in after lunch.

So they had a number of routines going on at once. The Engineering Team were the busiest, the outside staff were taking system readings around the boat, the Donk Shop Team were taking their monthly readings and the Polto had his lads taking bearing wear readings for the electrical rotating machines. It was all go, with a flood of messages coming into them to be recorded on the relevant sheets. Toby spent most of his time ensuring that this activity didn't over shadow the basics of their snort transit, in particular making sure that they kept well away from any contacts. Doing four knots does not give you much time to clear something coming close; early action and invariably a significant change of course was the only safe way to stay well clear.

He took another turn on the after scope, and was about to check their position on the LOP when the LRO came in with the signal log. There were a number of signals from the staff conducting the work up of the Frigates. Apparently of the original four they were due to "play" with, two had changed. The original ships had been diverted to another task, and one of the signals named the revised list including the replacements. The mini surface task force was now made up as follows: two were Rothsey Class Frigates, the third was a Daring Class Destroyer, and the fourth was that old warhorse HMS Wizard. Toby thought she had been paid off some time ago. When he had known her she had been in the Dartmouth training squadron. A first sea home for a number of cadets, fledgling naval officers experiencing life at sea as it had been with an open bridge and hammocks in the mess decks. Surely that couldn't still be the case? Simon and he were pretty familiar with all three types of escorts but he wasn't so sure of Steve. So to give him something of a change to his current routine tracing out their systems, Toby got down the chart table copy of *Jane's Fighting Ships.*

He took Steve aside and opened it up at the Rothsey Class Frigate.

"Steve have a good look at the three classes of skimmers we are going to be up against" Turning the page Toby pointed out the various features. "You will need to take in their overall structure, type of propulsion, armament and then imagine what they would look like through the periscope. Firstly, at a distance, what are the mast tops like? Are there any unusual radars? Remember you will have only a few feet height of eye. They will all have some of the standard radars, but what differentiates each one?" Steve took the heavy tomb from Toby and looked eagerly at the first one.

"Yes, I see" he replied.

"During our next watch, once you have a good feel, we'll send you into the Sound Room for a spell and get them to give you their take. So I suggest you make up a crib sheet which includes what we've discussed plus number of screws and other features which the lads listening in on our rotating dome sonar will want to take advantage of." Steve looked up captivated by the challenge and Toby passed him the signal to make his notes.

"Thanks, Toby. Are you happy for me to stand back and spend this last hour putting a crib sheet together? I'll keep out of the way in Fire Control corner." He replied and tucked himself away using the flat screen of the TCU as a make shift desk.

Toby turned back to concentrate on the Control Room. It had just turned 1200 and the watch handover was underway, a period when inadvertent mistakes were

A Rothesay Class Frigate

easily made, so they had to be closely engaged. In the background the smell of lunch, as the meals were transported from the galley to the various messes, started to get their taste buds working overtime. So with stomach rumbling Toby made some adjustments to the trim and kept a close eye as the afternoon watch settled down.

One more turn on the search periscope, and before Simon knew it the familiar west country accent of his favourite engineer told him his stint was up. He turned over to John. Little had changed, although only one fisherman was in sight now. So Steve left him circling slowly on the roundabout and joined Toby at the wardroom table for "Baby's Heads" with lashings of gravy.

Toby had just started to devour his favourite lunch when Simon came in.

"Toby, have you set out the bait yet?" Steve looked at them both with a questioning look on his face.

"Sorry, Simon, I forgot – I'll get one out once we have cleared lunch away. Steve don't look so worried, let me explain. During long periods of inactivity, particularly leading up to exercises, the Boss tends to get edgy and resolves it by finding extra things for us all to do. Our way of easing the situation is to leave Cowboy paperbacks lying around. He cannot resist them and devours them, reading all night if they are that good. He is occupied and we don't get any extra grief! A good, albeit underhand solution to a potentially sticky problem."

Steve just shook his head, wondering what would come up next.

ooOoo

1345 Tuesday 6 November

Toby got his head down after lunch, and to his surprise managed to get a few hours shuteye. It must have been John's absence and the lack of his blocked nasal passages with their incessant snoring that provided the peaceful atmosphere for some sweet dreams. Peter and Toby were becoming more and more convinced that John needed some serious drilling to sort them out. They hoped that he might actually see someone at the Royal Naval Hospital at Haslar about it one day. It had been very cold throughout the boat during the snort transit and the draught had cut a bitter chill throughout the boat. As a result Toby had reverted to wearing his long johns. Not a pretty sight, but it stopped the cramp he suffered from in his legs. Arising from his pit for tea there seemed little point in dressing formally. So when John and Peter came off watch he was given some serious ribbing about the standard of dress in the wardroom. In fact they wouldn't have noticed as he was seated the other side of the table and looked relatively normal from the waist up – but a disloyal Leading Steward had informed on him, believing officers should set better standards.

Frank, the TASO, and Julian the Fifth Hand, were in the control Room for the first dog watch, having taken an early tea. According to the fix and the subsequent dead reckoning, they had gradually made up some time and were slightly ahead of their planned position. As a result they had stopped snorting and were about to go deep. The diesels were now stopped - at last – and the crew felt them taking the boat down. After all the time they had spent either on the surface or at periscope depth snorting, it was quite eerie. The ventilation was still running so there was still a background hum. Slowly their black home started to tilt and they made their way gently into the depths.

"*Silent Routine*" came over the broadcast, and the fans stopped.

Everyone was awake, listening. The silence was deafening. They stayed like that for about thirty minutes then the fans were restarted. The Boss was giving the sound room every chance to get a solid plot established before the first run started at 1900. In the mean time Toby simply settled down with his latest paperback until it was time for Simon and him to gather themselves together and take over the last Dog Watch. Unlike their surface counterparts, splitting the Dogs made little difference to submariners as they continuously kept two hour watches dived. So at 1830 Simon, Steve and Toby gathered around the chart table to take over from Frank and Julian.

The short time silent hadn't given them many contacts. There was one distant fisherman, and a fast moving contact classified as one of the northern cross channel ferries, but no sign (or sound) of their potential adversaries. Unusual - but not uncommon. Simon and Toby laid out the exercise orders on the chart table as a last check that they were fulfilling their part of the script, and settled down to clockwork mouse and act out Orca's part. 1900 went by and still they had no warship contacts. So they kept to the script and continued around the race track they had been directed to follow. A steady four knots at 250 feet, with the northern and southern legs separated by a short cross leg of thirty minutes, to give a reasonable spread between the two major legs. Gradually the last Dog wore on and it wasn't long before

Simon, Steve and Toby were released for their late suppers. Given the circumstances and the anticipation of being embroiled in a hot pursuit, they had not planned to show any movies in the messes that evening. They needn't have bothered. There wasn't the merest hint of a contact. They began to wonder where the hell the skimmers had got to.

With the morning watch coming up Toby decided to get his head down early. No real problem other than it meant he had to ditch all the other wardroom sleeping bags on the deck in the corner of the wardroom so that he could occupy his berth. His bunk, being the top one of the three tier, was where they stowed their bedding. Nonetheless, being of sane mind, without a conscience, or any guilty thoughts in the world, Toby was soon dispatched into a deep slumber. He found himself floating in a deep, silent mist, desperate to avoid the nets deployed to entwine them as they kept circling in the depths.

"It's 0415, Sir. Your shake for the morning watch, or – your part of it." was the first thing he remembered since climbing up into his bunk. The Control Room messenger had been gentle in bringing him back to the land of the living. Pushing his feet, still enmeshed in his sleeping bag, out into the void and down to the deck of the wardroom, he dropped down and in one simple movement landed on his feet and allowed the sleeping bag to drop to the floor, enabling him to step out and sort himself out. This manoeuvre had taken some weeks to practice, but by now it had become second nature, gathering his cord jeans he pulled them up and donned his submarine sweater. At this depth the temperature in the boat was quite pleasant, but it was best to start off warm. The wardroom was in red lighting, so they didn't have to don the special red filter goggles to ensure they were night adjusted should they need to come up to the surface in emergency and use the scope. Julian disappeared and as they entered the Control Room gave them fresh cups of coffee. It was just what they needed, a strong shot of caffeine to get their minds sharpened for the task ahead. As ever, at such times, Toby wondered what the hell made him think that this was what he wanted to do with his life. "Oh, to be sane and sensible" – little chance to date he thought, perhaps a settled married life would bring him round. Putting such thoughts to the back of his mind he swigged back the coffee and staggered across to the chart table.

Simon had already arrived and was crouched over the plot, trying to focus on the pattern of exercise areas in the dim red lighting. Toby joined him, and together with Julian, they gathered around the chart table and took in the latest details of their position and the current state of the exercise. To their amazement, there still had been no contact with the Frigate Squadron. So they had come back up to Periscope Depth just after 0400. The last phase of the exercise as planned had completed at 2359, but without hide nor hair of their adversaries. It was rather baffling. Somewhat puzzled, they had no option but to continue with their orders. The next interaction was due at 0800, at the end of this watch. So in the mean time they would stay in their allotted area, separated by some ten miles from the frigates, before starting the transit into the interactive waters at 0700.

Simon and Toby moved over to the BOP and noticed that a few intermittent contacts had come and gone to the north of their track.

"Julian, what did the sound room make of these?" Simon asked pointing at them as Julian stepped over from the chart table.

"Not a lot, one was classified a fisherman, but the other was too intermittent to get any clear picture. With both of them being in our stern, and neither being visible, we didn't give them a high priority. Frankly, it's been very quiet throughout the watch. Frank took over the scope fifteen minutes ago and has had nothing in sight all that time."

"OK", said Simon "We have the watch. Toby you take over from Frank on the after periscope. I am going to clear the stern arcs first to ensure there is absolutely nothing astern."

"*Starboard fifteen; come right to 210. Sound room – clearing stern arcs, give us a précis of contacts on completion.*"

Toby took in the details of their position on the chart and leaving Simon to deal with the stern arc clearance, and with Steve checking that the trim was in good shape, he moved over to the slumped figure circling slowly round on the Search Periscope. Tapping Frank quietly on the shoulder, he interrupted his dark world to take over the Search Periscope.

"Morning Frank, still no contacts?" he quietly enquired, and with no obvious response shook him gently on the right shoulder. He gave a form of judder, shaking his shoulders, stretched his arms, and rubbing his bleary eyes slid off the roundabout seat.

"Not a bloody thing in sight; it's all yours. I really need my pit."

Toby put his settings on the eye pieces and clambered aboard the roundabout seat. It was a bit high for him, so making adjustments he settled down to look at the black void – and it was very black. The sea was a bit choppy and the scope was not that clear of the waves.

"*Depth?*"

"*Sixty five feet, Sir*"

"*Keep Sixty two*" he directed.

He decided to come really clear for a good look round. They had plenty of time before the re-start of the exercise when they would need minimal mast exposure. On the first quick all round look he could see very little with all the splashing over the scope.

"*Depth Sixty Two feet*" yelled out the after planesman.

"*Very Good*" replied Simon.

"*On course 210*"

"*Roger. - Sound room, I'll stay on a course of 210 for fifteen minutes, if that is not enough let me know.*" enquired Simon.

"*Will do, Sir.*" They responded.

They now had the chance to get a good picture of what was around. Toby still hadn't managed to focus on anything, but as he came around past the stern he could see the wash clearing down from the scope's face. Suddenly he could focus, and then he saw them. Two bloody great lights! …. first the green one and then the red …he actually had to look up at them either side of a dark bow cutting through the water like a sharp blade…."where the Christ had that come from???" It was heading straight for them. Trying impossibly to keep a cool head, he jumped into action. They all practiced this but this was far too real.

"*Full Ahead together … Flood Q … Keep one hundred and fifty feet …fifteen degrees bow down – no more.*" he shouted out into the Control Room.

Jumping off the roundabout seat he continued: *"Stop snorting ...down all masts"* Then, gritting his teeth, he grabbed the broadcast,

"Captain to the Control Room."

"Simon, I had Green and Red lights shining down my throat, something is coming straight at us. I didn't have long to look before the scope was covered but I think it is a warship."

"Sound room – close contact approaching from astern – report"

Simon took charge of the emergency dive, and they were just going through one hundred feet as the Boss rushed into the Control Room.

Down the Throat

"What is happening? Navigator?" He needed a succinct summary before judging what more needed doing.

Toby jumped in as Simon was simply reacting to the orders Toby had given. "I had a vessel closing fast from astern, Sir, coming straight at us. It was too close and I ordered an emergency change of depth."

"*Control - Sound Room. Contact approaching fast down Port side. Will be overhead directly.*"

The Boss jumped in: "*Half Ahead together – Revolutions 60. Bring the bubble level.*" As the revolutions came off, it became eerily quiet. Then they all started to hear the rush of their sudden visitor passing bloody close overhead. They leveled off just as it went over the top.

"Christ," Toby thought, "That was too close for comfort."

"*Depth 150 feet.*"

"*Roger depth. Sound room - target classification?*" demanded the CO.

"*Sir, two screws. Definite classified warship, probably a Frigate, rather than anything larger. We have recorded some lines I'll compare them to the data we have on our Exercise partners.*" Passed the Sonar Chief

"Do it as quickly as you can". Replied the CO.

As the sound of the twin screws biting their way through the water overhead started to recede away ahead of them, normality came back to the Control Room.

"*Vasco*, what other contacts do you have?" asked the CO, as he joined Toby on the plot.

"We had none, until our recent friend, Sir. We had just taken the watch and had started to clear stern arcs to confirm the two intermittent contacts TASO and the

Fifth Hand had earlier in their watch to the north had actually gone."

"In that case – Toby you carry on with the stern arc clearance. When it is complete, I'll take us back up to periscope depth. In the mean time, Simon let's see where we are in relation to the exercise areas. If that was one of them, and he believes he is in his perceived area, my guess is that it is us who are out of area, and not them. Their ability to fix their position is so much easier than ours as you are only too well aware."

Toby carried on with the current leg twenty degrees off to port of their course, until the Sound Room were happy that there were absolutely no contacts in that arc. Then he altered the same amount to starboard to check the other side. That was when they picked up the two warship contacts. Considering where they were, someone was definitely out of their appointed area. As the CO had said it was almost certainly Orca. Toby informed the CO and Simon as they continued wielding dividers and plotting error boundaries from the last fixes. Given Toby's jaundiced view, he was becoming more and more suspicious of that LORAN fix Simon had done with Steve. He was convinced that they had "situated the appreciation" despite the early warnings. It was so easy to do; it came down to pride, vanity, and the courage to accept that it only produced "cocked hat" fixes. He just hoped Simon wasn't in the pooh.

At last they finished the stern arc clearance and with the CO on the attack periscope came up to *PD*. All was clear and after a few more words with Simon he left them to start snorting and continue the transit, it was now only an hour until the start of the first serial in the exercises that day. Simon had briefed Toby that they had decided they were five miles inside the Frigate area, and as a result effectively only four miles from their chosen position for the start of the exercise. At least they now had some opposition. In fact they had concluded that the reason for Orca having no contacts the previous evening was that damned fix. He had had the courage to be direct with the CO and had suggested the fix as the cause of the predicament. They had played with all the potential compounded errors and agreed it was the cause. Simon had, true to form, taken it on the chin rather than dissemble.

The incident had brought most of the boat out of their bunks, in fact it had suddenly become quite crowded in the Control Room. Both the XO and Engineer, true to their own characters, had been on the scene very quickly. In fact, as regards officers, it was only the two watch predecessors that had remained in their pits oblivious to what had gone on.

Once the CO had departed, they both sidled up to Toby and asked who had been doing what. He realised what they were doing, it had already started to make him think. The stark question was – why hadn't Frank seen the Frigate before him? He guessed his sighting had been almost immediate on taking over the search periscope. Frank could have been unsighted because he had been a couple of feet deeper than Toby – who had brought the boat up so that he could see above the chop coming over the scope. However, none of them could stretch the truth that far. Their guess was that Frank had fallen asleep on the after periscope. It was easily done, going gently around with your foot fixed on the pedal to give a slow rotation, whilst your arms were akimbo on the periscope handles. Slouched down in that manner, no-one could tell whether the person on the scope was locked on and tracking or away in fantasy land. Toby knew that he had effectively been forced to shake Frank to get his attention to relieve him. Frank could be really in the shit.

Toby was aware that his actions had only just stopped all of them being in the shit, not just Frank. He declined to answer the sotto voce questions from the others, suggesting they talk once he and Simon were off watch. They accepted his response, but Peter suggested it could be better for them to talk before the CO called Toby in to see him. Toby was not sure.

Simon and Toby purposefully kept away from the subject until Peter and John came in to relieve them an hour later. By this time the exercise was underway, and they actually had contact on all four escorts – as originally planned. Peter and John took the watch from them, stopped snorting and took the boat deep for the first run. It was just what Simon and Toby needed for a good breakfast, peace and quiet, and a wardroom to themselves to gather their thoughts on a pretty dramatic two hours.

ooOoo

0900 Wednesday 7 November

As expected Simon and Toby were called in, in turn, to see the CO in his cabin as soon as they had finished eating. Simon came out looking flushed, but gave him a thumbs up as Toby passed him to pull back the CO's door curtain.

Before he could say anything the CO started, "Have a seat Toby. Firstly, well done for last night. Your speedy actions probably saved us from a very nasty accident, not that I would have expected any less of you."

Toby gave a mental sigh and waited for him to continue.

"Nonetheless, as you are aware, we need to go over what happened, make sure we understand if there were any mistakes, rectify them, and finally submit an incident report to SM1 when we get back. Simon has put it to me that the LORAN fix was probably the initial cause of our position error. Do you have any thoughts?" His voice was calm and measured, and put Toby at his ease.

"On reflection, Sir, I believe he is right. We all know how difficult it is to get more than an extended cocked hat from that set unless we have really strong signals. That and the significant tides we've experienced will have made our uncertainty area pretty large." He nodded in reply and then turned to the real reason for Toby being there.

"Now we need to understand what happened. I realise how difficult this is for you, but you know how important it is. Before you reply, I want you to know that I need to be able to separate facts from guesswork and speculation. I have asked to see TASO later this morning, but wanted to understand from both Simon and yourself what happened from the time you arrived to take over the watch."

Toby took a deep breath and after a short pause gave him chapter and verse from the time they both started the handover to his arrival in the Control Room. As regards his taking over from Frank on the Search Periscope – he played it straight – and told it as it happened, with no conjecture regarding the latter's physical state. Indeed, he made it clear that he could not say that he was asleep. The CO accepted his words and thanked him for an honest and considered reply. Toby left wondering what would come of it all.

ooOoo

0600 Friday 9 November

The next two days passed slowly with most of the time spent deep. None of them reflected on what had happened. Frank had his interview and said nothing to the rest of them, so they let it rest. This period, watchkeeping deep, allowed Steve and Toby to spend a number of hours going over his Part III efforts and work book. It was just what Steve needed to get a real feel for operating a Conventional Boat at sea. During the late night sessions to ring the changes and provide escape from his syllabus, they would sit around the search periscope well and. conduct quizzes based on the ships in Janes Fighting Ships. Anything to pass the time.

Meanwhile above them, the Frigate Squadron continued churning up the North Sea areas at a frenetic pace. No watch passed without Orca being submitted to the pinging of their active sonars. Those in the Control Room even started to recognise each of the surface ship sonar signatures and thus know exactly which ship was above them. As the serials progressed so they became more complex. The skimmers were clearly getting good value out of Orca's efforts, which by now were effectively "catch me if you can". It was all building up to the final twenty four hours of freeplay, when they would have a chance to fight back.

ooOoo

0015 Saturday 10 November

As he clambered down from his pit, still groggy and in need of the hot cup of Kai on the table, Toby realised that this was to be his last middle watch, well, at least for this period. After this all he had was the

0630 to 0830 morning watch, and then they would be on the surface with the seamen officers doing their stuff on the bridge. He was most certainly not going to do any bridge watchkeeping crossing the North Sea. Fortunately it was his choice, and he chose the warmth down below, even if it meant watching those ghastly movies.

Pulling his trollies over the long johns, he donned his submarine sweater, and finished off the Kai. He could see in the dark red lighting that Simon and Steve were ready to go out to the Control Room, so they all gritted their teeth, and set off for another two hours of fun and games. Toby was first out of the door and made his way along the short passage into the Control Room.

"What the bloody hell was going on?" he thought. There was not a sound, they were all concentrated on their respective tasks, but something was not right. The boat was still deep, but although visibility in the dark depths of deep red lighting was slight, he could tell something was wrong. It took him quite a while to realise what it was. Everyone, and it was everyone, was dressed in bras and knickers! "Jesus Christ was this a Panto? Or am I really going over the top?" thought Toby.

To their credit, neither Frank nor Julian were so dressed. So what was the story? The Second Cox'n was on the after planes, looking very fetching in a fulsome bra, and panties which he had been forced to stretch over his somewhat ample backside.

"What the hell is this about Second?" Toby demanded.

"Well Sir, the TI found a sack of rags which contained nothing but these rather fetching garments. You know, what we would have called "white rags". After a very short discussion in the Senior Rates Mess, we decided to put on a show. The lads were only too willing, so the only decider was whose watch. We chose yourself and the Navigator."

"Oh Christ," Toby thought – "Peter and the CO will go through the roof."

"Second, that's very flattering, but don't you think there is a time and a place for such goings on? Don't you think we've had too much excitement during our watches already?" Second knew what Toby was referring to.

"Not at all, Sir. We thought we all needed a light finale, one that would take our minds off those other events. The CO will want to get his own back on the Frigates later, and in preparation the TI has looked out a bevy of Green Grenades."

Simon and Toby looked at each other; they couldn't believe their eyes. They looked around, the senior figures all looked rather grim in their ill-fitting outfits, but a couple of the younger ratings actually looked pretty good. "Thank God the TI was not part of this watch, he'd be winking at us all and creating havoc." thought Toby.

Finally Simon took charge. "All right everyone, a great stunt. You have had your fun. We've got thirty minutes to the final run and the Captain intends to end our games with the Frigates in the traditional fashion – with a successful attack. So I want you all back to normal before I shake him at 0400."

There were grins all round, they understood. Toby just wished one of them had had a camera.

ooOoo

0740 Saturday 10 November

The last run started deep. After a deep sprint to clear their track, Orca was positioned such that she could penetrate the Frigate screen and have a good chance of attacking the main target, the Destroyer.

The attack teams closed up and the CO started to really enjoy himself. He quickly brought them up to periscope depth, with the closest Frigate only four cables away. Pretty tight, considering the targets were manoeuvring at fifteen knots. It put them in a plumb position. What followed was a classic periscope attack. They showed the minimum of attack periscope, just sufficient to get the data for the dummy three tube salvo. Finally they were in position, and as the CO called *"Fire One"* they launched the Green Grenade, the very visible announcement of a submarine's success, despite the four to one odds.

Daring Class Destroyer

Wreathed in a smile from ear to ear the CO announced, "*Green Grenade over the Target. Stand By to Surface.*"

As they broached and then began to roll around in the short chop, their playmates were regrouping only a few miles away. They quickly established a line astern formation behind their leader, and were soon head down, disappearing over the horizon for time alongside in Rosyth. They kindly sent a very warm signal thanking Orca for being such a good tame target, with all the drudgery that involved – it was kind of them to acknowledge the down side of the role. Although it was just as well they weren't fully in the picture.

So ended Orca's period of Clockwork Mousing. It had been a little more exciting than they had either expected, or indeed wanted.

Meanwhile, gathering their thoughts, they started to refocus on what lay ahead for the next few days. Thus, having *blown all round* to ensure maximum buoyancy, they set off south on passage for Sunderland. Four days *run ashore* in the land of Geordies - all those pubs, and lovely lasses in search of eligible young submariners – the messes were already starting to be full of pressed uniforms and the pungent smells of strong after shave wafted through the Control Room.

ooOoo

SUB MEN ARE SUPER

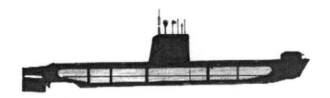

Missing Life in Submarines?

Lesson 6 on recapturing the old days:-

Renovate your Bathroom; build a wall across the centre of the shower, move the shower head down to chest level. Store beer barrels in the shower enclosure.

1025 Sunday 11 November

A formal visit to a town or port by a warship is not a casual affair. The basic planning is done some time ahead, but that is only the framework. There are a lot of advanced preparations and a number of final details which have to be brought together if it is to be a success and run smoothly. In a conventional submarine the burden is shouldered by the XO, with help from an unusual and surprisingly keen group of crew members. This group had been called together in the Junior Rates Mess to ensure the plan for the visit was ready. Peter had his timetable for Sunderland laid out in front of him.

- Day 1
  - 1000 – Alongside Corporation Quay
  - 1200 – CO calls on Mayor, followed by lunch with Council (CO and three officers)
  - 1830 – 2030 - Reception on board for 50 (guest list attached) – All Officers to attend
- Day 2
  - 1100 – 1700 - Submarine Open to Visitors – Duty Officer +1 & enhanced duty watch
- Day 3
  - 1500 – 1730 - Children's Party on board in For'd Mess – Volunteer Team of 12 + galley staff + enhanced duty watch
- Day 4
  - 1030 – 1230 - Visit to Local Hospital (6 ratings in uniform)
  - 1830 – Round Table Dinner (8 invited to attend – 2 Officers, 6 Senior rates)

- Day 5
  - 0900 - CO farewell call on Mayor
  - 1000 – Depart Corporation Quay

Peter had gathered them together at 0900 and had described the basic programme, but it was already coming on for 1030, and they needed to get on. He needed some help, so after a light nudge in his ribs, John politely interrupted the gathering.

"Peter, as the wine caterer for the wardroom, I'll take on the arrangements for the Cocktail Party on the first evening. If Toby and the Leading Steward can be my henchmen, we should be able to get it under control. On the first day you and two of the Seaman Officers should go to lunch with the Mayor, it will allow us then to prepare everything in the afternoon for that evening. I am duty that night as well, so it all fits." Peter was clearly grateful for the help, but didn't quite see it that way:

"John, that's great for the Party, but I think I would be happier to be around that first morning. In my experience that's when you get bounced with extra events and invitations. So I'll send Simon and Co, rather than go to the lunch myself. Before we carry on with your side, let me confirm a few details for the first morning. Simon, will we get a pilot off the mouth of the Wear estuary?"

"Yes, it is mandatory but we would have asked for one in any case because of the unusual tides at the river mouth. The CO and I will be on the bridge for the entry to come alongside at Corporation Quay, it's where all their visitors are berthed. We are also getting a tug to help us alongside, which is a nice change. The quay is outside the main commercial dock complex, and although it is the other side of the Wear to the main town, the routes in are pretty good and there is a standing taxi rank for visiting ships. So the lads will not find it too remote." He was clearly happy to join the CO for the lunch.

"Good. I'll start leave for those without other duties at 1330 each day. It means that everyone will be around to smarten the boat up each forenoon. Right then John, do you want to go into any of the details of the party?"

"Not really, we intend the normal fare of G & T's, with Horses Necks, and a few nibbles from the galley. I will have some wine out, but we need to be careful with that. Our standard financial allowance for a guest list of fifty only really allows for spirits at duty free prices, if too much wine and mixes are involved it will hit our mess bills hard. So don't ask them what they want simply give them a tray with shorts on it." He was serious, they had been badly clobbered after a visit to Norway four months ago. "We plan only using the Wardroom and Control Room with the normal layout and the exposed systems visibly tagged off."

"Good point John." Peter replied. " Cox'n can you ensure suitable lads in the duty watch are detailed off for escorting the guests on board" This was a veiled reference to ensuring that no lecherous sailor was based at the bottom of the vertical main access hatch, to look up the skirts of the all the young ladies as they showed their all coming on board. Going off was generally no problem; by then most of the ladies had enjoyed the party and were pretty keen.

"Lastly, Second Cox'n, please ensure the Ship's Bell is looking its' best, and put out the better of our Named Lifebelts on its' polished wooden stand at the end of the brow" Peter finished his list for day one.

"Already, in hand Sir" replied Second with a look which said volumes about sucking eggs.

Well that was the first day. The second, sadly, was Toby's. Open to visitors was something no-one volunteered for. Mind you there were a few of the lads that saw it as a source of *totty* for the rest of the visit. They had a routine for these days. It was a combination of giving the public a good tour and showing off their little home, while ensuring that no awkward or malicious bugger played around with the systems creating a safety and operational problem. Sometimes they were too remote from the town or city for many people to come over, but this time Toby thought it would be quite crowded.

After a very short discussion and a sympathetic look from those not involved they moved on.

Right, now the children's party. That's yours Leading Steward. Who do you have helping?" asked the XO

"Thank you, Sir. The Chief EA and the Second Coxn are my two leading helpers. You are aware this time it is going to be on board?" he asked.

"Yes, - unfortunately." The XO replied. They could see Peter was quite worried. Being unmarried and no offspring in sight, the thought of a mess full of four to seven year olds filled him with dread.

"It isn't that bad, Sir. In fact it makes it a lot easier for us all. Arranging the games, food and doing our party tricks is all much easier, and less expensive, when the party is on board. We've invited the TI to be "Father Neptune" and give out the pressies at the end. We couldn't find anyone uglier."

"Best you tell him that, not me" replied the XO. "Have the orphanages concerned confirmed numbers and transport?"

"Yes, Sir. I have written confirmation from both of them." He lifted the letters from a bunch of papers by his elbow. "Our party team is all sorted, both food and games. However, some help bringing the youngsters on board would be appreciated. I'd say four up top and two covering the main hatch. Would the duty watch be able to help out?" he finished.

"Yes, no problem. Toby, who is duty that day?"

Before he could answer Simon butted in, "It's me Sir. At least I'm not uglier than the TI. I'll make sure we have sufficient numbers up top and down below."

"Well we're almost there. Cox'n you are leading the team for the lunch with the Round Table. Who is going?"

The Cox'n read off a prepared list. "They've all volunteered, so we ought to make a good impression. A number of the Chiefs are Members in their own towns, so we know the score and should be able to make some good contacts."

Pausing and taking up another sheet of paper, he continued. "You've missed the Hospital visit, Sir. The volunteers for this are also lined up and the REA is leading. Given we will already have had the children's party, we have made it a visit to the Hospice rather than the hospital. They are actually next door and run by the same authority. We thought that a visit to the children's ward would effectively repeat the onboard party so we decided on the Hospice. Our Sound Room leader Chief Samuel actually comes from here and his Grandfather spent his last days in it."

"Well done, that sounds good. I know there is a lot of hard work going into these events, but I'm sure you'll all enjoy them. That leaves the goodies. Simon, can you pass up that bundle of bumper stickers. With Dolphin awash with these things at the moment I had no choice but to take a box full for our visit. Share them round. You'll be pleased to see that I only brought the one version. Frankly I couldn't stand some of the others, whoever thought of "Deep down you know it makes sense", must live in some isolated cage. So here is ours, one which will brighten your hearts - "Sub Men Are Super" - I'm sure most of the lads will want to spread them around the town???

There were moans around the table, although one or two quietly grabbed their own handfuls. The Cox'n said it all, noting how wonderful it was to be "Super"; it wasn't a term his wife had ever used towards him.

Orca's Bumper Stickers

ooOoo

0730 Monday 12November
They hadn't been close enough to the coast to actually see the outer areas of the river Tyne and Newcastle itself, but certainly noticed the marine traffic making its way to and fro as they steamed along on the surface to their rendezvous with the Pilot off the Wear. The North East had continued to be hard hit as ship building and the heavy industry in the area declined in the 50's and the early 60's. On the Naval side however, Swan Hunter still

continued to produce Frigates, the most recent notable ones being HMS Falmouth (a Rothesay Class) and HMS Galatea (a Leander Class),with Vickers building HMS Penelope (another Leander). The buzz was that they were also in the running for one or more of the new Aircraft Carriers.

Few of the crew had ever been to the north east but their perception was that Sunderland was the lesser sister. Nothing showed this more than the competition from their soccer teams. It was intense, the rivalry between the vertical black and red stripes being legendary.

At last they spotted her, the classic white topside and black hull of the Pilot tender, making an impressive wake towards them through the swell. The Pilot had been on the radio to the Bridge for some twenty minutes now, so there were no special formalities as he came alongside. Simon was quite impressed by the way the Pilot leapt onto the saddle tanks and was quickly up on the casing. It wasn't everyday you got to ride a submarine, and as explained earlier they weren't the safest things to jump onto at sea.

Simon escorted him up through the fin to the bridge, where he was met by the CO and a given a large mug of steaming Kai by the bridge messenger. It always paid to keep in with certain people, and on occasions such as this Pilots were top of the pile.

Down below there was an understandable air of expectation. When the crew had heard where the visit was going to be, they were surprised when they realised that only the only one among them who came from the northeast was the Sonar Chief. This visit was going to be new for almost all of them. The trip up the river was uneventful. Then the tug came up alongside, made itself fast, and started to ease them towards the jetty. Not something they were used to, and they found it rather pleasant being treated as special visitors. Up to this point the search periscope had been kept up, so the crew had been kept informed by a running commentary from whoever was manning it. There was quite a crowd on the quay. A large number were dock workers, goofing at the unusual visitor, but there were also a large group of smartly dressed people, presumably the welcome party.

Finally the mooring ropes were passed across and made fast, while a crane lifted a rather smart looking brow into place. By this time Peter was on the casing to meet the hoards coming on board. He urgently sent a message down for coffee for twenty in the wardroom, not that they could actually fit twenty in. John and Toby quickly adjusted the table setting, adding another pot of coffee and more fancy RN cups with those little fouled anchors on them. They would just have to spill over into the Control Room. Being mindful of the example they had to set, it had been agreed that the single malts were not appropriate. They had even dressed up. Gone were the steaming sweaters - all the wardroom were dressed in No 5's – full uniform with white shirts and ties. Not necessarily their best ones but at least good "steaming ones". The stripes on Toby's working jacket had started to fade and were a bit green in places. He wasn't concerned, as he felt he could at least use it to break the ice as a lead in to a nautical dit or two.

To everyone's surprise the first one down was an RN Commander, a pompous individual who started giving them all orders. John bravely grabbed his elbow, stating that the Wardroom was for the Mayor's guests and steered him into the Control Room. Here he immediately bashed his head on the overhead pipes and crashed into the for'd periscope (which was fully down) and covered his very smart doeskin uniform in oil. He was not a happy bunny.

Leaving him to Julian (the Fifth Hand), John returned to the Wardroom just as the Mayor and a group of senior citizens staggered in. The latter team turned out to be from the Submarine Old Comrades Association. No one had mentioned a branch in Sunderland, so the Wardroom team were caught somewhat on the back foot. Fiercely supportive of anything to do with submarines these guys had a well deserved reputation for looking after submariners during any visit. As the CO made the introductions, John gave Toby a knowing look. He understood, and immediately raided the bar to bring out a couple of bottles of Grouse. These guys were old stagers and knew the routine, the least those in Orca could do was to maintain submarine standards. They were very kind and with polite smiles accepted a small tipple as their duty, no more. Sadly that couldn't be said of the full gathering. Toby was just pouring some into the last two glasses, when the Mayor leaned across and grabbed the un-opened bottle.

"Thank you lads, I guess this one is mine on the Queen." So saying the bottle was slipped into his briefcase to the astonishment of all around the table. The CO was absolutely livid and fast turning a dark shade of purple. Seeing this, Peter took him firmly by the arm and led him away to his cabin, excusing his leaving on the need to change for the lunch. It gave them both the necessary breathing space. John continued his stalwart hosting role, and the episode was set aside, although clearly not forgotten. Finally the Mayor decided it was time for his formal lunch, and the lunch party left, with CO, NO and TASO in tow.

As soon as they had left one of the ex-submariners stood up and apologized for the Mayor's behaviour.

"That was more than bad manners. He's let all good, generous, Geordies down. You lads did brilliantly to hold yourselves back and not give him one. It was clear what your CO wanted to do. But don't you worry, we'll see the crew has a great time. The town is really looking forward to meeting them. Many thanks for the coffee and the wee dram. We'll be away now, but we've left some addresses and literature on the town with the Cox'n"

So saying, they staggered off and managed to clamber up the main hatch surprisingly nimbly, despite their old legs.

Peter, John and Toby cleared up the Wardroom. It had been a mixed start, but they had enjoyed the genuine warmth from the Submarine Old Comrade team.

"Who was that Commander?" Peter asked John, "I didn't see him go, is he still onboard?"

"I never found out. After bashing his nut and then covering himself in oil, he disappeared, although I never actually saw him leave. Leading Steward could you ask the trot sentry if he saw him leave?"

They carried on clearing up and it transpired that the RN visitor had left. He turned out to be a Supply Officer who also covered RN liaison with the North East. He had left his contact number and departed rather abruptly. Peter guessed he would be back for the party that evening. The consensus was that it had been a reasonable start despite the incident with the Mayor. So they sat down to a light lunch, and once leave had been granted, John having the duty was left to hold the fort.

Peter and Toby made their farewells and using the car that had been provided for the wardroom (the CO had been given his own) drove with their kit over to the hotel to check in. It was quite smart, an enjoyable change to their normal surroundings, and well placed north of the river for the centre of town.

Toby decided to give himself a small treat and luxuriated in the bath with a gin and tonic, laying there until the water started to turn cold. Wrapping a towel around his damp form, he grabbed the phone and put through a call to Judy at work. She didn't like him calling the office, but it was a while since they had spoken, and being back in the land of the living he wanted to hear her lisping voice. She answered straight away in formal business tones, but was genuinely delighted to realise who it was on the other end. He gave a brief synopsis of their travels since they had last spoken. It sounded quite grand, blowing up cliffs, the trip around Northern Scotland, plus all the adventures in the North Sea. There was little he could say as yet about Sunderland, but she laughed at the Mayor's antics. Ten minutes passed quickly and then she said she sadly had to do some work, and asked him to ring back mid-evening. Her last words bemoaned the Cocktail Party, such events were her scene and she loved showing off her long legs on the ladder, overtly enjoying his discomfort. It would have been great to have her with him, but having planned for her to join them at Dartmouth during their next running period, it was not to be. So, feeling pretty good, he slumped on the bed for a power nap before it was time to change for the party on board.

ooOoo

1745 Monday 12 November

Having scrubbed up well and cutting a dash in his best uniform, Toby strolled through the hotel foyer to meet the others in the bar as they had agreed. They had yet to arrive, so he engaged the very attentive barmaid in a conversation on the delights and nightlife of Sunderland. To his pleasant surprise it sounded quite promising. Fortunately it wasn't all pubs. They were not really his scene. A dislike of beer and a preference for female company had inevitably led him towards social events centred on good food and live music in rather smarter venues. Perhaps this was going to be one of the better runs ashore, he certainly hoped so.

Peter and Simon arrived together just in time to stop him weakening and having that early drink. There would be enough imbibing that evening and he needed to pace himself. The car was outside and it didn't take long to meander through the streets back to Corporation Quay. As they arrived Peter couldn't help scanning the boat to see if any small things were out of place. He thought it looked pretty good. The entrance to the brow was impressive with their immaculate named lifebelt standing out on its varnished stand at the shore end. Each side was decked with bunting and illuminated with spotlights. The whole thing was welcoming and rather festive – just the touch for a Naval party aimed at impressing the natives.

Down below was equally imposing. With subtle use of the dimmed red lighting, and gentle jazz music coming over the broadcast, the overall atmosphere was that of a smooth night spot. The chart table was now a well stocked bar, and nibbles were arranged on various cabinets around the space. To stop repeats of the visiting Commander's fate, ribbons had been tied to the lowest of the overhead pipes. A good idea, which enhanced the party feel, and which would hopefully stop further bloodshed.

The Leading Steward had co-opted a number of the lads to help him out. They were all smartly turned out and well briefed on their roles. John had decided to hold fort in the Wardroom - it was where the VIP guests would be hosted. The mini bar was decked out to match that in the Control Room, and John showed Toby his hidden stock of wines for those who really could not take the hard stuff. The table had been removed, and it was surprising how spacious their little home now looked. The lighting also matched that in the Control Room, as they were able to take advantage of the common system in both spaces which prepared those who manned the periscopes to be light adjusted before going on watch. John had even set aside a couple of bunks in the passage for coats. All they needed now were a few guests.

Toby was just about to give in and start a weak horse's neck, when the broadcast came alive, "Wardroom – Trot Sentry, visitor for the Engineer Officer on the casing." How odd! The guys up top had been told to usher the guests straight down as they arrived. With a quizzical look, John made his way up top. He wasn't away long and after only a few minutes re-entered the Wardroom carrying a package.

With a full grin on across his face he asked "Where is the Boss, Toby?"

"In his cabin, I think" Toby replied

"Do me a favour and ask him to join us" he winked at me. Wondering what was up Toby knocked on the CO's cabin door and said John had asked if he would be kind enough to join us. He had caught him reading his latest cowboy paperback, so putting this aside he willingly followed him back into the Wardroom.

As he entered John offered him the package, adding "A very kind gift from the Submarine Old Comrades, Sir." Passing it across he continued, "You can feel what it is." Peter and Toby stood back unaware, then as the wrapping paper came off, they all understood. The Old Comrades had sent down a very special bottle of Oban Ten year old Single Malt. It was their way of putting to rights the behaviour of the Mayor, a simple gesture which made them all feel rather humble.

The Boss was really overcome, "Perfect timing for a perfect gift. Those gentlemen have turned the day around for me and I now feel ready to actually welcome our guests." He turned, put their special prize on the bunk in his cabin, and strolled into the Control Room just as the first guests appeared at the bottom of the ladder.

The delightful Mayor was in the first group, although his presence was mollified by the entertaining crowd of Councillors he had brought with him. They had also brought a number of council employees, all very shapely and rather attractive - most of the typing pool was Peter's rather sexist guess. The drinks were passed around and it already looked crowded. John voiced his concerns to Peter, wondering whether they would need to take over the for'd mess as an overflow. Peter was well into his hosting mode and told John not to worry, his view was that the best parties needed to be squashed!

Toby was bringing drinks to more guests when he recognised the Liaison Commander from the morning amongst them. This time he was not in uniform, so his recall helped to ease the awkward feelings following the Commander's somewhat bloody adventure. He was some six inches taller than Toby and the only way he could stand comfortably was finding one of the gaps in the deckhead piping. So, with his head somewhat figuratively in the clouds, Toby broke the ice and asked him where he was based and how he came to have such an unusual role. As often in such situations, he turned out to be a very pleasant person. He had felt out of his depth (almost literally) that morning, never actually having been on an RN submarine before. Toby then explained that he had to circulate, but was thanked by the Commander who said that he would send a welcome pack, on the city and the local spots of interest, down first thing in the morning as a number of visiting warships had found it useful - a warm handshake of farewell and Toby turned to scan the scene.

In fact it was now so crowded that he could do little more than engage with the group of three that had been just behind him. They were crowded around the two Planesmen's seats, which one of the two very elegant ladies had sensibly occupied. They introduced themselves, and Toby explained his role. The guy was an accountant and both the ladies were lawyers, the three representing the professional business community. The conversation started with them asking why an apparently normal person like himself wanted to spend his working life in such an appalling environment. Normally the first question is about claustrophobia, so this was slightly different and probably more rational. Toby explained about the timing of Dennis Healey's Aircraft Carrier cancellation and his change of direction. That didn't satisfy the seated lady, who stretching out a seriously disturbing pair of legs, stood up, and with her ample bosom only inches from him, stated that she didn't believe a word of it.

"I know the real reason – you and probably most of the crew have a fetish for being covered in oil all the time."

Toby needed help keeping a straight face. "How did you guess?" he replied, as the others burst into laughter and she wiped one of her fingers for effect along the after planes tapper bar. She was very good and he was already captivated by her spell, but decided to take it a little further.

"That's uncanny, I didn't think many outsiders knew about our favourite game – we call it "Chase the Greasy Engineer". When the Control Room is a little less crowded (and it's all the home team), we take one engineer, strip him, cover him in oil and grease, and then try and catch him. It is impossible to get any real grip on him so it takes quite a time. He just slips through your fingers, it's a most exciting feeling. But we always get our man in the end." Their open mouthed reactions held about as long as his attempt at a serious face, then they all broke down laughing.

"Fifteen all" she replied.

"That's the best response in years to one of Sophie's outlandish comments." said the chap whose name was Robin.

They were great, and Toby collared the Leading Steward to refill their glasses. He let slip that the Mayor and company were about to leave the Wardroom so suggested that they all decamp to less oily surroundings before they lost their self control and started playing the game. It was a good move. John, having saluted the Mayor and company off the brow, had quickly returned down below to continue as Master of Ceremonies. Despite the duty he was thoroughly enjoying himself, and actually allowed Toby to change Sophie's drink for a glass of their hidden chilled white wine. It was clearly more to her taste than the shorts. Toby presented John and explained that as the Engineer Officer, keen to keep morale high, he had introduced the game Toby had just described. They all looked at him with added respect, albeit John was slightly nonplussed until Toby recounted Sophie's view of their career motives. By this time the masses were thinning, and those groups remaining were a mixture of the home crowd and guests who were teaming up for a night on the town. Robin suggested what they all needed was a good meal before they consumed much more alcohol, and recommended that they all decamped to "Othello's", his favourite eating hole. Simon and four more guests were also keen, so John passed Robin the Wardroom phone and he immediately booked a large table.

It had been a good party, and they reluctantly left John to lead the clearing up. Few of them were fit to drive so they took advantage of the loaned car and had one of the lads drive them all to the hotel, to enable Simon and Toby change out of uniform. There were some suggestions that they looked pretty good as they were, but neither of them had any intention of doing the town in uniform. From there it didn't take them long, and a short cab ride later found them all seated in Othello's at a large and rather grand table. Robin's choice looked spot on. Simon and Toby were placed at the centre of each side, and to their delight the ladies were ushered either side, with Sophie on Toby's left. Choosing their courses was not easy, the menu was not large but very good. Toby finally went for a seafood starter, and duck for the main course. They were a good crowd and they all got to know each other quite quickly. Simon and Toby's questions on where to focus the short time they had during the visit, gave rise to two main suggestions: Sunderland for the evening nightspots, and Hadrian's Wall for at least one of the days off.

The starter was good, but Toby found it difficult to concentrate on anything but Sophie's excitingly warm leg placed firmly against his under the table. His attempts to be a witty diner rather naturally began to stall given the circumstances. It became even worse when Simon, tongue in cheek, brought out the bumper stickers Peter had distributed. To their joint amazement they went down really well, with the ladies that is. They all promised to display them on the back windows of their cars, even in the face of opposition from some of the boyfriends. During the pause between courses it became very apparent that they weren't just being polite about their suggested visit proposals, but actively discussed a group day out to show them the countryside and this end of Hadrian's Wall. Toby explained that he had drawn the short straw the following day, Tuesday, for the "Open to Visitors" duty, but he would understand if there was no real alternative. "No problem", was Robin's retort: "if you are both free on Wednesday, let's make that firm." Toby thought Simon had the duty then, but perhaps it was flexible. Anyway they both agreed and it was fixed.

During the main course Sophie explained that she was in fact South African. Toby thought there had been a slight accent, but not being able to place it, hadn't commented. She had come over to Edinburgh University and then joined a legal firm with offices across the North East. She had only been in Sunderland for six months but had settled down and begun to enjoy it. Over the last summer her favourite outings had been exploring

Northumberland, which she found dramatic – both the scenery and the fantastic castles. As they tucked into the main course the conversation drifted back to the boat and those unusual careers, not that either of them really considered it a career, as yet. Toby let them all know that it was to be his pleasure to host a thousand or so visitors the following afternoon, but if any of them were really interested he would happily provide them with a personal tour and a glass of refreshment on completion. A number were really keen and he agreed to take them round in the early evening once the public open to visitors came to a close at 1800.

It was a great impromptu evening and it was past 2300 by the time they had asked for the bill. Although a number still wanted to paint the town Toby knew he had to call it a night. He was lucky that he could fall fast asleep at a moment's notice, and generally survive the "two on, four off" watch keeping routine pretty well. Nonetheless, he did need his sleep. With a demanding day to-morrow it was time to be sensible and make his way back to the hotel and that warm, clean bed. As he made his farewells, he was tempted to stick his neck out with Sophie, but discretion prevailed. After a warm cheek to cheek farewell and a promise to see him for that personal tour the next evening, he left her, Simon and the others to the delights of Sunderland's night life.

ooOoo

0745 Tuesday 13 November

It's only when you miss it, that you realise what a treat it is to sleep in a proper bed. Toby had gone down into a deep sleep within seconds of his head hitting the pillow. To bring himself round in the morning, he staggered out and had yet another bath – what luxury. He then donned his working No 5's and had a long call home to Judy. It was partly a feeling of guilt from the night before, not that he had really done anything to feel guilty for. Nonetheless, it was a good way to start the day for them both. She was still in bed, and her infectious laugh made him really miss her. So with randy thoughts that had no chance of being realised, he had a light breakfast, and got himself driven back to the boat. It was just before 0900, and some dockers were laying out railings under the guidance of the Second Cox'n, in preparation for the queues they anticipated having later. Experience had made them very aware that in managing a large number of people, especially families, it was essential for them to have a good time and yet accept the inevitable long wait in the queue. Toby stepped aside as some of the lads brought onto the jetty some folding boards which had details of the boat and its history. It would be something to wet the appetite of the visitors before actually coming across the brow and climbing down into the mysterious black tube.

John was in the wardroom, ready for the handover. He had made sure that last night's party had been wrapped up and fully cleared away before anyone had hit their bunks. So the on board team were all handing over a very clean boat. The previous night had not been totally duty for John. Apart from having a bloody good time, he had been invited to join some of the party guests in an entertainment box at Sunderland's ground for the mid week game on Wednesday. He wasn't sure who they were playing but it sounded really good. It included an early dinner before the game started and then drinks at half-time and again on completion. Toby felt quite envious. Both of them were soccer fans, and had played soccer for their respective training establishments, and Sunderland were doing pretty well this year. John's luck was in.

John quickly departed for the hotel so that he could have time for a tour of the city centre before joining some other guests that evening, and Toby focused on the day's priorities. The duty donk shop chief and his outside partner popped their heads in to let him know that they were about to start the full tag-out check. This would ensure all the systems were safely shut down, and marked accordingly with coloured tags, so that no mischievous visitor could inadvertently do something stupid like raising a periscope. Although in this case they intended having the search periscope raised – so that the punters could all take turns to look through it. While they were doing that the fore ends LWEM and Duty Watch were opening the torpedo loading hatch and rigging the sloping ladder. The plan was to use this as the entry point, and its' respective partner in the after ends as the exit route. With extra brows going directly across the casing to each hatch they could create a flow through the boat from for'd to aft for the visitors – and still have their normal main hatch free (with its' own brow) for emergencies. Straightforward, but still a good plan.

By 1030 they had just about finished. Toby made up some mugs of coffee and gathered the duty senior rates in the wardroom for a final brief. Frankly, they didn't need briefing, all he was doing was checking that they had completed their preparations and not inadvertently missed anything. For these open days they had to enhance the Duty Watch to ensure they had every compartment manned, with a shore team and some reserves should anything go awry. Everyone was happy and they all understood their respective roles, so they split up and the Second Cox'n, being duty PO, and Toby did a final walk through starting ashore. They purposefully followed the route the visitors would take, so that they could see it from the visitor's viewpoint. The view in the donk shop was a real surprise, the Engineering team had done a great job and it was sparkling. As Sophie would have remarked it was still oily, but it was clean oil.

Everything was all set and they were just going through the after ends when Toby noticed a little sign on a bunk with a very clean and new looking sleeping bag on it. "View the Golden Rivet". Good try you crafty buggers he thought. That old weaze, get the young lassies to lie down supposedly looking for this special rivet cherished since build ...and you can imagine the

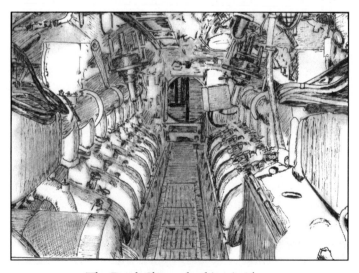

The Donk Shop – looking its' best

rest. Few were taken in, but a surprising number actually played along and enjoyed it.

Toby turned to his companion whose face had lit up, "Second, ask them to take it down. A grand way to trap the crumpet, but it's going to be too busy"

"Yes, you're right Sir – shame though. It has been nicely done."

They climbed up through the after hatch and finished on the jetty. All was ready for the hordes, and with less than an hour to opening time they returned on board to their respective messes for an early lunch.

ooOoo

1200 Tuesday 13 November

The queue was several hundred yards long when at 1200, they opened the for'd brow. Fortunately, it was a dry, mild, afternoon so those waiting were able to cheerfully await their turn. The main challenge was keeping the flow going, everyone was asking questions, and the lads were doing their best. Keeping a balance so that the punters had their money's worth (not that they were charged), and yet didn't linger too long, was difficult. As they entered the first compartment - the for'd torpedo space - despite the size of it, they found themselves constrained to the central aisle, and as a result were kept moving aft. Then through the bulkhead, with Grannies slowing things down, while the youngsters rushed into the ratings mess, charging around with new found freedom. A bit chaotic, but fun. The entrance to the Senior Rates mess was kept open with the curtains drawn back, so that everyone could look in, but the door to the Chief's Mess had been shut to allow somewhere for the Chiefs to hide away and grab a cup of tea. Then there was the

Wardroom. Toby knew from experience that it was inevitable that many would open the door to have a peep in if it was shut, so he accepted his fate and left it open. It made him feel very much like a creature in a zoo, but almost all the visitors were pleasant and cheerful, and to his embarrassment most of them called him Sir.

The Control Room was where most of the interest lay, with almost all the visitors wanting to look through the periscope, sit on the helmsman's seat, and try a valve or two … the crew had their work cut out. It was extremely busy, but everyone was cheerful. Toby actually started to enjoy the day and found himself talking to all as they passed, and then fully joining in, rather than remaining somewhat pompously like a part of an exhibit in the Wardroom. He ended up joining the flow and must have done five or six circuits through the boat as the afternoon went on. There were a couple of lost youngsters, but Toby had them taken back into the Wardroom. Using the broadcast to call their families added to the reality of the day for the guests. It also helped reduce the concern of the anxious parents, having a cup of tea or squash in the wardroom seemed a real prize to those who ended up there.

Finally at 1800 they had to shut the brows. They managed this by stopping entry through the gate into the jetty area, so those already in the queue weren't let down. There were still a few guests, where the messes had asked permission for them to remain on board for tea and cakes – already produced by the galley in anticipation. The long afternoon was over and the Duty Watch could settle down to a quiet evening. The trot sentry on the for'd brow had been counting those that came onboard. He was staggered to find they'd had two thousand three hundred and twelve. All in six hours. That was almost twice the figure from the recent visit to Norway. Mind you Sunderland had a much bigger population, over three hundred thousand they had been told. It had been an eye opener in more ways than one, most of the visitors were real working people. From Toby's narrow perspective he couldn't see many doing the jobs asked of the lads. It certainly made him think how privileged and perhaps protected they were. Strange thoughts, as he reflected on his upbringing in a council estate pre-fab, but it still looked very different.

The boat needed a thorough clean, and they decided to get it done before the evening meal. They de-rigged part of the rails and ladders so they could shut the weapon loading hatches for'd and aft. The full reversion back to the operational line up they decided to leave to the next duty watch the following day. The main action was a scrub right through the spaces. Each group did their own space and with a final effort the Second Cox'n and Toby did rounds at 1930. The spaces hadn't been bad but that number of people couldn't help filling up the gash bags and making the floor tiles mucky. The lads had done well and Toby happily released those that had been co-opted to aid the normal duty watch to go ashore on leave.

He was about to have his supper when a call from the trot sentry told him that the team from last night (or at least those that had been keen for a guided tour) had arrived and were waiting on the jetty. Putting his supper back in the slow oven in the galley, he donned his jacket and made his way up to meet them. Six had arrived and this time the girls had wisely donned trousers. Robin seemed to be the leader of this little social set, and they were all in fine, cheerful, form. A kiss from each of the ladies and handshakes all round, and he led them back down below. With the table replaced in the wardroom they realized just how small it really was. Cozy was the word, and they were soon snuggly cramped in place, each with a full glass.

"Are we sitting comfortably?" Toby requested, and had an instant reply of "Yes, Mummy" and a couple even stuck their thumbs in their mouths! They were in the right mood.

"I thought it would help if I gave you the basics of the boat as a whole sitting in here, it will put the individual bits into context." So saying he grabbed a large sheet of paper showing a simple layout of the boat which was used on open days to help the visitors.

"The beast isn't that big, it's about 2000 tonnes on the surface and 2500 tonnes dived. As you can see from the sketch it has five main compartments, each is separated by four main watertight bulkheads, numbered: 34, 49, 77, and 103." Toby directed them to each area.

"I won't take you down into the lower spaces, they are very cramped, wet and oily ... especially you Sophie, you might get carried away and start playing our game. The battery tanks are big and specially sealed in case any acid leaks, but as each two volt cell is two feet square and

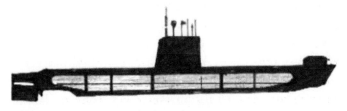

The boat layout

stands up to chest height, all we have is a crawl way for access with about three feet head room."

"Come on then we'll start up front, those of you taller than me will have to watch your heads, or you'll bash them on the overhead pipes and cables." Toby led them to the fore-ends and, ducking through 34 bulkhead watertight door, they assembled on the walkway between the stowage racks. The struggle through the door caused some amusement, with the odd shin getting a scrape. As they assembled it actually looked quite empty. He told them about their antics with the four wire-guided practice weapons used on the range and then the excitement of the LIVEX off Cape Wrath. Robin noticed the rider's bunk still fitted on one of the port side racks, so he had to try it for size. He was a big chap and it was a little too snug, but he thought he might be able to adjust for a short trip. Toby explained how they loaded the fish and then showed them the escape tower and kit. One or two had heard of the training tower at Dolphin and were interested to hear that all had to go through it before qualifying. A look at the tubes and Toby could see that the ladies were starting to shiver, it was always cold and damp up there, so he suggested they return to the accommodation spaces.

The junior rates space was virtually empty except for two lads playing a board game in one corner. "Isn't that ludo?" asked Diana, Sophie's pal. Toby smiled and explained that she was close; it was what they affectionately called "Uckers" a distorted RN version. Then they noticed all the black -out curtains, and as they passed further aft Diana getting into the swing of it asked him "What were all the shelves for?" Toby smiled and had to explain that these were the bunks. He then went on to add that a number of the junior lads up here had to hot bunk. "No it wasn't sharing in those terms, we have rules about that. There just aren't enough to go around, especially when we have a number of trainees on board. Remember no-one undresses to go to bed; we have to be able to jump out and deal with any emergency. So you can imagine one young lad waking up in his overalls, and turning over a nice warm pit to his counterpart. They do at least have their own sleeping bags."

Next were the senior rates messes, with actual beer barrels in the showers. By this time it was getting close to sunset, so Toby ushered them back into the wardroom and went up to do his duty. It didn't take him long and he returned to find them in the Control Room, gathered around the search periscope, taking turns to do an all round look. Fortunately Simon had just come on board to recharge his blue liner cigarette supplies, and had kindly continued the tour. None of them had seen RN ciggies before, so he had been forced to pass them round. The quality was quite a surprise, nothing but the best for the Senior Service. As they left he showed them the plush ablutions block, with those rather famous heads known as submarine traps. Toby told them the tale of the wardroom "stalagmite", to looks that clearly thought he was telling yet another tall tale. He assured them it was absolutely true, ask any of the crew. By this time they were becoming a little shell shocked walking through this machine, which just went on and on. So Toby increased the pace a little and took them on through 77 bulkhead into the donk shop – more grease and oil. It was a slightly false image, as the two mighty diesels stood dormant. He explained how the noise in here affected those not used to it, and Robin likened it to being inside an enormous car bonnet - not a bad analogy. Toby continued by explaining that unlike the old WWII submarines the diesels weren't directly connected (albeit via clutches) to the two shafts and screws. In Orca's case they drove the generators which charged the batteries. The batteries then provided power to the motors which did drive the screws. Its' fancy name was the Ward Leonard System, which allowed the boat to be almost silent when on battery power. To emphasise his point, Toby informed them that if they ever wanted to sink a US Aircraft Carrier (a natural everyday desire); the best vessel to do it would be a good conventional submarine. Not as often put across in the press, one of those noisy new nuclear boats. They all looked at him with an increasing awareness of his insanity as they arrived in the Motor Room. Here, to Toby's surprise, he found the Polto appearing out from the back of the switchboard.

"Polto, what brings you back on board?" he enquired.

He turned and answered, "I thought I'd better scrub myself up and put on something a little smarter – the Cox'n and I are being taken out by the Submarine Old Comrades. They're due here in twenty minutes" As a diversion Toby showed his guests the private wardrobe he and the Electrical Senior Rates had created behind the switchgear. They just couldn't believe it.

"We simply have to use every inch of space" he told them. "I haven't shown you what I call my office, but to you it would probably be a few shelves over our main gyroscope with a bigger shelf which is just enough to write on. Come on, this last area is where all the engineering lads reside. This is the most cramped space on board – yet they love it, and other crew members are only allowed in by invitation. It's quite a privilege to be invited back here when they are all in residence." Toby turned and led them through 103 bulkhead, where the *Stokers* and *Greenies* co-habited happily together. The back spaces in the wing bilges of this mess were affectionately known as the swamp because they were always damp, and you could feel it. The group worked their way around the after planes hydraulic actuators, and finally came to the two warshot Type 20 torpedoes stored in front of the two after tubes. These were effectively decoys, with the real hardware up the front. A totally cramped space, with machinery impacting every inch, but home to a bright band of stalwarts.

So ended the grand tour. Despite his best efforts they had scraped a few shins and bashed a couple of heads, and really deserved some well earned further refreshment. In the chat as they returned, the notion of living in a machine came across strongly - this was nothing like any ships of their experience.

It was now well past eight and regrettably he had no ability to offer them anything other than more alcohol, so they said their farewells and promised to meet both he and Simon at the hotel at 0930 in the morning. He was reminded to come prepared to do some serious walking. It being a Wednesday, the traffic could be heavy and they expected to start the first walk along the wall by 1100 at the latest. Escorting them up onto the casing Toby made a show and saluted them all off, winning broad smiles from both the ladies. It made him grin, his supper was going to be somewhat dried up, but he was really looking forward to the trip in the morning.

ooOoo

0630 Wednesday 14 November

Toby was shaken by the *LRO* somewhat earlier than he had intended to get up the next morning. At least the latter had had the courtesy to do so with a cup of tea in his hand. Even the fact that it was tea was thoughtful, Toby couldn't stand coffee first thing in the morning. But, like all shakes, there was a reason. They had received a number of signals early that morning, and a number weren't routine. He dropped down out of his pit and sat at the table, a pretty sight in his t-shirt and long johns. It was turning bloody cold, and despite all the visitors the previous day, the atmosphere on the boat was cold and damp. Toby hastily slipped his submarine sweater over the t-shirt and with the steaming tea doing its stuff had a closer look at the signal log. There were a dozen new signals, but only three needed some action, the rest could be left to later for the XO to handle.

There was clearly something about this running period, every time they thought they knew what they were doing, a change would come out of the blue. This time it was the Royal Marines or *Booties,* as they were affectionately called. An exercise with them had been planned for the previous running period, but had been cancelled (by the Booties) at short notice. As a result Orca had ended up returning to Dolphin a couple of days early, a real bonus as it turned out. This was pay-back time, and 45 Commando wanted to re-instate an exercise, somewhat similar to the cancelled one, at the end of this trip. To add insult to injury, SM1, being mindful of our extra time alongside after the previous cancellation, had readily accepted the Booties' proposal. The CO was not going to be pleased. Toby put the log down and taking the wardroom phone called the CO at the hotel. He was already having breakfast in the dining room, so it took a few minutes to find him. He was always approachable, and ever the gentleman, so Toby had no qualms in calling that early. Once he had come to the phone Toby explained that they had three signals that he needed to be aware of, and before Toby could offer any veiled description of their content, the CO said he'd be onboard within the hour. Before he rang off, Toby suggested Simon join them. The CO was bound to get him involved in re-planning the rest of the running period, and knowing that Simon was keen to come on the day out with the local team, an early debate would avert any disruption of their day.

If this was not to upset the planned day out Toby knew that he had to get his skates on. So, a quick scrape of the chin, and he was soon regaled in his No 5's having breakfast. Then it was time to say good morning to the Queen. He rushed up top and with a bitter wind blowing onto the berth had conducted *Colours* before much of Sunderland was about. That done he got together his gear for the day out, stuffing his pusser's grip with *steaming bats*, thick red socks, a clean pair of *No 8 trousers*, and an old rugby shirt, with a relatively new submarine sweater. Not a bad impromptu hiking outfit. In preparation for the Boss and Simon he laid out some mugs and asked the galley for a fresh pot of coffee. Then he got together the charts he and Simon would need, and had the Comms office produce another set of the signals on their gestetner machine. It was a bit of a bum's rush, but he made it. Their arrival was announced by the Trot Sentry just as the coffee was brought in, and timing the pouring of the three mugs perfectly, they both walked in.

"Morning, Sir. Sorry to start Sunday off like this. It's the Booties, they have asked for their joint exercise to be re-instated at the end of this period, and SM1 have agreed." Toby passed him the signal log and let Simon see the copies.

"I had a feeling this might happen, but thought that it was probably too late for this period." The CO replied "Let's see what they propose?" It took them both a few minutes to read through the signals.

"Well, Sir. It is effectively the same plan as before, with the only change being the moving of the exercise target site from Dartmouth to Portland. It is at least slightly closer to home for us," opened Simon, as he turned to the charts Toby had laid out on the table. "They have also allowed us a faster transit time on leaving here. That should save us half a day. As before, the actual time of the insertion is up to us, within the three day window."

"Yes" replied the CO, "We still have the original exercise orders, and as you say this hasn't changed those. So we shouldn't have a lot to do to re-plan our bit. In simple terms it's goes like this: a covert photo recce of Portland harbour, insertion of the Bootie SBS team, they demolish the defended target and withdraw, finally we pick them up and take them back to Dolphin with us. The exercise debrief is three days later, which allows us to retain our return long week-end. At least Captain SM fixed that for us. I'll give him a call today before I send our reply signals" he drained his coffee and drew the Portland chart towards him for a closer look.

Simon looked at Toby "We have reasonable water off Portland Bill, it's just the ferry and warship movements in Weymouth bay to be wary of – and the famous tidal race around the Shambles and the Bill. That will be a factor for the Booties getting in and out."

"Yes, I agree Simon. Toby, thanks for giving me the early heads up. I think other than my call to Captain SM there is little we need to do today. You get your handover completed and head off. Are you taking the duty Simon?"

"No, Sir. Frank has agreed to swop. Toby and I have been invited out for a trek along Hadrian's Wall with a pub lunch halfway."

"Sounds pretty good. In that case once you've handed over I'll give you both a lift back to the hotel." As the CO finished Frank stuck his head around the curtain and suggested they do the formalities in the Control Room. It didn't take long and with what Toby loosely described as hiking gear in his pusser's grip, they all piled into the Boss's car for the short trip back across the river to the hotel.

ooOoo

0930 Wednesday 14 November

They came in two cars. Toby found himself being driven by Robin in his Mini with Sophie and Diana in the back. It was very snug, and the girls made rude noises whenever they hit any significant bumps. Simon and his crowd followed in an old Landrover with potentially more space but there were five of them. The weather looked increasingly menacing, the wind was significantly more biting than normal for that time of year, and some ugly looking dark clouds were forming up ahead.

It didn't take long for them to clear the town outskirts. Robin's route was to take them west towards Washington and then get the A1 north, bypassing Newcastle. The intent was to get to Corbridge as early as possible, have a look around the Roman Town and then head on to the length of the wall between Housesteads and Chesters.

These two famous forts had some wonderful stretches of wall remains stretching out between them. Mini's are great little cars, Toby had owned one when Judy and he had first got married at the end of his time at RNEC Manadon. With wear and tear the front seats had collapsed, which made driving it quite exciting. They had even taken it up to Rochdale for his Industrial time with Whipp & Bournes (the heavy electrics manufacturers). It finally gave in and was traded for an MG – not that he got very much for it. This one was in good shape – but they are still very small. So after an hour they all needed a break, and were relieved as they entered the outskirts of Prudhoe and saw the signs to Corbridge.

Corbridge is a pleasant market town on the banks of the South Tyne, famous for the remains of the Roman Town about half a mile away. This was Simon and Toby's first taste and it was impressive. A whistle stop tour covered the main area with its' granaries, aqueduct, barracks and workshops. It had been the main garrison town for the forays of the Roman Legions into the dark areas beyond the northern edge of the world as was. Huddled together against the cold, the group braved the increasingly bitter weather and then sought refuge in the museum. It contained some unusual stuff which allowed them to peek back at life as it had been.

Robin only allowed them forty five minutes and they were off again. His ambitious intent had been to go to Chesters Fort and then take the cars to Housesteads, leaving one there, so they could walk the thirteen or so miles between the two. A one way hike, with transport at each end. After Corbridge, the girls decided that this was too ambitious given the nasty weather so they decided to take charge. Robin was told to pull over and

Sophie got out to negotiate with those in the Landrover. They didn't need much persuading, and she returned to direct Robin to Housesteads. The consensus was still to give Simon and Toby the best possible views of the Wall, but without freezing their bits off. So the new plan was for a couple of Wall stops with views over the moors and then a warming pub lunch, with Housesteads Fort somewhat later in mid afternoon. It sounded a good plan and Robin agreed. They set off again with the mini's little heater going full blast for those in the back.

Their first stop was in the middle of nowhere, with a well preserved section of the wall only a field away. It was an amazing sight, snaking its' way across the hill side. Toby was surprised how much was still in existence. The team explained that over the years a great deal of the stone had been "reworked" to produce some impressive buildings. A number of the Reever's Castles on the border had only been possible using this stuff. They had all learnt about Hadrian's wall as children, and Toby vaguely remembered sketches of it at primary school. There was now a strong movement to preserve what was left. They took it in turns to have some pictures taken, not that it was easy with the light but it did make the shots atmospheric. They clambered back into Robin's little beast and set off for the next installment.

They had another short stop by the remains of a tower, and headed off to a village which Toby understood to be called "Once Brewed". He was not sure because the Pub was apparently called "Twice Brewed" and there was a debate about the names. That aside, it was really warm inside. They were met by a warm fire, piled high with logs, and after a round on Simon settled down to choose lunch. Toby offered to buy some wine but most of the guys preferred the ale, so it was just he and Sophie to share a rather heavy red. The food was soon with them and he had one of those northern specialities, a large Yorkshire Pud with the works inside it, together with lashings of gravy. It was not bad and certainly improved the taste of the vino. It also fortified him against the bracing afternoon ahead.

Housesteads Fort was only just up the road. He could see why they were so keen to come here. It had it all. It was perched high on the exposed escarpment of Whin Sill, and as they wandered around a strong gust actually brought in the first snow flakes. He made a comment wondering how the Romans had survived up there, and Diana informed them that records had shown that most of the legionnaires had actually come from Belgium. They were probably hardy Gauls, well used to such climes. Toby was really taken with the place. They started at the east gate where the cart ruts had carved into the road stone and gradually worked their way down the hill slope past the barracks and hospital. Their numbers had gradually depleted by this stage, with all but Sophie and Toby retreating to the museum to get out of the snow. The last building was amazing - the renowned multi-seated latrine. The pair of them just had to sit down and try it despite the snow now falling in large flakes. Sitting there, they imagined those soldiers doing their business, as freezing water flowed beneath their feet. How they were able to use the sponges and dip them in the icy water to clean up the mess, didn't bear thinking about. It was as crazy as the supposedly modern variants on board the boat. Sophie commented that in brass monkey weather like this, the Romans would have rubbed off their numb bits with the solid frozen sponges. At least it would have reduced the rape and pillage they would have inflicted on the locals. A nice thought - she certainly had a way of expressing herself.

A great place, but it was now bloody cold. Toby helped her to get to her feet to return to the museum. It was a moment they both knew was coming. She clung onto his arm and pushed her head into his shoulder to shelter from the wind. Neither of them could resist, and they just gave in. She brushed the snow off his face and brought her lips up to his, the salty warmth simply consumed him. Wonderful, and absolutely frightening, but at that moment he simply didn't have the courage to stop it happening. Neither of them said anything as they turned back up the hill, arm in arm to the museum, the snow descending and a dramatic silence enveloping them.

Opening the door, they shared a knowing look, and she let go of his arm before they rejoined the others, who having given in to the weather, had ordered steaming mugs of tea. It was just what they needed, so Sophie and Toby joined in, the hot liquid helping to bring them back to an even keel.

The journey back was difficult because of the ghastly weather. It had turned to sleet and the roads were awash with spray coming at them from all sides. Robin needed to concentrate and the lack of chat was probably just as well, covering the un-natural silence that had fallen over the back seat. The team arrived back in Sunderland at 1830, and Toby asked them to drop himself and Simon at the boat, as they had to meet the CO to discuss the new programme.

He offered an early evening drink, but the others could see that he and Simon would be busy, and with most of them having commitments for the evening, they made their farewells. Toby and Simon thanked them for a great day out despite the weather. Sophie gave Toby their host's numbers so that a final night out could be arranged for the Friday before the boat departed on the Saturday morning. Toby waved them off, noticing that Sophie was quietly hidden in the back of the Mini.

ooOoo

1700 Thursday 15 November

The CO had called Captain SM and within the constraints of the public phone system had established that the timing of the joint exercise with the Booties would be the same. The new target was Portland, but that aside, the main problem was getting them and their equipment to Orca. The CO had explained in the call that if they had to go alongside at Dolphin, or any other suitable port on the south coast, it would mean extending the running period – with difficulties for the forthcoming maintenance and docking period. After a further exchange of more calls, it was finally agreed that the Bootie team would bring their gear up to the boat at Sunderland. They would set out on Friday and be with Orca first thing Saturday morning with all their gear, so sailing would only be delayed by a few hours. After the preparations that had been made under the casing for the cancelled exercise, the Squadron anticipated few problems. So stowing the kayaks and the rest of their gear would simply follow the original plan.

"Sounds fine to me. Any problems you two can think of?" asked the CO.

"No, Sir" replied Simon, "I'll get the Passage Plan and the large scale charts for Portland ready for review."

"No need for that to-day, it's Thursday and I'm sure you can find better things to do. Late morning tomorrow will be OK, and we'll go over them as a team after lunch. How about you Toby?" he asked.

"The only thing that has occurred to me is the problem we had with the directing gear for the *187 set*. You will remember that it kept sticking during the last exercise runs with the Frigates. The *REA* had a look a look at it and changed some servos, but I'm not certain it is fixed. We'll need it to be fault free to track the boats as we retrieve them at close range" Toby replied.

"Good point. Let me know how it progresses."

At this point a weary Leading Steward came in with a tray of nibbles. He had just finished clearing up from the Children's party. It had been a hoot and the TI, dressed in his weirdest outfit including some seaweed with a home-made trident in hand, had made a great Neptune. The youngsters hadn't been able to finish off all the food, so he had dispatched the leftover cake and cookies back to the children's homes, but still had a lot of crisps and such left over – this was their share.

"Well done, Leader – it sounds as if you gave them a wonderful afternoon, I heard the excited shrieks way back in the Control Room. Is anything left of the for'd mess?" joked the CO.

"It's all still there, Sir – scrubbed clean of sticky cake and back to some order." he replied and staggered off to have a well earned break.

Simon sought out Frank to take back the duty, not that he had really had it that long, and Toby made his way back to the hotel to clean up and change out of his rather fetching hiking gear. By now Judy would be back from work, so he phoned home to make one of those "check reports".

It sounded as if the weather down south hadn't been anywhere near as bad as Toby had experienced, but it had still been a chilly afternoon. She had spent it in one of the "frost bite" races held at the sailing club. She had then stopped over to see their American friend whose idea of English afternoon teas, was serving gin and tonics with cheese and biscuits. A genteel way of ending a day's sailing which Judy thoroughly enjoyed. Toby managed to keep the pangs of guilt out of his voice and they spent a good hour on the phone, chatting and ignoring the hotel bill. They said their goodbyes and he sat there for some time feeling his stomach churning. In the end, he finally plucked up the courage to call Sophie.

"You took your time" was her reply but rather than getting himself lost in a web of lies, he bit the bullet and suggested they go out to dinner for the evening. It was the right move, she said she would book her favourite place and be over to collect him in an hour. So the die was cast.

Later, when looking back he thought it could have gone either way. His trouble was being too honest, sometimes unnecessarily so. It had the makings of a good evening, but he couldn't hold back any longer, and in the pause following the starters he finally told her that he was married.

"I am not surprised, and guessed as much from your behavior," she said sighing. "But I still think you have beautiful blue eyes!"

His confession turned the corner and they had a good evening, fortified by a good bottle of vino, telling each other their life stories. It seemed quite unreal, being so intimate and openly relaxed together. It became a supper to savour, and ended up with a heart-stopping farewell embrace and a warm but final goodbye.

One of life's "if only" moments.

ooOoo

1830 Friday 16 November

Toby spent the next day busying himself around the boat and ensuring that everything was ready for the Booties' arrival the following morning.

The REA was not a happy bunny when he called him back on board to sort out the 187 sonar. He was probably the biggest guy on board – in fact being honest – the fattest guy on board. Despite his seniority he was also a shirker, avoiding any extra responsibility like the plague. So having Toby on his back, particularly during a port visit, went down like a lead balloon. Finally, after four hours of effort he came back to the wardroom and reported that he had done all that was possible and hoped that the sonar would function correctly and not stick when they tested it during the next dive. Toby had just finished thanking him for his efforts, without obvious sarcasm, when the Cox'n popped his head around the door curtain.

"Afternoon, Sir. I see you've been giving "Rolly" a hard time. Well done – he's needed a kick up the arse for a while." … and disappeared as quickly as he had arrived. Little got missed in a close community like Orca.

The Booties duly arrived the following day, and much to the delight of the locals, unloaded kayaks and a whole host of gear on the quayside which then slowly disappeared into the depths of the boat. In fact, it only took just over three hours from their arrival to having all the gear properly stowed and ready for sea. On completion the drivers were given an early lunch and then their fleet of trucks departed en route back down south.

So ended the Visit. Being a Saturday morning the town's hosts and a surprising number of locals, particularly young ladies, were gathered on the jetty to wave farewell. It was all smiles as the last rope was slipped and Orca made her way down the river. Below, it was definitely quieter than usual with many of the crew nursing thick heads, and just a few reflecting on some rather special broken hearts.

ooOoo

FUN WITH THE BOOTIES

Missing Life in Submarines?

Lesson 7 on recapturing the old days:-

Don't watch TV except movies in the middle of the night. For added realism have your family vote for which movie they want to see; then select a different one.

1336 Saturday 17 November

After a warm farewell, they dropped the pilot off, and turned the speed up to a credible twelve knots for the long surface passage down the east coast to the channel bottleneck off the Dover/Calais narrows. The Royal Marine visitors were busy sorting and stowing all their gear up in the fore-ends, and it wasn't until late afternoon that Toby actually met their leader Lieutenant Mike Thornton RM.

The Booties had always been slightly different. Firstly, their ranks didn't equate to the same titles in the army - each one in the RM was the equivalent to the next one up in the army - so a Lieutenant equated to a Captain, a Captain to a Major and so on. They did, of course, belong to the Navy not the Army, so Lieutenants in each of these were equal in rank. Toby perceived that there was a logic there somewhere.

Mike was a quiet chap, slightly taller than Toby, but no great hulk, in fact he looked perfectly normal, and without knowing what he did for a living you would be forgiven for not noticing him. Perhaps it was part of the training within the Special Boat Service (affectionately known as the SBS – cohorts and counterparts to the army's SAS) to meld into the background. Mike explained that there were eight of them in the team for the exercise, himself, a Sergeant who had been taken in by the Senior Rates mess, and six marines who were based in the for'd mess, and sleeping on temporary racks in the fore-ends.

They were quite an experienced team and were really looking forward to the trip. All of them were underwater experts, and as a result hadn't done a covert surface entry for a time. They looked on this as a trip down memory lane, a traditional exercise in the old reliable canoes. As Mike explained, despite the significant developments in underwater gear, little could replace fabric canoes for a covert surface entry. They had no radar signature, kept low in the water, and were almost silent. If it got a little too hot they could even launch small mortars from them. Toby looked at him, imagining the impact of a mortar on such a flimsy craft.

The crew's afternoon catch-up activity was about complete and as Toby wasn't doing any watches up top on this trip, he offered to show Mike around once the delayed lunch was over. Quiet would have descended on the boat by then, with most of the crew bedded down. Mike accepted, and Toby introduced him to the Wardroom team as they all gradually assembled for lunch. Peter was the last down, as he and Simon had both been up top for the exit from the Wear estuary, with Peter then continuing the watch. So Toby repeated the formalities, introducing Mike to the XO. They all decided to save any debate on the exercise for to-morrow's forenoon, so turning to a lighter topic, Peter decided that good manners demanded that they entertain their special visitor with a mess dinner at sea.

"Leading Steward", Peter called "Have a chat with the PO Cook and let me know whether you need 24 hours to prepare something special - we only have tonight or to-morrow - can the pair of you come in and discuss it once lunch is over?"

"I'll let him know, Sir." The Leading Steward replied while juggling a jug of custard and plates of figgy duff.

"Thanks." said the XO, "We haven't had a dinner at sea for some time. It will get us back in the right mindset, after all the indulgence during the visit. Good idea Toby?"

"Definitely." he replied. "It will also give us a chance to show off our most recently won colours"

"Colours? What do you mean?" asked Mike.

"It's all these frivolous young officers." replied John. "What Toby is keen to show off is his latest tie. With the dress hems of the wives and girlfriends disappearing up their bums as a result of modern fashions, many of them have been literally cutting them off to create mini-skirts and dresses. The throw away bits have been made into ties for their respective beaux. Toby, et al, like showing them off with their No 5's – sorry - our smartest uniform. It looks good, particularly with winged collars, even I have been forced to follow suit."

Mike grinned "It all sounds very fetching, I can't wait to see you in all your glory."

ooOoo

1430 Saturday 17 November

Once lunch was over Toby took Mike on a tour of the boat. He was well informed, having done some previous exercises in an uprated O boat, which was very similar. They took their time and chatted as they went through, finally ending up in the fore-ends, where Mike was able to reciprocate and show Toby his gear.

"These are the kayaks. We transport them in two halves. It means a two man team could, if necessary, carry them across country. As I said earlier, they haven't changed much from the earliest days. The material is more modern, but their main feature is that they have virtually no radar signature. We tried various lightweight metal skins for the boats, but they stood out like a sore thumb."

He pulled one over for Toby to feel the material. It was very smooth, but had some depth to it and was rubber lined on the inside which gave it a degree of thermal insulation. Turning to another kitbag, Mike pulled out a cylinder attached to a rope, which looked as though it was used underwater.

"You probably won't have seen one of these, it's one of our latest toys." He passed it across - it was quite heavy - but Toby was none the wiser.

"Haven't a clue" Toby replied.

"This is what we have dubbed a *Trongle*." He looked quite serious, but Toby was not sure whether it was a front. Continuing he asked "Do you remember the *Bongles*?"

"No ...?"

"Ah ... let me explain. On previous covert surface insertion operations it has always been difficult for us to find the retrieving submarine. Even when they are surfaced, their dull black paintwork makes them merge into the darkness. So one of our more experienced teams started to rattle tin cans full of stones. They held them just under the surface, and it helped the submerged boats locate us using their sonar. It worked so well, that we eventually made something akin to it into a formal device, and called it the *Bongle*."

"Sounds fascinating"

"Yes, but the plot didn't stop there. Given the rise in technology and the transistor era, the Admiralty Underwater Weapons Establishment (*AUWE*) at Portland, decided to bring us into the modern world and created this. It's a transistorised version, so we have called it a *Trongle*."

"That sounds pretty dubious particularly as it involves AUWE, but I guess from the expression on your face, you must be serious."

"I'm afraid so, it's the latest product of dedication and innovation from that font of learning." Mike looked as doubtful as Toby did. He introduced him to the rest of his team and then they made their way back to the Wardroom.

Mike's interesting explanation had reminded Toby of the problem with the 187 sonar. He knew that they should really get it checked out early, but they could only do it dived. The Boss was understandably keen to get on with the surface passage, but finding out they had a problem with the main sonar at the last moment when they dived for the exercise itself was the last thing they needed. Toby went to find Simon.

As ever, he was lounging over the chart table. "Where else would you find the Navigator?" thought Toby. He explained his dilemma, and the doubts he had about the REA's judgement as to it being fixed. There were a couple of options, they could dive before they were off East Anglia, but it was pretty shallow, or they could wait until they were through the Dover Straits and off the south coast. Toby told Simon that they only had to get wet. Although, saying that, he was being somewhat misleading. The only part which flooded was the array within its dome which allowed the heavy sound pulses emitting from it to be radiated into the sea. The rest of the kit, comprising the drive servos and head amplifiers, was in a pressurized mini-hull under the casing, with high pressure glands feeding the signal cables down into the actual hull. Toby felt they needed to test the gear as soon as possible, and it was agreed that they raise it with the Boss at tea.

It was just as well that they hadn't left this issue any later. The CO agreed and made it clear that diving once off the Wash was not an option. It was decided to carry out the evolution during the Second Dog Watch, well before sunset and well clear of any of the North Sea ferries. It was planned to be just a quick dip, although yet again it took them a while to sort out the trim. The XO thought his problems were less about the extra Bootie gear on board and more about the different level of salinity in this part of the North Sea. Whatever it was, it took some time. Unfortunately, Toby's fears were well grounded. As soon as they started to rotate the 187, even without transmitting, it started to stick again. It was almost as if it was held back by extra drag in one sector. "Thank God I hadn't just accepted the REA's assurances." thought Toby, as he took the REA aside once again. The latter was very embarrassed, as he disliked being in the spotlight. To save exposing their dirty washing in public Toby took him up to the sound room and sat him down for a heart to heart.

"Look, let's forget about blame and kudos, all we want is to clear the fault, so where do we go from here?" said Toby as the REA sat down opposite him, with the Sonar Chief beside him.

"I frankly don't know, Sir. The only thing I can think of as a last resort is if I went into the 187 pressure hull and we dived to create a realistic operating environment. Then I could check out all the servos and see where the fault is. One of them must be subject to a high resistance once under sea pressure and then it starts to stick."

"Yes, that might highlight it." Toby thought that this was more like it, the REA was at last being honest with himself. "However, I don't think you should go on your own. How much room is there inside its mini pressure hull, would there be room for two? If so, I'll come with you. It's not that I believe what you are proposing is unsafe, but if anything untoward were to happen, two pairs of hands will be better than one. The other thing I would suggest is that you audit what spares we carry for the directing gear in the dome, and that we take a selection down with us. That way we might not have to repeat the exercise."

"I'll get on to that straight away, Sir" he replied.

"One last thing, is there a comms box or phone link inside the dome? Presumably you need one when doing routine maintenance alongside."

"Yes, Sir. There is a sound powered phone which goes to both the Control Room and the Sound Room." he replied.

"Good, at least we wouldn't be totally cut off and would be able to keep the Control Room aware of what we were doing." Toby reflected. They broke up and Toby went off to find the CO. By the time they had come to this conclusion the boat was back on the surface and continuing the charge south at twelve knots. The CO was in his cabin going through a selection of ties. He hadn't realised that Peter's impromptu dinner was on for that evening. So confirming his attendance at the dinner with the Leading Steward he invited Toby to sit down and go over the options with the sonar. Toby put everything as straight as he could. There was no guarantee it would work but the suggested dive was the most credible thing they could do without reverting to a full strip down alongside. If the fault wasn't fixed the exercise with the Royal Marines would have to be cancelled, and after all the recent extra effort that would be extremely embarrassing. The CO decided they should wait until they were just past the Isle of Wight before conducting the special dive. That way they would be in familiar local waters, and if it didn't work they would just have to go back into Dolphin and do a full strip of it alongside. It was decided – they would dive around 1600 the following day. That gave the REA and Toby plenty of time to ensure they had everything ready.

ooOoo

1900 Saturday 17 November

Having a Mess Dinner at sea is a pretty rare event. Simon had drawn the short straw for the watch that evening and was the one who would miss out. In fact Steve was good enough to volunteer to do the watch with him, which saved some embarrassment as otherwise they would not have all fitted around the table. The Leading Steward still had to seat seven, a squeeze at the best of times, which they normally overcame by staggering their meals.

The respective rigs were impressive. From the waist down nothing much changed. Toby retained his cord jeans and steaming cowboy boots, his variation of the Pirate Rig. From the waist up it was a different thing. Starched white shirts with wing collars and some amazing ties, the gaudier the better, topped over with their No 5 steaming jackets. Images to impress a number of ladies, but sadly not a one was in sight or likely to be so. In Toby's case the tie Judy had made had come from the hem of a bright floral dress with strong blues and reds and a hint of green. It sounded dreadful, but in fact it made a rather fetching tie. As they were on the surface, they gathered in the Control Room for a pre-dinner cocktail. Not quite the same as their surface counterparts on their quarterdecks, with silk handkerchiefs blowing in the breeze from top pockets, but the Orca team did their best. The cocktails had been specially created by John for the occasion. They were pretty good, albeit alcohol free given where they were. Mike, the guest, wasn't able to cut quite such a dash, but he didn't do badly having borrowed a tie from Frank.

After fifteen minutes the CO joined them and they made their way into the wardroom which the Leading Steward had really set up for the occasion. In the centre of the table were the few trophies owned by the boat; pieces of silverware and a small fruit bowl in which were embedded supposed Orca teeth. They were definitely teeth, but none of them had ever been close enough to an actual Orca to validate the claim. They sat down to a splendid table and the Leading Steward served the first course, kidney's on a salad base, not quite "Shit on a Raft", but almost, as they did have croutons to go with them. They also treated themselves to small glasses of wine, without which the evening would have been somehow incomplete. The chat flowed and Toby got Mike to tell the assembly about his exciting new Trongle. You could tell by the askance looks around the table that they were all absolutely captivated. Peter started to recount a similar occasion when he had hosted a Captain from the Horse Guards. The chap had been very impressed and kept asking questions about having *Sergeant Johnnies* who understood all this machinery. He also actually used the phrase about chaps "living well in the field".

In response Mike asked us if we had heard the story of the two officers having breakfast. "One was a Guards Officer and the other a Royal Marine. They were sitting together having breakfast after a mess dinner. The Guardsman looked extremely jaded, and to make matters worse had his cap on. It looked rather ridiculous, but the fellow was not looking well and clearly didn't want to chat. Anyway the Royal Marine went to the table laid out with the cereals to get some corn flakes. Having filled his bowl he returned, sat down and asked the fellow to pass the milk. He was just simply ignored. Try as he might he couldn't get him to pass the milk. In the end he lost his temper and swore at his neighbour to "Show some manners and pass the Bloody Milk ..." This at last achieved a reaction. A somewhat bucolic Guardsman responded to the Royal Marine and with an arrogance that he just could not believe, turned to him, begrudgingly passed the milk and stated, "When a Guards Officer has his cap on at breakfast it means he doesn't want to be spoken to." Quick as a flash the Royal Marine lifted up his foot and put his boot in his corn flakes and responded "When a Royal Marine puts his boot in his cornflakes .... He bloody well wants you to pass the milk."

They all just fell about in fits. A brilliant story, clearly Mike wasn't as quiet as he looked. John joined in but the grin on his face showed that he had heard that one before.

The steaks arrived and all went quiet for a while. Then Peter turned to John, "As our local senior citizen I think it is your turn to regale us with a tale of daring do, or failing that one of your dits. Come on John tell us about the delights of running out of Singapore."

"Delights? Not quite the term I would have used. Perhaps you would all benefit from a true tale, one that is a lesson to all young aspiring officers wanting to cover themselves in glory, and avoid ending up deep in the S,H, one T." he replied.

"Some of you may recall that I had almost a full commission running an A-boat out of Singapore. Well, about halfway through my time out there we had an extended maintenance period which included a docking. Most of you are aware that, like us, A-boats had two shafts. Well, one of the major activities during the docking was to replace the old screws with the newer ones which had composite inserts to reduce the singing at certain revs. Despite the heat, the work went well, and we managed to complete on time. Our CO was a well known officer whose casual attire frequently included him sporting rather dashing bow-ties. No names, no pack drill, but you know who I am referring to. We were a happy band of brothers and having partied out at the end of the maintenance period, eventually accepted that we had to go back to sea. Departure day was the normal grand affair with Captain SM and his team on the jetty, and the Engineers Officers on the casing giving their positive reports to the CO before he made his way up to the bridge. I had only just made it down into the Control Room as he ordered "*Slow Ahead together*". The screws started to bight and then we heard "*Stop together.*" …rather unusual … but it was quickly followed by "*Slow Astern Together*". I didn't really take in what was happening, but became aware that we were still going astern without any change of orders. Then I was called to the Search Periscope and was stunned to see that we were making our way out into the middle of the channel …going ahead. Oh Christ! It hit me almost at once … we had put the screws on the opposite shafts and everything was arse about face. Well, to cut a long story short, the Boss had realised almost at once what was wrong and had the wits to order astern. He took us calmly out into the middle of the channel, turned around and brought us back alongside to the puzzled faces of the Squadron

Officers who were still there. It cost me a fortune in drinks. We had to go back in the dock and swop them over. To add to my embarrassment he had a metal deck chair welded to the after casing, while we were in the dry dock, and forced me to sit in it as the screws were swopped, thereby ensuring that this time they were on the correct shafts. A salutary lesson to all confident young officers – beware being too complacent!"

They all looked at him somewhat mesmerized. Mike wasn't sure he should really believe him, "was he pulling their guest's leg?" That grin raised some doubt and a number of question marks. None of them were ever really sure that John's dits actually happened, but they were bloody good.

"Come on Toby, it's your turn for a last dit before the pudding" directed the XO.

"Peter, you know I'm no good at telling jokes" he replied, but it was to no avail so he wracked his grey cells for something appropriate, even if the outcome did make him feel somewhat of a prat.

"Ah, I know. Have you heard about the Officer who in a single evening watch took the most amazing fix and then broke the record for the longest ship report on record?"

Before they could respond he continued. "Mike you will probably be familiar with the rudimentary navigation we adopt when close to the coast, taking fixes about every hour or so, sometimes more frequently if there is a strong tide. We use a compass on the bridge and as each bearing is taken the officer of the watch calls them out down the voice pipe to the helmsman, who repeats them for the on watch Petty Officer to plot them on the chart table. It is simple but effective and invariably produces good three point fixes. Like all things in the service there is a ritual and this one starts with the order from the bridge of "*Stand by Bearings*"

Mike replied that he understood our system, but had not actually been on the bridge when any fixes had been taken.

"Well this time it was a little different. A certain rather talented officer was on watch one evening in a boat which had left Portland and was starting to make its way across Lyme Bay. It was a gorgeous evening, he'd had a good supper, and could see a couple of elegant old square rigged sailing vessels with the southerly wind on their beam making good progress across the bay some five miles ahead. Being a keen sailor with a desire to have his own small yacht one day he thought a reasonably close look would not be amiss. Anyway, having turned the corner around Portland Bill, the Petty Officer on the plot called up to the bridge for the first of what was to be a series of fixes.

"*A good three pointer while we are close in Sir, to give us a reference across the bay*" was his request.

So the aforementioned officer duly set up the pelorus on the Bridge and moving over to the voice pipe gave the order:

"*Stand By Bearings*"

The helmsman dutifully repeated the order "*Stand by Bearings, Sir*" and continued to lean awkwardly to his left, ear wedged firmly against the bottom bellows opening of the voice pipe, awaiting the bearings to call them out to the PO on the plot. As he sat there a feeling that all was not well gradually came upon him, and some background noise down the voice pipe gradually became a slow rumble, which quickly turned into a violent noisy eruption. Heads turned towards him as, too late he realised what was happening ... and three ball bearings burst out of the pipe before he could take his ear away!"

Silence reigned around the table and at last Peter said, "Who was it?"

Before Toby could reply the CO, with a big grin on his face, said he had been the XO at the time and again "No names no pack drill", but he could confirm it as a true dit.

So Toby continued ... "Well gentleman, my story of this watch isn't quite complete. The said officer had the gall to then take a proper fix and pass the bearings down to a very distrusting helmsman. However, by now he was very much aware that a somewhat uncertain fate would greet him when he turned over the watch and made his way below into the control room, so he decided to go for broke. The two square riggers, in full sail, looked absolutely wonderful as the sun began to go down. He had recognized them and knew that they were actually the two old French vessels the Belle Poule and the Petite Etoile, both in excellent condition. So he called down to the plot *"Stand by Ship report"*.

The unsuspecting reply came back *"Stand by Ship report, Sir"*

"Tell the Captain I have two vessels at six thousand yards, they are fifteen degrees off the port bow, bearing moving slowly aft. The first one is the Belle Poule on a broad reach with the following sails set ...." he continued to describe each and every sail set. It took about seven minutes. He then repeated the whole thing for the Petite Etoile. Finally he had the cheek to ask the plot to read the report back to him to ensure that no errors had been made in the translation. The whole ship report took more

than a page in the log and some twenty minutes overall. At least that watch went by quickly, and he wasn't lynched on coming back down into the Control Room. Self preservation had motivated him to get the lookout to pass a message from him proposing beers all round for the watch below, and a special drink of his choice for the helmsman when next ashore." Toby finished his tale and noted the grins and nod from the CO.

"Well done Toby, after that we definitely need the Pud" said Peter with a wave to the Leading Steward.

They demolished a rather fine tarte tatin, and then eased their chairs back for the cheese and the inevitable glass of Port. It was a very special evening and they rounded it off in the traditional Naval fashion with the Loyal Toast, seated, and raising their glasses of Port to "The Queen". Dinners like this were few and far between given their cramped life, and the routine and operating they had to undertake. In their last two years on board they had only achieved three. Mind you they had made up for it with a number of parties on board while tied up alongside. All in all, it had been a great way to pass the passage out of the Wash and down around East Anglia.

ooOoo

2030 Sunday 18 November

They continued south over the next twenty four hours. As they joined the transit lanes to get through the Channel narrows they gave a very good impression of a cyclist on a Motorway. A very small and slow craft surrounded by giant supertankers charging along with no chance of changing course or stopping to avoid this little black shape designed to merge into the background with the additional menace of the cross channel ferries dashing between the gaps in the lines of the enormous tankers and container vessels. It all created a pretty hairy scenario.

For once the Seamen earned their money. Peter recounted the story of a Destroyer Captain he knew telling him that the only way to go through the narrows was to do thirty knots so that the only concern you had was running into the ships ahead of you. However, in the case of Orca, a mere 2,500 tonnes of small conventional submarine, only able to maintain twelve knots as a credible surface passage speed, painted black and low in the water meant it was a nightmare. The CO stayed up for the whole transit, and the XO and NO took it in turns on the bridge with him. By the time Orca turned out of the lanes to edge closer to the Sussex coast, heading to clear St Catherine's Point on the southern tip of the Isle of Wight, they were all pretty exhausted. So much so that John and Toby rejoined the bridge watchkeeping roster and did the middle (midnight to 0400) and morning (0400 to 0800) night watches to give them all a rest.

The result was that they ended up in the exercise areas SE of the Isle of Wight with a bubbling bevy of Seamen fresh and ready to go, and two somewhat jaded Engineers, of whom one did not at all fancy his post breakfast activity of diving in the Sonar 187 pressurised dome space with a rather fat and smelly REA.

1000 Monday 19 November

At 1000 Toby and the REA gathered the spares and tools they would need for the repair escapade in plastic bags, put them into two mail bags, and deposited them below the tower ready for their little jaunt. After a coffee to warm their insides they presented themselves ready to go to the XO in the Control Room. The second Cox'n kitted them out with life jackets and safety lines and they closed up around the chart table to go over the plan. It was relatively straightforward and with the CO, Peter, and the Sonar Chief assembled Toby gave them a rundown of what they planned to do once they were in position. The important thing was to establish and maintain the comms link. No-one had dived with the 187 Sonar chamber manned before, so although it should be a safe evolution, none of them knew for certain. Once everyone was clear on the order of events and the options once the pair were in place, the CO declared himself happy.

He then took the broadcast *"Bridge, Captain, take the way off the submarine and have the casing manned when safe to do so."*

The TASO had the watch on the bridge, and rang down the engine orders to take the way off the boat.

The 187 Sonar Dome

It took a few minutes for the boat to slow down and then he ordered

"Second Cox'n and party, the casing is clear. There is only a slight chop but beware of any wash. You are clear to man the fin, open the fin door and repair onto the casing. Report when ready to open the for'd casing doors for entry down to the Sonar Chamber"

"Aye, aye, Sir." replied the Second Cox'n and started up the ladder into the fin closely followed by his casing party.

Once they had opened up the fin door and rigged the safety lines they called down to the pair of them to make their way up and join them. With only a small chop running they were able to make their way up through the fin, open the fin door, and assemble on the casing without getting drenched. They all fixed their safety lines to the casing roller. It wouldn't stop them getting wet but would prevent them slipping off should any wash, or large wave, rock the boat. The REA and Toby waited on the casing while Second and his team of two reported up to the Bridge and received permission to open up the access down into the casing free-flood area. This was the path down into the 187 Sonar Chamber. It took some time to tie back the plates and clear a way down through the undercasing area. With so much being tied down to stop any underwater noise they were forced to remove some of the lashings to create a route through to the chamber access. Even then it was not easy. They took it together, slipping and sliding with their backs bent double and feet awash from the occasional waves, which albeit small, eased up over the main pressure hull and filled their boots. For the last stretch they had to crawl on all fours and it wasn't long before they were soaked from the waist down.

Under the Casing

Finally they arrived at the Sonar Chamber access hatch and, after a great heave with a two foot wrench, cracked it open. The REA clambered inside and with the casing party passing down the gear Toby relayed it on to him in the chamber. He could see there wasn't going to be much room, but thought, "so far so good, even if they were both very wet and getting quite cold."

The chamber was no more than five feet in diameter and about eight feet long, with the majority of the space being filled by the directing gear and the sonar signal head amplifiers. The transducers were assembled in a big array above this in the dome, which was a free flood area, within which they rotated to either receive passive noise signals or transmit, depending on the mode they were using. So with little room to spare the REA squeezed his cumbersome frame around the directing gear to the other side of the chamber and started to take out some of the tools. "Not yet" Toby thought, and brought him up short, telling him to check the sound powered phone before they went any further, that vital comms link to the Control Room and Sound Room. The last thing Toby wanted was to find a fault in the link after they had dived. He clambered in and settled down on the other side. The comms link was good, so Toby gave a thumbs up to the casing team, and managed to turn so that he could shut and clip the door behind them.

Neither of them enjoyed that final moment shut in that damp space waiting for the boat to dive. Toby had every finger and toe crossed and wondered "what for the love of .... had made me think I should be here with the REA." They heard the casing team shutting down the casing doors to the free flood area, and then an eerie silence enveloped them. They must have sat there for some minutes before the sound powered phone went again. It was the Sonar Chief in the Sound Room who had the presence of mind to understand that what they needed was a continuous commentary telling them what was happening in the Control Room. So, by his good thinking, the unfolding events were relayed to them as the TASO went below and the XO dived the boat. It all seemed to take a hell of a long time. To make matters worse, the REA's body odour, as he bathed in his own sweat, was becoming so strong that Toby found himself unable to think of little else.

Then the boat started to dive. Toby could see that the REA was as scared as him, as his face had turned white, so Toby started a verbal exchange, initially checking for leaks, making sure that the pressure wasn't going up, thereby indicating a leak with water coming in even if they couldn't see it. Toby then got him to man the phone and to ask what was happening at the other end, getting him to make continuous reports back via the Sonar Chief of what was happening to the boat and the general state of play.

It worked for them both and they gradually got into a rhythm which took their minds off their precarious situation. Altogether it must have taken some twenty minutes or so from starting to dive for the boat to settle at depth - it never seemed that long when they were in the Control Room. Then at last the Sonar Chief told them he had been ordered to operate the 187. This was it, they had the gear out and an Avo was connected to the first drive servo. To give the REA room to take the readings they swopped roles and Toby took the phone.

"*Ready in the Sonar Chamber*" he reported.

The Sonar Chief replied "*Enabling the Directing Gear now.*"

The Array began rotating and a low hum began, it was louder than they expected and they had to raise their voices to hear each other. Before long they were shouting despite the close confines of their little tomb. The REA began taking impedance measurements but after a few minutes Toby noticed a smell which he recognized immediately as that of electrical burning. Then smoke started to seep out of one of the drive servos. It was right in front of him.

"*Stop rotating*" he ordered.

"*It looks as though one of the Servos has started to overheat and smoke is coming from it. Give us a few minutes and we will report back.*"

It didn't take long to confirm what they could see. In the short time the set had been rotating this servo had all but burnt out. It must have been starting to go for some time. Fortunately for them it decided to call it a day right in front of Toby's nose. Well, it wasn't exactly high brow fault finding. They just followed the smoke! It took the REA about ten minutes to replace the servo – fortunately it was a spare they carried and had put into the mail bags. The biggest hurdle was swopping positions in the cramped space. Eventually they were ready to try again. Hopefully that was it but you never could tell. Something else could have easily caused the problem; fault finding was always a juggle between cause and effect.

"*Sound Room – Sonar Chamber, we have replaced the servo. Restart the directing gear.*" Toby ordered.

Well, it had worked. The array started to rotate, there was no more sticking or slipping, the hum had stopped, and no sign of any more smoke. They reported the success back down the chain, although they assumed the Sound Room could see that the set was working normally now. The Sonar Chief passed the traditional "well done", a *Bravo Zulu,* from the Control Room and Toby and the REA started to put the covers back on the directing gear.

The boat surfaced about thirty minutes later, and after another ten minutes the pair heard a knocking on the chamber door. Toby guessed that the time locked in the chamber must have been well over an hour, long enough for him to no longer be aware of the REA's BO. The return trip across the casing was uneventful, but their arrival in the Control Room was very much a surprise. AS two very wet and jaded bodies appeared down the ladder the CO clapped them both on the back and warmly shook each of them by the hand as they stepped down the ladder from the fin. It was so unexpected, being treated as returning heroes was hardly what they felt they deserved. However, the idea of diving in that little black space hadn't appealed to any of them. Now his nose was back in working order Toby also wondered how he had survived – "Christ the REA stank" he thought. Thus ended their little adventure, with fault finding by following the smoke - so much for top flight technical analysis.

ooOoo

1300 Monday 19 November

After using all that nervous energy Toby gorged himself over his late lunch and then settled down for an afternoon in his pit. He went out like a light, and the first he knew was being shaken for tea by which time most of the wardroom were seated and tucking into the last cake, saved up by the Leading Steward for their trip up the channel before getting home to HMS Dolphin. He had decided to ignore the added exercise and was heard muttering something about "making the best of it". It was a really moist fruit cake and the guys had been kind enough to save Toby a large piece.

They were making good progress along the Channel and expected to pass St Catherine's point, the southern tip of the Isle of Wight, before midnight. That would give them plenty of time to get into the Portland areas, dive for their covert entry and undertake the photo recce in the early hours but with the sun well up.

The plan was then to sneak out, analyse the photo shoot, and return in the evening to release the Booties. With most of the crew kicking their heels, and an early night looming before the games in the early hours, they were all at a loose end so Toby suggested they had a Dog Watch movie. He fancied a Michael Caine movie, but was outvoted and they ended up choosing the Beatles' movie "Help". John and he rigged up the Bell & Howells projector, and were just fitting the first reel when Mike came in. Not having seen a movie in a boat before he couldn't believe how much gear they needed just to project such a small picture on the chart pinned to the wall.

"Why don't you join the for'd mess and show the films there, you'd have a much bigger picture and you could all share them" he declared.

"No. Film shows are intimate mess events." replied Peter "The Chiefs and Senior Rates would feel just the same. Although I will admit that some of us have joined in at the odd time. It depends on our watch routine and the boat's activities."

So they snuggled down, squeezing six of them around the projector, and with small beers all round, focused on the 18 inch size screen and enjoyed the film's zany plot. It wasn't a bad choice, Toby thought they'd all seen it before, but it was good value and kept their spirits up as they headed west some miles off the entry into Portsmouth Harbour, with home slowly disappearing astern.

With an hour or so before dinner Toby grabbed Steve, the Part III trainee, to further his training. With the Leading Writer in tow they went down into the AMS below the Control Room, gathered around Toby's small home-made desk area, and mustered all the kit they would need for the following evening's photo recce. Despite the potential value of the final product, the gear they were provided with was fairly basic. The 35mm camera, with the necessary fitments to go onto the periscope, were good quality, but the outfit provided to develop the films at sea was less than basic. It gave Toby the impression that the intent was to discourage them from actually developing the films themselves. That was probably a reasonable proposition for the real thing, but in a covert deployment, whether for real or exercise, they would have no choice. Having mustered all the kit and chemicals they went back up to the Control Room and made their way aft into the Officers Head's. This was to be the Dark Room.

The Dark Room!

They started by converting the light fittings to dark red lighting, then set out the trays for the chemicals using masking tape to hold them into place. Several strands of a mini washing line were set out to hang the prints on, albeit at head height right over where they would have to stand. The problem was the pressure hull curvature. A normal height crew member had to lean slightly back to have a pee, so you could imagine their difficulty. The biggest challenge was setting out the enlarger, which could take the 35mm negatives and focus them on A4/A5 paper to enable a good resolution of the target areas. It ended up on the toilet seat.

They covered all the gaps around the door and between the adjacent traps with masking tape to ensure that no light leakage would upset their determined efforts to produce a credible panorama. Finally to put the Dark Room to the test they took some shots inside the boat and put them through their innovative production process. Much to their satisfaction and surprise they turned out pretty well. They then shut down the Heads and installed an impromptu Dark Room sign on the door.

Steve hadn't come across this part of an Electrical Officer's duties before so Toby took him back to the Wardroom and showed him some of the more exciting shots they had in the boat's portfolio. The most exciting was from a SINKEX which Orca had been privileged to undertake some eighteen months ago. Toby had only been on board six months and the CO had joined three weeks before that. It was their baptism of fire in more ways than one. The target had been an old destroyer and she had gone down incredibly quickly once the salvo of Mk VIII's had hit their mark.

Steve was beginning to get the feel for the wider responsibilities of the job and once they had finished borrowed the slim volume which offered guidance on photo recce's – not that there was much. No sooner had he settled at the Wardroom table than the Leading Steward came in to lay up for dinner. Tonight's effort was to be a much more sober affair, with most of them wanting a good meal then sleep before the early morning efforts got underway. It may well have been an exercise, but they were still taking Orca into a fairly hairy area with significant sea traffic. The hope was that at 0400 in the morning nothing would be about, but you never knew. They had a quiet supper with little of the usual banter. The CO and Simon were the first to finish and departed without staying for any pud. They headed for the chart table and laid out the larger scale charts to go over the morning's covert entry around Portland Bill and in towards the Breakwater. The Booties' target was the strange building which appeared to have a mast and cage at the western end of the breakwater. This was their "target demolition" point. How close they took the boat for the photo shots was down to luck in terms of fishing and other small craft around at that time of the morning and the safety margin in terms of depth of water. They also had to be mindful of the various wrecks in the area, a number having been used to block the Western Breakwater entry. Not that they intended to get that close. Portland was a safe haven under normal routine but it was a different matter for a covert entry.

ooOoo

0230 Tuesday 20 November

Orca dived at 0230 with the Shambles light to the west of them. The idea was to have as much water as possible available to enable them to get into their routine - dive, catch the trim and start the transit into the Breakwater without any untoward pressures. The problem was that they had to be in position as the sun was rising to have any chance of getting reasonable shots of the Portland Breakwater and the potential target. The plan was that the first rays of the sun would give them what they wanted as it rose in the east and illuminated the target area. In theory all was in their favour - the uncertainty was the level of defence forces that might be deployed. The Booties had no idea whether this exercise was simply a pull through one for them alone, or whether a defensive force had been prepared and was to be part of the action. They simply had to be prepared for the latter, even if it didn't materialise. They closed up in a form of Action Stations with the CO on the attack scope guiding them into the increasingly shallow waters as they approached the eastern side of Portland Bill.

The Shambles Bank also made the room for manoeuvre somewhat restricted, nonetheless they kept it to the west and headed north parallel to the eastern shore of the Bill keeping well clear of the hazardous rocky shoreline and the ferry entry channel into Weymouth. They had also scrutinized the tides to make sure that the famous Tide Race was not going to embarrass them. They crept slowly north doing about four knots with the dark shadow of Portland Island looming to the west. The idea was to keep well outside the twenty fathom line, not a lot of water but enough to give them some room to avoid any early pre-sunrise traffic.

Some familiar sights passed as they made their way along. The CO kept them informed as he spotted well known landmarks appearing in the distance out of the gloom. Initially the Lighthouse at the Bill, and then as they passed the silhouette of the steep sides of the Island he reported seeing the old but rather grand buildings of the HMS Osprey base Wardroom hanging onto the sides of the cliff. At last the Breakwater started to appear, and with it the first rays of the morning sun. At this point Toby took over on the search periscope and they started taking the overlapping shots for the recce photo spread.

He had only taken about six shots when the Boss reported a fast Rib (potentially a patrol boat) travelling at speed inside the southern entrance. They knew that nothing of any size could use that entrance, and fortunately the Rib continued across the inner harbour, albeit at some 20 knots. Nonetheless, it confirmed that there was some activity even at this time in the morning. Trying not to be distracted Toby continued taking shots. His goal was to ensure that he maintained an overlap between successive shots and at the same time kept the quality of the shots up to the mark. He had to concentrate and put all the other data being passed around to one side so that he wasn't distracted. It was not easy as they pushed further and further into the shallower areas which gave views of the main Portland Harbour entry. Toby did recall the overlapping shots containing the Booties' Breakwater target, but little else as they made their painfully slow progress into danger.

The rising sun was now lighting everything up and it was becoming time for them to withdraw. Finally Toby reported completion of coverage of the main entrance and the CO decided to call it a day. Retrieving the camera,

Toby had the search periscope lowered, and the CO ordered a slow turn to make their way back out to and beyond the Shambles. It was still pretty tense, the tide was about to turn and another twenty minutes or so and the Portland Race would be starting to run strongly. Slowly but surely they crept back out, with just the foot or so of the attack periscope marking their covert progress.

They stayed at Action Stations the whole way, but despite the Control Room being filled with some twenty bodies you could have heard a pin drop. At last with the Shambles astern they were able to go deep and finally return to watch diving. So far so good, the real action was to be on the morrow and this had in effect just been a rehearsal. Rehearsal or not they had all felt it, and now Toby's small team had to do their stuff in the home made dark room. There really wasn't room for Steve so Toby had to ask him to leave the task to himself and the Leading Writer. They set out the trays and filled them with fresh developing solution. Toby took every precaution against their lack of experience so that there was least chance of a ball's up. As they removed the film from the camera he had all his fingers crossed. If the pair of them were to mess it up now the last few tense hours would have been a waste of time. They processed the film following the directions laid down using a timer they had borrowed from the galley, and then hung the roll up to dry. Under the dim red light they could see the negatives looking pretty crisp, but the real test would be once they were dry and they could put them into the combined enlarger/developer. There was nothing they could do for a while now, so they left the make-shift dark room and each made his way back to their respective messes to have breakfast.

Meanwhile, the CO and Mike were reflecting on the options for putting the SBS team ashore. It was clear that going in that close and surfacing to release the teams in their canoes was not credible, so they were ensconced around the far end of the table looking in detail at the local tides. As the discussion continued it became evident that they were trying to use the tides so that the canoe entry could take advantage of having the flow with them around the Bill, then turn so that it would also aide them for the exit. The variables were the distances from drop-off to the target and then out to the pick-up zone, and the time they would need to place and set the charges. The only way they could get nature and their goals to match was with the boat coming in much closer than was either normal or safe for these operations, as the water was pretty shallow that close to Portland.

The debate continued. Toby had already managed to devour his eggs and bacon and was happily digging in to a plate of toast and jam, (sadly without marmalade which had run out over a week ago). As John had said "one has to make some sacrifices in life". Having studied their dilemma Toby decided to offer a way out.

"Have you considered coming in to the west side of Portland Bill, Sir? Mike and his team could be dropped off in the lee of the Island off Chesil Beach where it is reasonably deep. It has the advantage of being quieter than the east side with its' entrances to both Portland and Weymouth harbours. It also has fewer lights and boats can easily merge into the background. Finally it is not that far for the SBS team to paddle before they catch the tide and are carried around the Bill on their way into the Breakwater. It could also be a potential loiter area for us. There is much more water that side, there would be less surface traffic with the ferries and most of the yachts on the other side and the bonus is that we could then be close at hand to aide their exit if needed. The down side is that we would be screened by the island from any Bongle /Trongle transmissions. Mike, are they credibly used at a distance or just for a relatively close rendezvous?"

"Only short range, we never use much power otherwise we would simply advertise our presence." Mike replied.

"Toby, I think you have hit on the answer" declared the CO. "It would solve the entry challenge, and we could achieve a rendezvous in relatively benign conditions protected from the strong tides, so that a tow out beyond visible range of the shore would allow us to surface and recover the team with less risk. What do you think Mike?"

"I think it sounds like a plan." He turned and checked with Simon that the tide rip around the Bill was not going to be more than they could take. "Yes, that looks manageable."

Toby didn't expect his off the cuff idea to be so readily accepted, but they were both experienced players in their respective roles and would have been aware of any draw backs. Anyway, the overall game plan was set out and all Toby had to do now was produce the visible data on the target. So, excusing himself from the breakfast table he returned to the "dark room".

The Leading Writer was still enjoying his breakfast, but as the negatives were now dry, Toby decided to try printing the first shot. He had plenty of photographic paper in various sizes and decided to go for an A5. He set it up and it was soon evident that the shot was pretty good quality with a sharp focus, which bode well for the rest of them. So he proceeded to shoot each negative in turn. Before long there was little room left on the washing line set up to dry the exposures, even at A5 size, and he accepted the need for another break before completing the task. On his way back to the wardroom he gave the CO an update on the recce results and they agreed to gather in the wardroom at 1130 to look at the resulting panorama.

With thirty minutes or so to waste he decided to button-hole Mike and get the frequency range his "Trongle" would be operating at, so that the Sonar Chief and his sound room crew were in the picture. With the 187 sonar now fully functional, the chance of a timely rendezvous with the SBS team, using all the aids, looked good.

By the time he returned to the "dark room" the Leading Writer had taken down the first set of prints and was well underway finishing off the rest of the film. They had done pretty well and the result was looking quite good. Another fifteen minutes and the last of the prints were dry, so they could now set up the panorama. Toby left him to it and went off to find Simon so that he could borrow an old chart on which to set out the overlapping shots. The goal had been for a thirty per cent overlap, the shot timing based on a range of about 4000 yards to the breakwater. Looking at the track it was probably a bit more but the quality of the shots more than made up for the slight increase in range.

Toby had taken the first batch and as he was gathering them up together with the old chart, the Leading Writer arrived with the rest of the prints. The chart table was needed by the Watch Dived team, so they gathered up their photos and took them into the wardroom. The panorama looked pretty good. The significant overlap had allowed them to use the sharpest of the shots to good effect. With scissors and sello-tape they set to and before long the Breakwater with Portland Harbour in the background began to unfold across the wardroom table. Once the set was complete Toby went off and returned with the chart they had actually used for the entry. The two together showed the visual scene and the planned overlaps with the boat's position plotted every ten minutes. It was good stuff and would meet the needs of the team at 1130. Finally, Simon brought in the charts showing the overall exercise areas and the details of the west side of the island and the Chesil Beach cove. A pot of coffee and half a dozen mugs and they were ready for the gathering.

They assembled as planned, the CO, Peter, Simon and Mike who had brought along his Sergeant. Clearly this was a somewhat false exercise as almost all of them had a fairly intimate knowledge of Portland and its harbour area. Nonetheless, it was surprisingly instructive to get a feel of how much data could actually be gleaned from such an exercise. The quality of the shots of the breakwater were good but the lesser quality of the distant harbour facilities, and the lack of data for the east shoreline of Portland Island, made them realise that a real operation would need a much more comprehensive set of shots.

They reviewed the current plan on the charts and noted the hazardous areas for the Booties in their canoes and the boat during the entry and when on the surface. The key was timing to take advantage of the tides, but also keeping outside the time span of the full force of the race off the Bill. Finally they vacated the wardroom so that Mike could bring his complete team in to view the data at first hand and ensure each and every one of them had the full picture. They split up just before twelve and as a finale Mike had a final chat with the CO, TASO, the Sonar Chief and Toby on the operation of the Trongle. Hopefully it would provide them with a relatively covert homing signal and lead Orca down onto the canoes in the pitch black night they were all anticipating. It was going to be a long haul so food and sleep were the immediate priorities, and it wasn't long before the boat gradually shut down, with those on Watch Dived going about their business in hushed tones.

ooOoo

1600 Wednesday 21 November

At 1600 the Booties started assembling their canoes in the fore-ends and setting out their kit for the Sergeant to inspect prior to packing it into sealed waterproof packets. These, together with their respective weapons, would be placed in the bows and sterns of the canoes once they had been man-handled onto the casing.

They approached to a position about ten miles off the start of Lyme Bay and the great spread of Chesil Beach. They were well clear of the cross channel ferries and yachts plying out from Weymouth, and somewhat to the west of the Shambles shallows. The intent was to close into the drop-off point in the shadows to the west of Portland, maintaining a slow four knots at periscope depth. They started in at 2230. Fortunately, although it was a very dark night, the lights from the shore and Portland Bill lighthouse made it easier to take regular fixes. With a heading of 020 they made their way into the lee of the Bill, the lights of Weymouth fading from view and Orca disappearing into the shadows on the quiet west side of the island. Mike had voiced a concern that his team could have been lit up by the lighthouse. Fortunately they had realised that after going around the Bill, by keeping close to the east coast of the Island under the overhang of the cliffs, the SBS canoes would be in the shadows and effectively hidden from the loom of the light shining out above them.

The SBS team had laid all their gear out along the main passage, with the canoes fully assembled. They looked every inch the part in camouflaged fatigues, faces streaked to break up the image, and canoe skirts around their waists. The Second Cox'n was perched at the top of the access ladder into the tower with two of his lads close behind. Hands on the hatch lever, he and his team were ready to open up, make their way along the casing, and once safe to do so open the main access hatch and help the SBS team get their gear onto the casing. Silence and speed were essential. All they needed now was confirmation that there were no contacts either visually or on the sonar. There wasn't a sound in the boat.

"*Sonar – Control Room, no contacts.*" the Sonar Chief reported over the broadcast.

The CO did a last all round look, flipped the periscope hand grips up and stood back as the mast was lowered. He turned to the XO and in a calm voice ordered "*Surface*".

From then on it was all action. The roar of the air rushing into the tanks drowned most of the noise. Orca popped straight up and the blower was started up to ensure stable buoyancy. The CO was locked back onto the attack periscope and once he was satisfied that the casing was dry he ordered the casing team up into the fin and out onto the after casing deck. It was pitch black up there and you could only make out the sketchiest view of what was unfolding. Two heavy taps from up top on the main access hatch was the signal to open it up from below. It flew open and the bow of the first canoe immediately came into view followed by two dark shapes pulling up the next one and the canvas bags containing the gear. From the passage below it seemed eerily quiet, no normal sounds of frenetic activity, just the occasional scrape and rubbing sound as the boats were eased over the side. The weather could not have been better, a little chop but no real waves, and the sky covered by low cloud.

At last the Booties were all launched and underway. The canoes disappeared slowly south towards the shadows of the coast, the Booties determined to catch the start of the tidal race and hopefully the free ride around the Bill. The boat quietly dived and turned to clear the outer reaches of Lyme Bay and the tidal race before they found themselves caught in it. Although the depth of water that side of the Bill was reasonable, the Island blanked most of the sonar contacts, so they remained at periscope depth and relied on their eyes to keep out of trouble. It was now 0200 and they had a couple of hours to wait and ensure that they had thoroughly sanitised the recovery area. It was one of those periods when playing the waiting game certainly seemed harder than actually undertaking the dangerous operation itself. With the Boss sitting quietly on a stool by the chart table, they maintained concentration and kept a close, but quiet, control over the evolving plot. Once clear of land the sonar began picking up a large number of contacts. Sorting out the wheat from the chaff was a continuing challenge. Sitting on the edge of the English Channel with

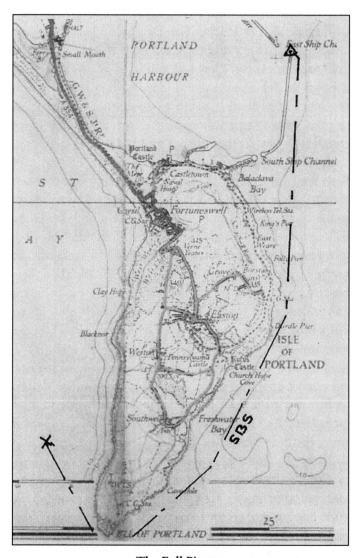

The Full Picture

the vast number of ships plying up and down, at all hours of day and night, meant that the sonar was becoming swamped with contacts. The *Bearings Only Plot* was looking pretty busy and yet visually there appeared to be little to worry them. They just had to ensure that nothing slipped under their mental radar and caught them unawares. Continuing south at four knots they began to gain increasing confidence that there were no close contacts to impact the exercise.

At 0230 Simon and Toby took over the watch from Peter and John, not that any of them had actually been able to sleep. There had been a couple of contacts on sonar to the east, which had initially been classified as fishing boats, and finally their mast head lights had come into view. They were obviously working in tandem, just to the south of the Shambles bank. Peter had taken their bearings and they were moving slowly right. No problem as yet, but they would have to be watched closely. As Toby took over the periscope the Boss joined Peter on the plot and they decided it was time to turn back in for the rendezvous. They were some way off the race so the tide rip wasn't affecting them, but a slight chop had started to increase to a level where individual waves could be identified. Any more and the recovery would become a little testing. The turn back to the north east was deliberately slow, to ensure that there was no danger of dipping the scope as they went around. Once they had steadied on course Toby did another all round look and then went straight back to the fishing boats. They had turned almost 180 degrees and were now heading directly across the Shambles for the Weymouth entry channel between the bank and the Bill. This had the potential to become embarrassing. Toby reported the change in their course and the CO came over and took the scope for a closer look.

Concentrating on them for a short while he then did another all round look and summarised his view. "It depends how far over they come. If they turn back to Weymouth up the channel we should be OK. Just as well we decided to put our tow-point RV the other side of the Bill. Keep us posted on their progress Toby."

"Aye, aye. Sir." he responded, taking the scope back. Despite the enveloping darkness it was becoming easier to make out the land features as the lights on the coast started to come back into view. Even so the chances of seeing their Bootie colleagues at any range were pretty slim. Mind you, that was meant to be the idea.

Time appeared to be going very slowly, but before any of them realised it was 0400. The CO turned to Simon and calmly asked him to close up at Action Stations. It was all done very quietly. Toby had been once again on the scope, and after giving it up to TASO, took up his normal position on the Fire Control console. The fishing boats were still coming towards the Bill, and as a precaution their settings were put onto the system, and updated with regular visual bearings and estimated ranges. Once they were all settled down the CO called for silence.

"Gentlemen, we are about to undertake a very risky procedure, with the lives of our Bootie colleagues very much dependent on our patience and skill. The plan is for us to rendezvous with them in the next hour. They have a device which should help us to track them. Once we have their position, the intent is for us to remain dived and transit as slowly as we are able up to them. At the RV they will be spread out line abreast with each canoe joined via

a stout lightweight hawser to make a chain. We will then pass between them and tow them clear of Portland into the quiet of Lyme Bay. At a suitable point we will then surface and recover them."

"In the case of any emergency they will release the tow." he added.

Turning to the Outside Wrecker he continued, *"Firstly we need a stop trim, to allow us to start the tow as slowly as possible, and thereafter, concentration from us all. Just stay calm and on the ball. Our prime interaction with them will be visual, so reports from the scope as ever take priority."*

"Carry on Number One, reduce speed as required for a stop trim."

The CO took over the attack periscope, the search scope was lowered, and Peter started a staged reduction of the speed, making increasingly finer changes to the trim as they slowly came to the hover. They never quite made it. He was getting close when the CO announced yet another change of course for the fishing boats. The boat was taken back up to four knots and Toby put the new target data for the fishing boats on the Fire Control system. The pair had reached the start of the channel between the Bill and the Shambles and as expected had turned to follow the coast north probably heading for Weymouth and the early fish market. The crew kept their fingers crossed that all had gone to plan for the canoes, and they were catching the last of the return tide in the shadows of the east coast, well clear of these two. The covert passage to the RV off Lyme Bay, took Orca more and more to the west of the Bill and they finally lost sight of the two vessels. It was 0430 now and about the time when the Booties should be starting to transmit on their Trongle.

A quick visual fix showed that the tide was having more effect on them than they had anticipated, and they were in danger of over-reaching the RV with the island blanking any chance of using the Trongle to home in on the canoes. After the problems with fixing off the east coast of Scotland the last thing they wanted was another balls-up. So the CO's order to turn to port and execute a 360 turn, putting them back on their original planned approach, was greeted with some relief.

It was just as well that the CO was a cool character. The continued lack of the homing beacon signal, and the evident impenetrable gloom up top, was starting to raise the tension in the Control Room. There was a very real danger of coming upon them with no notice, and a resulting collision or capsize.

"*Navigator, take the attack periscope from me, my eyes need a rest.*" Simon quickly took over and the CO called the Sound Room for the latest close contacts.

"*Nothing close, and no beacon transmissions, Sir. We have been getting some interference from about 025 since we did our loop. It is a crackling noise and sounds almost like a very large and loud group of shrimp or perhaps something dragging underwater.*"

"*Which contact is it on the BoP?*"

"*This one here, Sir*" replied TASO indicating the short term contact which had a slight closing movement.

"*Navigator, I'll take back the scope. TASO guide me onto that contact. My guess is that it might be our team. XO reduce speed to two knots if you are able - but keep us on depth*"

They crept ever closer. The "interference" gradually got louder and the confidence that it was the Booties slowly mounted.

Finally, the Boss shouted *"Stop Together, starboard ten ...no decrease to five. I have them in sight a cable on our starboard bow."*

"Heading now?"

"016, Sir."

"Steer that, we are about to engage the hawser and take up the tow"

They managed to slow down to below two knots for the impact, which understandably they never felt. The only indication was the CO slewing the periscope around to look astern as the chain of canoes were pulled together. He kept up his commentary telling the guys in the Control Room that he could see the first two canoes, which were slewing about quite violently, and that he simply had to rely on the fact that they hadn't broken away from the tow to assume that the other two were there as well.

They raised the scope another foot to ensure that the tow bight around it was secure, and then gradually turned in small five degree steps to make their way clear of the coast. After forty minutes they had cleared the recovery area and the CO decided they had achieved all the objectives of the exercise. With nothing further to be gained, the for'd scope was raised to full height (the signal to the SBS teams to disengage) and then lowered, leaving them to drift a short way astern. Putting the mast back up to check they were well clear, Orca surfaced and a weary, wet team of Booties closed in to be recovered.

The rendezvous marked the end of the exercise so everyone took their time. The Control Room blew round to achieve full buoyancy, and eventually the Second Cox'ns team had all four canoes laid out on the casing. Mike and his team decided that it would be easier to re-stow the canoes if they were split into their separate halves, and they set to spanners in hand. In parallel the casing party gathered the remaining gear together, and carefully passed it all down the hatch for the Watch below to carry through the boat into the fore-ends. Finally the canoe halves followed and the casing was shut down ready to get underway.

The Booties were desperate for showers, clean clothes and a mega breakfast, and those of the crew who had spent most of the night on their feet were all pretty exhausted. As this was the last sortie before returning home John allowed the SBS team the special privilege of a full fresh water shower at sea, a first as far as most of the crew could remember in a conventional submarine. For the rest of the crew, food was the main priority and the galley served them well. Mike eventually joined those in the Wardroom for his delayed breakfast, bringing a bucket and some other odds and ends. John gave him a quizzical look and he simply replied "Props for later".

By the time Mike had emptied his plate, the disparate members of the Wardroom had begun to gather for the Post Exercise Wash-Up. Simon had to write up the narrative and lessons learnt that morning or the pressures of the return home would take charge and any retrospective report would be of little value. As ever, yet another fresh pot of coffee was produced and they were joined by Mike's Sergeant, the Sonar Chief, and the TI.

Peter kicked off by going through the basics of the photo recce. Little comment there other than the realities of peacetime exercising in an area with so little manoeuvre room and significantly shallow water. Then the covert deployment, again no major issues, although the casing team came up with some useful proposals for

The Booties coming home

rigging the casing to get the manned boats into the water with less risk of incident, particularly in higher sea states. At this point Mike took up the tale. The plan to make use of the tidal race had actually worked. They had made good progress down the east side of the Island, often being able to get in under the shadows of the cliffs to avoid any chance of being seen. They had made good time, which was just as well. On reaching the start of the Breakwater they had decided to move inside through the southern entrance, which although blocked for normal access, presented no problem to them.

However, halfway down the next stretch they were forced to retreat when two fast RiBs appeared from the Naval Base heading for Alpha Point and the exit to Weymouth Bay. In fact once the Ribs had reached the exit they had stopped, loitered for a few minutes and returned whence they had come. The incident had held the SBS team up for about twenty minutes which had given little time in hand had there been any more delays. In the event, they had made the target without further incident and the dummy charge package had been put in place and set to transmit from 0600.

The return trip had started well. Knowing that time was pressing, they had set off at a good pace, accepting that the transit back to Orca would not be quite so covert. They were approaching the cliffs immediately below the lighthouse when they saw the two fishing vessels heading straight towards them from the direction of the Shambles bank. It must have been at about the same time that Orca had lost them when approaching the west side of the Bill. They had decided it was too risky to continue and had opted to shelter in the lee of the rocks just below the light, albeit hidden from the loom. So the second hold-up had blown the RV time. Once the fishing boats had passed they set off at a cracking pace, but to add insult to injury, the chop in the Race began to tell and they began to take in too much water. Finally, albeit an hour or so behind the curve, they reached the RV and deployed the Trongle. At this point Mike got up, went to the bucket, and retrieved a small object. It was a small transistor radio, which he switched on.

"Gentlemen, Trongles are like transistor radios" and so saying he dropped it in the bucket of water soaking Peter and John with some effect ... "... they don't work in water!"

There was a pregnant, and somewhat indignant pause, particularly from the wetter members around the table, and then a grin started to spread over the CO's face as we all suddenly understood what had happened. "So the strange noise we were tracking was your home made Bongle ..." smiled the Boss.

A fitting innovative conclusion to our playtime with the Booties.

ooOoo

HOMEWARD BOUND

Missing Life in Submarines?

Lesson 8 on recapturing the old days:-

*Install a small fluorescent light tube under your coffee
table; then lie under the table to read books.*

1130 Thursday 22 November

The fore-ends were a bloody mess, not that you could blame the Booties. They had done their best but the delays had forced them to go flat out to make the RV, and all you could see of them at the moment were their arms and legs dangling over the edge of their impromptu pits lying on the racks between the torpedoes. It was clear that the TI and his team would have to leave them to get their well earned rest before starting the job of getting the compartment back up to standard for the return home.

Despite the long night they had a lot to do before they got back alongside. Orca's upcoming six week maintenance period was to include three weeks in a dry dock, which meant going over to the main part of Portsmouth Naval Base. An inconvenience for access to facilities and workshops in HMS Dolphin, but a blessing for getting home as most of the crew lived in married quarters on the Portsmouth side of the harbour.

Toby was returning to the Wardroom for the planning meeting, which John had called, when the CO popped his head out of his cabin and called him in.

"Toby, I've just had a signal from Sea Lion. She has just got back to Dolphin ahead of us and reports that on turning into Haslar Creek around Fort Blockhouse she had to take avoiding action to stop ramming into a yacht which was adrift, and with the tide behind her, was surging out of the creek causing mayhem to all the local boat traffic. The main point was that their Navigator Peter Alsop thinks it was your boat "Colonsay."

"Oh, Christ, Sir. I hope not. I use one of the Naval moorings which should be pretty secure. Could you send a signal to the squadron to ask them to check it out?"

"I'll do that. You carry on with John's meeting and I'll keep you informed."

"Many thanks, Sir. I'll be in the Wardroom."

That was the last thing Toby needed so close to home, but he realised there was nothing he could do until they were alongside so he pushed into the Wardroom, filled a mug with fresh coffee, and sat down to listen to John and the assembled team. John had called the gathering of his and Toby's senior teams to go over the plan for the period so that they all understood what they had on their plates. It was also a leave period and ensuring that they had coverage and the specialists would be available at the right time was never easy given the small size of the crew. They also had too many lone specialists who needed their leave as much as everyone else and just couldn't be there around the clock. So they had to call on squadron and workshop back-up quite often. John and Toby worked a scheme whereby John and Chief Connelly (Toby's senior Chief), or Toby and the Chief Tiff (John's senior man CPO Johnny Knox) were always paired up during leave periods. The two Chiefs were very good and they'd never had any problems.

As they had found too often for comfort, planning for such events in a conventional submarine meant two things. You were the lowest priority in the Dockyard and the plan changed every day. Nonetheless, they had to have a framework which they all understood. So they took over the wardroom and with schedules held up by sticky tape covering two walls, grabbed cups of coffee and started the tedious job of going through it. Peter stuck his head in, feeling that he should be there to co-ordinate, but quickly appreciated that they had to sort out all the conflicting needs before any rough plan could be realised. So he excused himself and left them to get down to bare tacks.

Fortunately the major conflicting items had little flexibility, and once they had identified those that had to be done in the dry dock, a credible pattern began to emerge. The key to success was the availability of the SM1 specialist technical staff. At least that made them independent of the dockyard, or they would have been up the creek. John's main themes were the major rebuild of the two donks and his need to check or change a number of hull fittings to continue the "safe to dive" criteria. Toby's were a weapons alignment check in the dock, the change of one of the underwater telephone hydrophones and exchanging two duff cells in the for'd battery. On top of all that they had the usual plethora of maintenance routines across all the systems with the odd mast exchange and a gyro rebuild just to mention a few. It promised to be quite a busy six weeks.

One thing was on Toby's side, John was going on leave first. They both knew second leave was best, it allowed you to get stuck in and tackle the challenges once the return long week-end was over. Then you had the benefit of an almost normal life going home each evening. Finally you had your leave and could actually forget work and not have it play on your mind, so Judy and he would have time to get used to each other again, before going off for some sun and beach. He was definitely ready, but accepted running the technical activities for the first two weeks was a necessary evil.

By lunch time a credible plan had been achieved and they split up to leave the senior technical chiefs to top and tail it. Toby's next challenge was to attempt to finish all his personnel reports before they were back alongside. Of the nineteen on his plate he had fully completed fifteen, not a bad effort. They were a good bunch and fully deserved any extra effort on his part. He'd never been a tick in the box type, and tried hard to reflect their personal qualities in fully rounded reports without too much stylisation or pigeon-holing. Two more were almost there and he could finish them off in the Dogs. Then there was LREM Best. He needed to make some calls to draftee and HMS Collingwood once they were back alongside if he was to achieve his proposal of getting him on the next POREL's course.

Finally he had Chief Nunn, his Upper Yardman candidate for promotion to officer. This particular report was really important, it would either get him firmly on the road to becoming an Officer, or leave him as an "almost but not quite". The report was complex, and comprehensive, and to complete it he needed John's and the Boss's guidance as to how to position it. He knew that he would also have to gauge the squadron's view, after all Nunn would be competing with a number of other good candidates across the squadron. So he was in for a busy time that evening on the two reports, and then would have to follow up on some significant actions on Nunn's behalf once they were alongside in the home base at Dolphin.

After the prolonged time loitering on the surface in Lyme Bay, Toby had no real feel as to the time they actually started the passage home and therefore what time they would get to tie up alongside. Lunch wasn't ready yet, so he ambled into the Control Room to have a look at the chart. They were further adrift than he had expected. Clearly it had taken a fair time to get all the SBS gear back onboard and stowed down below.

They must have left close to 1030, and with about eighty miles passage back and around the Isle of Wight, they wouldn't be back until around 1830. That said, arriving out of normal working hours was not a bad thing. It meant less hassle on arrival and a chance to have a quiet evening at home. With his long weekend coming up it all fitted in rather well. The arrival would be fairly low key, although Captain SM1 would probably welcome them back. He'd know how keen they would all be to get home to their families, and would be the last person to inadvertently hold up the reunions. The other good scheme was the arrangement whereby the Wardroom Hall Porters at Dolphin were given advance notice of each boat's return and made a point of personally phoning the wives of all the officers to let them know the anticipated time alongside. It worked so well that, without fail, those wives and girlfriends that could get away were invariably waiting on the jetty as they came in. It was a little thing but a great morale booster.

In the boat the crew were actively engaged in what he could only describe as a frenetic "Spring Clean". The Control Room had already been scrubbed out and as he went for'd each of the messes was being thoroughly cleaned with copious applications of water and a lot of elbow grease.

As he was passing through the Control Room, the Boss who had been leaning over the plot turned and gave him a signal from the squadron. It set out the next scene in the Colonsay saga. It was definitely Toby's small yacht – 27 footer. The MoD police launch, in an attempt to give a clear passage to the berth for Sea Lion had been forced to physically push the yacht clear and once Sea Lion had successfully tied up had gone out to look for the rogue yacht only to find that a passing motor boat had taken it in tow and was pulling it back up to the moorings in Haslar Creek. So far so good, at least Toby felt that there was a good chance no damage had been done. It was good of the power boat to help out.

Thus reassured he continued on to the fore ends. The SBS team were now up and about and collecting all their gear together. They were being somewhat hassled by the TI, who wanted to ensure his space was up to scratch, thus they were being objectively forced to get their act together and remove all the evidence of their impromptu stay. Toby had gone up there to gather up the log books of the various fish they had discharged. The TI had filled out the relevant parts and, having checked them over, Toby took custody of them so that he could return them to the Squadron Staff once Orca was back alongside. It had been a good haul for a single running period, four warshot Mk IX's (or Mk VIII equivalents as he preferred to call them), and another four practice Mk 23 wire guided fish. Mind you they had fired enough over the last eighteen months, particularly during the time in Norway, to realise that in anger the only reliable fish were the old straight runners. All hopes for a good homing weapon really rested on the new ones under development now. Toby gathered the log books up and returned to the Wardroom, laying them on his bunk together with the increasing bundle of Squadron returns. Time for the final lunch on board for the next few weeks. Sadly it wasn't a very social affair as everyone was preparing for the return. As the last plates were cleared away, it seemed rather strange that the usual activity of putting up the bunks just did not happen, there was no chance of any sluggard getting into a pit, there was far too much to do.

Toby set to with his papers laid out on the Wardroom table and managed to finish off those last two reports over the next hour. This left him with his final paper exercise. Having been Steve Frankham's mentor during his Part III time under training with them, it was his duty to bring together Steve's work book and certificates. Toby found him in the Control Room and got him to bring along all his workbooks and logs. They went through it all together to ensure that he hadn't missed any systems, or counter signatures for the all the tasks that had been listed to complete. There were a couple of signatures missing, but as these were only oversights as he had done the actual drills, they were soon able to chase the relevant chaps up and add their signatures to the Part III log. Finally Steve needed a draft report which Toby would then offer to the Boss for his final assessment and sign off as a fully trained submariner. They discussed his performance and had a general chat about his time on board and wishes for the future. He had clearly enjoyed the freedom of being on a conventional boat, but was still keen to move onto a nuclear one. The reality of starting off as an assistant to a head of department, rather than immediately running his own one in either an "O" or "P" Class Boat, did not turn him off. He had this strange idea that Nuclears were the way of the future, and didn't see the idea of stepping straight into the hot seat as quite so appealing. Strange chap, but it took all types. He then left Toby to draft the words which didn't take too long.

Finally with his fully completed pack under his arm Toby knocked on the Boss's cabin door and sat down with him to go over the results. Steve had clearly impressed and with a few minor changes the words were accepted. So Toby took them away, quickly typed them up, and had the final signatures added. For Steve this was a significant milestone. He was now classified as a fully trained submariner, and would get the "Submariner's Pay" premium from then on. Yet little was made of the transition, it would be a few years before the introduction of the Submarine Badge and the pomp and ceremony that would follow at such times for Steve's successors. They did, however, give him first choice of a cake (which Toby had asked the galley to bake) at tea that afternoon to mark the occasion. His three weeks with them had been pretty dramatic, what with the live firings, the time with the frigates and the fun with the Booties. It was three weeks he wouldn't forget.

It was time to get Toby's kit together. This trip had been a long one and he needed to give everything a good dhobying, even the special set of sea going plain clothes he normally kept on board for the odd run ashore. He had purposefully kept this outfit to the minimum to ensure that as few of his clothes as possible were permanently tainted with the stench of diesel. This time even that set needed to go the cleaners. So he gathered them all together and stuffed as much as he could into his pusser's grip. The others he put into a number of suit covers, and then laid it all out on his bunk. He changed into his sea going No 5's and strolled into the Control Room to see how far they had to go.

They had just rounded St Catherine's point at the southern tip of the Isle of Wight. Up ahead was Bembridge Ledge, that legendary submariner's hazard to navigation. Not that long ago, after a large submarine exercise involving a number of boats, two A-class submarines were racing each other back to Dolphin, each keen to beat the other to the favoured alongside berth. One went too close and ended up aground on the ledge. Embarrassingly it had had to await a spring tide a couple of days later before it could be floated off and had been featured in the press high and dry for all to see. The CO up to that point had been quite a star, but few survive a "Collisions and Groundings" incident. The finger only points one way. So, realising that his impressive career had come to an end, legend has it that he sent out a signal asking for details of "Farms for Sale in the West Country". A fittingly simple way of accepting the blame without excuses.

Not long to go now. John had come back into the wardroom and they prepared for their normal role as VIP hosts, while the seamen ensured they got alongside without incident or any scratching of the paintwork. No food or nibbles this time, just a quick nip for presentation's sake and then the haste to get away. The boat was looking good. All the efforts to clean her up had been worth it. Each mess was laid out with rows of pusser's grips awaiting that first night "up homers". Those left behind to take the duty would accept their fate and meld into the silent boat. Invariably the bachelors in the crew took the duty on such nights. It was a fair balance, they'd all done it in their time.

Finally just as they sensed the speed coming off as they made their way into Portsmouth Harbour, one of the comms team put his head into the wardroom and passed another signal to Toby.

"God John, it's just getting worse. Look the buggers in the power boat weren't helping out, but pinching Colonsay for salvage. Apparently they contacted Judy, who had the presence of mind to contact the Squadron and who have taken it on and are calling in the MoD police."

"Well, at least you now have the "heavy mob" taking charge. Captain SM won't take any prisoners. My guess is that it will all be over before he comes on board in a few minutes" John gave Toby a reassuring smile and continued to get the bar ready for our home team VIP visitors. Then with hard astern revolutions on the port side they felt the boat being pulled around the corner into Haslar creek. The manoeuvre was always a bit iffy, the tide tended to grab the stern and swing them further around than they intended. Mistakes in full view of the squadron hierarchy understandably did not impress. This time, however, all was well and they started the final manoeuvring to come outboard of a P-boat, achieving the gentlest of nudges as they came alongside. It turned out to be Sea Lion; they were once more happily tucked up in the bosom of the squadron again, it was good to be back.

Although reasonably late both Captain and Commander SM had come down to welcome them home. As soon as the brow was across they were on their way, quickly down the ladder and into the Wardroom for a small one before ushering everyone off to their nearest and dearest. The Great Britain round trip had been of great interest in itself without adding on the myriad activities they had been involved in. Some of these had been pretty special if not unique. While the Squadron staff received the potted version Toby was given a final brief on his boat by Commander SM. All was well and his boat was now tied up alongside the yacht moorings and the "privateers" had been informed about the actual rules for claiming salvage, and formally warned about their conduct. Judy was up to speed and would fill in all the details.

Despite their obvious interest in hearing more about the trip the VIP team managed to stand back and allow the crew to start contacting their loved ones and make arrangements to get home. For most of them this meant the trek from Gosport back around the northern reaches of Portsmouth Harbour to the married patch in Farlington Avenue close to Havant. They had only been alongside for some ten minutes when the Wardroom phone became connected and a stream of phone calls started, either from the Hall Porter, reporting the times of arrivals for the respective ladies, or from the girls themselves arranging individual pick-ups. It actually became somewhat chaotic. Finally Captain SM, knowing that they all needed to get home, kindly said his farewells. He turned, raised his glass and congratulated Orca on a very successful "Routine Running Period". A purposefully tongue in cheek description recognizing all they had been through. Then he quickly departed leaving them to continue their frantic efforts to get away.

To add an air of formality, leave was then piped over the main broadcast by the Cox'n. It allowed the crew to change gear mentally and they all started to gather the weekend basics and carry them in their pusser's grips off the boat to await their lifts ashore. Those in the Wardroom started to head ashore to the Dolphin Wardroom. In simple terms moving from one bar to another, with the benefit that the inboard one was by the car park and the Hall Porter's office so calls could be answered straight away.

In Toby's case having cleared the jetty, grip in hand, he rounded the corner thinking he would have time for a quick horse's neck before Judy arrived. Then he heard that familiar deep throated gurgle approaching behind him. He turned and there she was, Judy with her familiar smile lighting up the evening, driving their eye-catching MGB with its classic red body and chrome bumpers.

She had just turned in from the beach road when they spotted each other. Toby stuck his thumb out mimicking the need for a lift, and playing her part she stopped beside him, wound down the window and with a sparkle in her eye said: "Hey Sailor, looking for a lift?" with all the innuendo that simple statement implied.

It was great to be with her again, and after a quick kiss through the car window, she turned the beast around and parked it by the front lawn. He went around the back, opened the boot and squeezed the grip inside. The apology for a boot had very little room and he only just managed to get the lid to shut. Then he was in the car and they just held each other. Words weren't needed, it had been too long this time. Finally they let go and just looked at each other. After what seemed an age later, Judy put the car in gear and they set off, she recounting the recent events surrounding the rescue of their boat. She had had the presence of mind to contact the Receivers of Wrecks, within the Customs and Excise organization, and so had established that we could not be held for salvage without either requesting it or giving our consent. "What a star" Toby thought.

"Christ, you stink. I'd almost forgotten the appalling smell of diesel which that wretched black thing envelopes you all in. You need a damned good scrub" Judy interrupted his thoughts.

"Yes, please" Toby replied, in eager anticipation. After that gentle riposte, they got into the journey and he gave her a brief account of his adventures since they had last chatted on the phone. She thought the idea of meeting and playing with hunky SBS types sounded rather appealing, particularly if, like Toby, living in Orca had covered them in a thin film of oil. He patted her knee, noticing just how short her skirt was, and told her to calm down.

At this time of night the rush hour had just about finished so they made good time. That journey was always deceptive; it was always seemed longer than Toby remembered. At last they turned into their road and parked outside the married quarter. He grabbed his gear and Judy locked the car and led him up to the front door.

Turning she said "Look, I know the hall is a bit chilly but you aren't to go anywhere until all your contaminated clothes are de-fumigating on the washing line. They'll need at least twenty four hours before they are fit to go in my washing machine"

"OK Lass, I know the drill … but don't be long - I will literally be freezing my bollocks off"

So saying she turned the key in the lock and they both stepped inside. He passed her his grip and she disappeared to hang it all out on the line. In the mean time he started to undress, finally taking his underpants off and, standing in the all together, threw the last bundle at her as she came back.

"Don't get cold, I won't be long" she grinned as he stood there. Christ he felt randy, and at last she came back in. His feelings were overtly clear when Judy returned. She came slowly up to him, grasped his arm and turned to lead him up stairs.

"I promised you a good scrubbing" she said "Then, once you are fit to devour, the fizz is on ice and I've got a little surprise for you … and remember, it's my turn to be on top".

He meekly followed, knowing he was about to go up to heaven.

Annex A - H.M.S. ORCA

CAVE QUAM MORSUS
(Fear us lest we bite)

HMS ORCA *on the Clyde*

HMS ORCA	
Launched	1960 – Barrow-in-Furness
Commissioned	28th Sept 1961
General characteristics	
Displacement:	2,080 tons surfaced 2,450 tons submerged
Length:	290 ft (88 m)
Beam:	26 ft 7 in (8.10 m)
Draught:	18 ft (5.5 m)
Propulsion:	2 × Admiralty Standard range diesel generators, 1,650 hp (1.230 MW) 2 × English Electric main motors, 12,000 hp (8.95 MW) 2 shafts
Speed:	12 kn (22 km/h) surfaced 17 kn (31 km/h)submerged
Range:	9,000 nmi (17,000 km) at 12 kn (22 km/h)
Complement:	71
Armament:	8 × 21 in torpedo tubes, 6 bow, 2 stern; 30 × Mk8 or Mk23 torpedoes, later the Mk 24

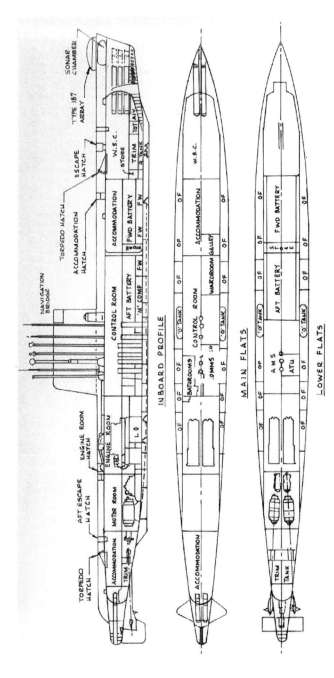

SONAR CHAMBER

TYPE 187 ARRAY

ESCAPE HATCH

W.S.C. STORE

TORPEDO HATCH

ACCOMMODATION HATCH

NAVIGATION BRIDGE

AFT ESCAPE HATCH

ENGINE ROOM HATCH

ENGINE ROOM

MOTOR ROOM

TORPEDO HATCH

TRIM TANK

ACCOMMODATION

CONTROL ROOM

AFT BATTERY

'M' COMP

FWD BATTERY

ACCOMMODATION

INBOARD PROFILE

W.S.C.

ACCOMMODATION

OF

WARDROOM GALLEY

OF

CONTROL ROOM

OF

'O' TANK

OF

BATHROOMS

OF

ACCOMMODATION

MAIN FLATS

OF

OF

FWD BATTERY

OF

AFT BATTERY

STORE

OF

'O' TANK

AMS

ATU

'O' TANK

TRIM TANK

LOWER FLATS

Internal Breakdown

Annex B - GLOSSARY of TERMS

AMS – Auxiliary Machinery Space

Appointer – Officer who allocates jobs to the RN officer corps

Avalon – Name of the DSRV (USS Avalon)

AUWE Portland – Admiralty Underwater Weapons Establishment Portland.

AWEO – Assistant Weapon Electrical Officer

Baby's Head – Individual Steak and Kidney suet pudding

Blown All Round – Using the Blower (high pressure fan) to pump air into the ballast tanks to assure full buoyancy

Bongle – Shaker used to make a noise for Submarines to find Royal Marine swimmers

Bootie (Bootneck) – Royal Marine

Bomber – SSBN – Polaris Submarine carrying Nuclear missiles

Boomer – US term for SSBN

BOP – Bearings Only Plot

Bravo Zulu – Well Done – Flag signal congratulating another ship. A real accolade in the RN.

BRNC – Brittania Royal Naval College based at Dartmouth in Devon. School for all RN initial officer training

Clockwork Mousing – Acing as a target for surface ships

Cocked Hat Fix – Inaccurate three point fix, where bearings from each source fail to produce a single position

Colours – Raising the White ensign each morning (or saying Good Morning to the Queen)

Coulport – Royal Naval Armament Depot at Coulport on Loch Long

CSST- Captain Submarine Sea Training

Daring Class Destroyer – Last of the old post WWII destroyers; fitted with significant gunnery

Dhobi – standard tri-service term for washing clothes; from the Indian.

Dogs – The Dog watches – split into 1st and 2nd dog watches from 1600 to 1800 and 1800 to 2000 respectively

Donk & Donk Shop – Diesel engine and Engine Room

DSRV – Deep Submersible Rescue Vessel

Escape Tank – Tank in HMS Dolphin where submarines practice escape drills

Faslane – Submarine base on the Clyde. Originally based on a submarine depot ship, but expanded into a shore base to encompass SM3 and SM10

Fast Cruise – Training cruise whereby submarine pretends to be at sea but stays alongside. Can last several continuous days.

Greenies – Electrical staff – named after the Green stripe which used to be between the gold ones for early Electrical Officers

Haslar – The RN Hospital just outside HMS Dolphin

HMS DOLPHIN – home of :-

- the 1ST Submarine Squadron in Gosport – **SM1**
- **FOSM** – Flag Officer Submarines
- Submarine Training and escape schools

HMS ACHERON – A Class Submarine. Last WWII design with emphasis on long surface passages in the Pacific. Last submarines to have a gun fitted on the casing.

HMS Neptune – Shore establishment at Faslane Naval Base

HMS ORCA – The fictional submarine around which this tale is based,

as one of the first O Class submarines, build standard before modernisation

HMS PORPOISE – First Submarine of the *Porpoise* Class (*P - Boats*). The pathfinder design for the *Oberon* Class (*O – Boats*) which came later. Essentially the same design but with differing steels for the pressure hull. These had a lesser specification steel so were built with additional deep eighteen inch t-frames every sixth frame to provide required hull strength. This gave them slightly less internal space to the later *O- boats*.

Horse's Neck – Brandy & Dry Ginger

Janes – Jane's Fighting Ships – catalogue of warships worldwide

Janner – Person from the West Country

Kai Submarine brand of Hot Chocolate

LEANDER Class – Frigates: workhorses of the surface fleet.

Lecky – Nickname for the Electrical Officer

Lines – Sonar tonals; used to differentiate targets

LIVEX – Live firing exercise

LOP – Local Operations Plot

LREM – Leading Radio Electrical Mechanic

LRO – Leading Radio Operator

Mk 8 (Mk VIII) – Submarine launched, gyro angled, straight running torpedo

Mk 9 (Mk IX) – Surface ship launched gyro angled, straight running torpedo

Mk 23 – Mk 23 wire guided Torpedo.

NO – Navigating Officer

No 2, 400hz machine – Electrical generator providing power to weapon fire control equipment

No 5's – Officers full uniform; in the 60's and 70's worn as a working uniform with a best one saved for formal occasions. Now replaced by a sweater, with shirt and tie, plus trousers as a working rig.

No 8 Trousers –Dark blue working trousers – formally matched with light blue shirts. Today's "Action Rig"

Nuclear Hunter/Killers – Nuclear Attack Submarine

Nuckie Pooh – RN personnel serving in Nuclear Submarines

Oberon Class Submarine – Follow-on RN new design conventional submarine to Porpoise Class (Designs of both almost the same but with upgrades of material and equipment)

OPDEF – Operational Defect

Outside Wrecker – CPO Artificer responsible for the mechanical systems in a submarine (outside the engine room)

Part III – The third practical on the job part of training to become a qualified submariner. Used as jargon to refer to all trainees.

PD –Periscope Depth

Perisher – Commanding Officer's Qualifying Course for Submarines

Petrol Budgie – helicopter

Polto – Petty Officer Electrician; responsible for high power electrics in the submarine.

Pongo – Naval term for a soldier

Porpoise Class Submarine – First RN new design conventional submarine after WWII

Plumber – mechanical engineers (not plumbers!)

Pusser's Grip – RN canvas holdall

Radar Shack – very small space which housed our navaids and radar sets

REA – Radio Electrical Artificer – looked after radio and sonar gear

Rider - A submarine visitor (trainer or trials staff)

RNEC Manadon – Royal Naval Engineering College Manadon; on the outskirts of Plymouth (no longer exists)

Roundabout – The fixed seat and motorised drive which enables the Search Periscope to be used for prolonged periods.

Run Ashore – Ashore leave

RV – Rendezvous

Second Cox'n – Seaman Petty Officer in charge of external evolutions and maintenance. Includes berthing; anchoring; painting external casing & fin. Leads the team of quartermasters.

Sergeant Johnnies – Non Commissioned Army Officers who know how things work

Shit on a Raft – Kidneys on fried bread

Skimmer –Submarine nickname for those in surface warships

SINKEX – Live firing exercise against a hulk

Steaming Bats – Heavy boots worn generally at sea, and especially in magazines

Stokers - Engineering Mechanics – related back to the original ratings who used to feed the boilers.

SM2 – Second Submarine Squadron based at Devonport. Comprised a mixture of Conventional and Nuclear Hunter Killer Class submarines.

SM3 – Third Submarine Squadron based at Faslane on the Gare Loch. Comprises a mixture of Conventional and Nuclear Hunter Killer Class submarines.

SM10 – Tenth Submarine Squadron based at Faslane on Garloch, Comprises the four Polaris Nuclear submarines

Sound Room – Space for Sonar Cabinets & operation of Sonar sets.

SSD – Special Sea Dutymen

SSN – Nuclear Attack submarine sometimes called a Hunter Killer

S206 – Naval form for Officer's Reports

TASO – Torpedo and Anti Submarine Officer

TCC – Torpedo Control Console- previously called the "fruit machine"

TCU – Torpedo Control Unit

TI – The Torpedo Instructor

Totty – Young Ladies

ToT's – Torpedo Operating Tanks; used to automatically compensate for weight of torpedoes on discharge.

Trongle – same as a Bongle only Transistorised

Type 23 Frigate – forerunner to the Leander Class. First modern Anti-Submarine frigate

Vasco – Nickname for Navigator's across Navies. Based on Vasco de Gamma, early Portuguese explorer/navigator.

Water – area of sea allocated to a submarine with clearance for diving operations.

Yellow Peril – Smoked Haddock, usually served with a poached egg on top.

XO – First Lieutenant (Executive Officer)

187 Set – Sonar 187; the main rotating sonar sited in the bow dome above the casing.

Lightning Source UK Ltd.
Milton Keynes UK
UKOW05f2312130114

224542UK00001B/46/P